Miranda expected no reward for saving Charles Hastings's life from a gang of mysterious assailants. But she did not expect what she wound up with. She was left with this ungentlemanly gentleman on her hands. Not only on her hands, but in her house. And worse was still to come.

Mr. Hastings was in desperate need of a place to hide from his angry enemies until his wounds healed enough to let him resume the high-stakes game he was playing. And he had an idea that only a gamester as shockingly bold as he could conceive—much less propose.

"Where do you intend to go?" she asked him.

"Why the only place in the world I can go. The only place I will be totally safe," he replied. "Your bedchamber."

What was Miranda to do? Should she say no, she would be putting his life at risk. On the other hand, should she say yes to his outrageous intrusion, she herself would be hazarding what she understood to be more precious than life itself—and with this skilled and seductive libertine, so easily lost. . . .

Gamester's Lady

Gamester's Lady

by
Barbara Sherrod

A SIGNET BOOK

SIGNET
Published by the Penguin Group
Penguin Books USA Inc., 375 Hudson Street,
New York, New York 10014, U.S.A.
Penguin Books Ltd, 27 Wrights Lane,
London W8 5TZ, England
Penguin Books Australia Ltd, Ringwood,
Victoria, Australia
Penguin Books Canada Ltd, 10 Alcorn Avenue,
Toronto, Ontario, Canada M4V 3B2
Penguin Books (N.Z.) Ltd, 182–190 Wairau Road,
Auckland 10, New Zealand

Penguin Books Ltd, Registered Offices:
Harmondsworth, Middlesex, England

First published by Signet,
an imprint of Dutton Signet,
a division of Penguin Books USA Inc.

First Printing, September, 1994
10 9 8 7 6 5 4 3 2 1

ONE

An Ill Bird for Plucking

Hastings's First Principle of Gaming: Show me a
creature who will never punt and I shall show you a
dead bore.

Though he held a hand rich in court cards, Mr. Charles
Hastings frowned. Something, he sensed, was in the wind,
and it smelled of rotting fish. His hackles stood at attention
like a crack regiment. Glancing up, he studied the saloon,
as though the crimson walls and trompe l'oeil ceiling of
Mrs. Stout's gaming house might reveal the source of these
odd sensations. At last, his eyes fell on his opponent, the
lace-trimmed Lord Everard. Instantly he knew: the gentleman, if he could be called a gentleman, was dishing him.
For all his blood, title, and reputed wealth, his lordship was
no better than a Captain Sharp.

Mr. Hastings's large gray eyes began to shine. His severe
expression, which had ill suited his bonny complexion and
boyish face, now relaxed in a mischievous smile. To think,
he chided himself, only moments before, he had been
seized with a fit of yawning, certain that he would be hoary
with age before the tiresome game of piquet ended. No
wonder, he had told himself, one referred to establishments
such as Mrs. Stout's in St. James's as a gaming *hell*. To
Charles Hastings, boredom had ever been the worst hell on
earth. But now, thanks to Lord Everard's delusion that he
could be sharked, he was alive with interest. Even seeing
Everard add points for repique did not dampen his spirits.

The game ended, going to his lordship to the tune of a
hundred guineas. Mr. Hastings rose and proclaimed cheer-

fully, if unnecessarily, "You have the devil's own luck tonight, Everard!"

Everard acknowledged the observation with a nod, saying, "I trust it is not such a great loss that you mean to call a halt."

"I never call a halt while I play with the house's blunt, and as I still have my winnings from vingt-un, I am entirely at your service."

"I was afraid you meant to leave."

"Ordinarily in the hierarchy of pleasures, I count piquet first and palate second, but it is a maxim with me that to play on an empty stomach is to beg to be rubiconed. In a word, before we resume our game, I must go and avail myself of the delectables in Mrs. Stout's dining parlor."

Lord Everard's scowl indicated that he did not fancy losing his pigeon to smoked salmon and iced champagne. He shuffled his deck absently.

A brief survey of the fellow's hands informed Mr. Hastings that Everard had not cheated by dint of a wide shuffle. If he had, he would have formed the habit of holding the cards with a considerable space between his first and second fingers, the better to deal from the bottom. His lordship's fingers were as close as a miser's, proving he had used some other device. Mr. Hastings only hoped it would not be too easy to discover what it was. That would spoil the fun.

He laid a wager with himself, just to make the stakes as lively as possible: by the time the watch called out two-of-the-clock, he would be in a position to diddle the diddler and prevent his ever presuming again to serve a fellow gamester such a rascally turn. If he succeeded, he would buy himself the hunter he had admired recently at Tattersall's. If not, he would give over gaming for the remainder of the Season and confine himself to playing whist with his mother. This last thought gave him such a shudder that he was more determined than ever to succeed.

"I shall wait until you have supped," Everard said tightly.

Mr. Hastings performed an elegant bow. "I was certain I could depend upon you." On that, he made his way out of the parlor, past the faro table and down the crimson-carpeted steps.

Although it was Mr. Hastings's opinion that Mrs. Stout offered a bill of fare fit only for invalids and country squires, he smiled with delight upon entering the dining parlor, for poised in front of the table, sipping claret and licking his lips, was Felix DeWitt, an old and trusted acquaintance who was a good deal plumper in the cheeks than he was in the pockets and who was, at the moment, in Mr. Hastings's debt for several hundred guineas.

Clapping him on the shoulder, Mr. Hastings nearly caused Felix to spill his drink.

"Oh, it is you, Hastings!" he said. "I suppose you've wearied of winning and have come down to assist me in staining my coat."

"I am losing."

Felix eyed him. "You are gulling me."

"No. In point of fact, I am being gulled."

"The fellow doesn't exist who can gull you."

"If you come into the card room, you will see one who thinks he can."

"Who the deuce is he?"

"Everard."

"Never say so!"

"I am astonished as yourself. I never heard the fellow was rolled up. What do you suppose would induce him to rook me?"

Felix helped himself to a lemon tart from the table. As he tasted it, he closed his eyes, sighing with pleasure. "I expect that, like you, he is partial to winning."

Mr. Hastings laughed. "So much so that he risks being caught, exposed, expelled, and shunned?"

With lemon cream outlining his lips, Felix replied, "I expect it is his new squeeze, Mrs. Buxleigh."

"Never heard of her."

"An excessively handsome creature, and shockingly expensive."

"That description fits virtually all my acquaintance."

"She is devilishly fond of faro. Have you not met her?"

"I do not play faro. One has to deliver half of one's winnings to the bank. That goes much against the grain with me."

"She is playing faro now, if you wish to have a look at her."

"Do you mean Everard has brought her here?"

"I expect he could not keep her away. Though the lady is newly arrived from the rural regions, she has acquired London's vices so rapidly as to be thought a native."

As he pondered this information, Mr. Hastings helped himself to victuals from the table. The instant he tasted the leather which masqueraded as roast beef, he set down his plate. "Pray tell me, Felix, how do you contrive to eat this fodder?"

"Your taste is too nice," Felix said between swallows. It was clear from the rapturous tone of his grunts that he thought Mrs. Stout's table splendid.

"Do not be long in finishing your tart," Mr. Hastings said. "We are wanted in the card room."

Having washed down the tart with wine, Felix replied, "You know very well I do not fancy cards. I confine myself to E.O. I have no liking for games of chance that depend upon skill." He licked crumbs from his fingertips.

"It is not necessary that you fancy cards. It is enough that I do. I intend to catch Everard and expose him. To do so, I require a witness. You are so fortunate as to have been selected."

In alarm, Felix cried, "Gad, if I wished to put an untimely period to my life, I should eat myself to death, thank you very much. I have no wish to make my exit at Everard's hands."

"You disappoint me. I had no idea you were such a pudding-heart, and merely on account of his being an excellent shot."

"He is as prime with a pistol as you are with a deck of cards, and if you mean to call him a cheat to his face, you will have the proof of your own eyes, for he will call you out."

Mr. Hastings smiled and pointed a shapely finger at Felix. "Not if I have a witness."

"Should you produce a hundred witnesses, he will deny your charge. He always manages to prove himself in the right by the most persuasive of arguments—a well-aimed bullet."

With a bracing hand on his companion's shoulder, Mr. Hastings whispered enticingly. "Think of it, Felix." He gestured theatrically into the distance. "Think of the adventure of it. We shall be on our mettle to discover an ingenious chisel and expose the chiseler. Our wits shall be tested to the utmost. Is that not a delicious prospect? Are you not perishing to embark upon such a noble quest?"

"It sounds jolly, to be sure, but I am not perishing to perish, which I am certain to do if Everard is crossed."

"I take my oath, he will not shoot you. If he shoots anybody, it shall be me."

"I do not fancy seeing you killed either, Hastings. You may think otherwise, as I am in to you for a considerable sum and would be relieved of the debt if you were relieved of your life. But I am not so paltry a fellow as to wish it."

"Your loyalty touches me, Felix. I vow, if you go on in this vein, I shall dissolve in tears."

"Scoff if you like, but I think you are excessively amiable, when you are not bored and restless that is, and you are always willing to advance a fellow a bit of the ready. Your demise would rob me of appetite for days."

"If your devotion is sincere, then you will see to it that I do not get my head shot off. You will come with me and protect me from my own impetuosity."

By this time, Felix had devoured the lemon tart, along with a handful of dried fruit and sugared nuts. The table dishes had been picked fairly clean and the removes had not yet been brought out. As there was nothing more to eat, Felix shrugged. "Oh, very well, but you must take your oath you will not duel with Everard."

"To please you, my excellent friend, I shall give you my solemn promise. Nothing, not the threat of death upon the rack or boiling in oil or sitting down to whist with my mother, shall induce me to meet the fellow. You have my word." He put out his hand, and they shook on the bargain.

"I am relieved," Felix said with a sigh. "I was afraid you imagined I would act as your second, which is more than I engage for, I assure you. That sort of thing renders me so dyspeptic, I can scarcely digest a dish of porridge." He punctuated this assertion with a delicate burp behind his fingers.

Before they passed into the card room, the gentlemen paused at the faro table so that Felix might point out Mrs. Buxleigh from among the crowd. With a shift of his eyes, he indicated to Mr. Hastings that the lady in question was the one leaning eagerly over the table, the better to study the faro board. Her pose revealed a quantity of rosy bosom set off prettily in black lace and garnet necklaces. Mr. Hastings did not recognize the bosom or the dimpled face that accompanied it; however, he admired both. Even more admirable was the lady's spirited betting. She punted everything on the six of spades. The cards were dealt, and the lady lost. Nevertheless, she did not hesitate an instant to bet again as high as before. He could see that a man of weak character like Everard would be tempted to cheat at cards in order to frank the losses of such a pretty, engaging, and rash female.

But though the temptation was understandable, it could not be ignored. Everard must be caught, if only to protect one's brother gamesters. They both belonged to the same clubs—Brooks' and Boodle's—and one was obliged to protect the reputation of one's club. Even more, one was obliged to pursue one's own amusement, and nothing gave greater zest to life than a battle of wills, especially one which promised the additional spice of danger.

When Mr. Hastings entered the card room, Everard stood with stiff politeness. "Ah, so you have come back."

Mr. Hastings replied, "Did you think I would pull it?"

Nervously, Everard laughed. "No, no. I was certain you were a gentleman of your word."

Whipping up his coattails, Mr. Hastings sat and remarked, "Indeed, I am. And now we shall see what sort of gentleman *you* are."

Everard's head snapped up at this, but as Mr. Hastings made certain to maintain a bland expression, the fellow's alarms were somewhat quieted.

Felix entered and lounged against the wall. From that vantage point, he had an excellent view of the players. To Mr. Hastings's satisfaction, he folded his arms and fixed his eyes on the green-baize table.

Everard fiddled with his deck, shuffling the cards in a dilatory manner. After glancing unhappily at Felix once or twice, he said, "Does DeWitt mean to stay?"

"You have no objection, I trust?"

"As the other players have gone and we have the parlor to ourselves, I had thought this might be a private game between two gentlemen."

"And so it shall be, for Felix's presence is the equivalent of other men's absence. He is scarcely here at all, except as my bank."

At this compliment, Felix glowered.

Everard looked doubtful.

"If you take my vingt-un winnings," Mr. Hastings explained pleasantly, "I shall require a loan. Mr. DeWitt has kindly consented to supply any amount of brass I might require. Is that not correct, Felix?"

Felix bared his teeth in a brilliant smile. "How much do you require, Hastings? A thousand? Two thousand? Just name your sum."

"As you see," Mr. Hastings said, "he considers it an honor and a privilege to allow me to lose his pot, even though he is perfectly capable of losing it himself."

As Mr. Hastings had calculated, Lord Everard scarcely attended to this banter. His eyes glittered at the information just gleaned, to wit, that his pigeon meant to stick out the game to the finish and, more to the point, was already in a losing frame of mind.

"I say, this deck of mine is rather a tattered affair," Mr. Hastings remarked. "With your permission, Everard, I shall send the waiter to fetch a new one. May I fetch a new one for you as well?"

Without an instant's hesitation or change of expression, Everard agreed, handing over his deck.

When Mr. Hastings stepped to the door to summon the waiter, his eyes met Felix's. The glance they exchanged acknowledged that Everard had apparently not stooped to marking the cards. If he had, he would never have agreed so readily to a new deck. Felix shrugged, conveying to his friend that he was damned if he knew what the fellow's gambit was.

Mr. Hastings resumed his seat, and the game began. During its progress, he marveled at Everard's subtlety. His lordship seemed to know precisely what his opponent would declare and which cards the stock contained. He was so expert at sinking that Mr. Hastings's considerable winnings from vingt-un were soon exhausted.

Throughout the play, Mr. Hastings took careful account of Everard's every move. He did not permit the man to scratch his ear or twitch his nose without being thoroughly scrutinized. Nevertheless, at the end of half an hour, Mr. Hastings had ascertained only that his lordship was not using the customary means of cheating. He was not palming knaves or shaving the ends of queens or producing kings out of his boot; his strength was too consistent for any of that. Furthermore, he appeared to know what tricks Mr. Hastings would take before he knew himself. Mr. Hastings racked his brain to discover how he did it, but though he had been taught cards at the hands of London's most skilled sharps, he was now in to him for five hundred pounds and no closer to smoking the swindle.

He was certain of one thing only: ordinarily in piquet, the dealer was at a disadvantage while the elder had the advantage. In his game with Everard, the opposite was true. Each time his lordship dealt, he gained a pique, a repique, or both. Indeed, the only time Mr. Hastings won a hand was when he was the younger. Somehow, Everard had contrived to turn piquet on its ear. Such a feat could only be accomplished if the dealer knew in advance what cards he was dealing.

Mr. Hastings drew out his watch and clicked it open. It read a quarter until the hour of two. He had fifteen minutes. All his amusement for the next eight months depended on his making haste. If he failed, he would be condemned to play whist with a woman whom he loved with all his heart but who scarcely knew a slam from a slowtop or a ruff from a rum touch. His mother's capacities suited her for no more than an undemanding game of quadrille. However, as whist was all the crack, the dear lady felt compelled to play it, much to the chagrin of anybody who was so unfortunate as to serve as her partner. To make matters worse, she did not like to play for money. She preferred the stakes to be raisins, nuts, or, devil take it, buttons!

Shuddering, he cast a glance at Felix. All he got for his trouble was a baffled shrug. Poor Felix was growing heavy-lidded with watching. Mr. Hastings sighed at the sight. He had put his friend to prodigious trouble for nothing, for it seemed as though he was about to rise from the table not only no richer but also no wiser than when he had first sat down. Such a catastrophe had never befallen Charles Hastings in his life. He had lived thirty-one years without ever being humbled.

Up to that moment, Mr. Hastings had betrayed no hint of uneasiness. He had successfully concealed his intentions behind his face, which was so boyish and sweet as to beguile any onlooker. Because of his smooth complexion, his chestnut curls, and his large gray eyes, his countenance was the envy of every cardplayer in Town. It had won him the admiration of women old and young whose maternal instincts were roused by his deceptively ingenuous expression. More important, it had been the means by which he had undone a parade of cheats and braggarts. However, his youthful good looks appeared to be doing him precious little good in this instance.

He put his hand to his temple. His eyes ached. His neck was stiff and sore, and his leg was numb from sitting too long. Even so, he was not about to fold. He still had a few minutes left. He would uncover the deception, he vowed, though it might cost him a hole in his skull. An impulse seized him to take Everard by the throat and accuse him to his face, but all at once he was struck by a light, not the light of a clever notion, but the light of Everard's ring.

It was a ruse he had heard of but had never seen. Nobody to his knowledge had ever been so impudent or so mad as to employ it. He sat back, stretching his legs, spreading his cards in an even fan, smiling to himself. Another glance across the table confirmed his suspicion. Everard was wearing a shiner. It was a broad-band ring worn on the third finger of his right hand. The side of the band opposite the sapphire setting was polished so that it approximated the surface of a looking glass. As he dealt each card, taking it between his right thumb and forefinger, Everard was able to read its value. No wonder the blackguard knew what cards he dealt.

It was all Mr. Hastings could do to keep from sending up a laugh of triumph. Once more, he pulled out his watch. He had found out the device with a minute to spare. Now he could buy himself that sleek hunter.

His satisfaction was brief, however. The question remained: what was he to do about Everard? He had given Felix his word that he would not engage in a duel, and truth to tell, he himself was not greatly enamored of the idea of shooting at another man while being shot at in his turn. Grass before breakfast had appealed to him when he was eighteen and a greenhorn. Now he found it a dead bore.

He did not fear for his person; his ear, shoulder, chest, foot, and both arms bore the proofs of his manly courage. These scars of honor he had acquired before he was twenty-five, so that neither man nor woman could dare to call him coward. However, he had lately come to regard these marks with more irony than pride. They represented, in his view, a youthful dedication to folly. Had he really been a man in those days, he told himself, he would not have felt the need to puff himself up at the peril of another man's life, or his own. The only good to have come out of those escapades, he believed, was that he had never actually killed anybody.

He further objected to dueling because he had come to regard it as ridiculous. What fool would willingly wake at an ungodly hour of the morning when he might sleep until three? To engage in a duel, one was expected to count off twenty paces in all seriousness and then march about in a damp field, catching one's death and wondering whether one's dicing hand was about to be blown to pieces. Not only was it absurd, it was sadly lacking in imagination. It had been done to death, so to speak. What Mr. Hastings required was amusement, and experience had taught him not to look for it in dueling.

He must find another way, an *interesting* way, of teaching Everard a lesson. He laid a wager with himself: before November was out, he would have his revenge—and without the expenditure of a single bullet. If he won, he would buy himself a new watch. He had looked at his present one so often in the last hour that he had come to find it drab. On the other hand, if he lost, he would spend a month in Bath with his mother playing whist, and he would nobly refrain from uttering a single sarcastic shot when she ate all the nuts and raisins he won from her.

TWO

Improvements

We have just come from Blaise, where everybody
excepting myself sang the praises of its castle.
Though I failed to fall into raptures over the folly, I
could not help but admire the grounds. I daresay, it
was not the first time I had beheld imposing rocks,
deep woods, steep ravines, and winding streams; it
was only the first time I condescended to notice! The
Guide attributes the beauty of the estate to Mr.
Repton, the landscape gardener. One cannot live in
England above two minutes without hearing that
name extolled, but I never knew its significance until
today. His eye, his taste, his sympathy quite
overpowered me. Because I was unable to express
such sentiments to my companions, who would talk
of nothing but the folly, I have had recourse to this
journal. I am curious to know more of Mr. Repton
and his work. What a gratifying calling it must be to
labor in concert with nature, not to tame or correct
her but to draw her forth through art.

The wind drove the rain in slanted sheets. It was morning,
but the clouds and biting chill had darkened the sky. Because Miranda Troy could scarcely make out the Greek
temple in the distance, she put her hand to her eyes to
shield them from the downpour. Her hooded cloak was
soaked, as were her gloves. Droplets ran down her cheeks,
which were rosy and fine in the best of weather and were
now whipped into a glow by intermittent blasts of wind. In
spite of the elements, she kept her eyes fixed on the temple.

It was, Miranda concluded, an eyesore. What was the use
of it, when not twenty feet away there was a ruin—not a

constructed ruin but a real one, from the days when monks inhabited the abbey? Her grandfather had made the mistake of playing amateur improver, and the temple had been the result. Had it graced the banks of a pond, so that its reflection in the water might please the eye, it would have been charming, but no attempt had been made to unite it with the landscape. Its purpose had been to afford her grandfather something picturesque to view from the terrace, but, in fact, because it had been erected on a hollow instead of a rise, it was scarcely visible. Moreover, the manner in which it had been placed on the expanse of bare lawn, without vines or shrubs to twine through its pillars, gave it the appearance of an eruption, like a boil on an otherwise silken complexion.

Six weeks earlier, Miranda would have found the temple perfectly harmless. Indeed, six weeks earlier, she would have had the bad taste to like it. But having lately enjoyed a visit to Blaise estate and viewed Mr. Repton's improvements, she had returned home to Arundel Abbey a changed creature.

Her fingers itched to get to work. Because winter was approaching, improvements to the landscape were out of the question. But there was much she could do inside the house. It had been built in the early seventeenth century at some distance from the abbey ruins and, except for the addition of water closets and bake ovens, was ill suited to a family of the modern age. Mr. Repton's principles of landscape design—neatness, elegance, and comfort—applied equally to interiors. The first thing she would do, she resolved, was transform the old-fashioned cedar parlor into a living room.

The sound of her name carried on the wet wind broke her reverie. She looked around to see Ragstone, the ancient butler, coming toward her, carrying an umbrella and calling to her.

"Miss Miranda, her ladyship wishes to speak with you."

Miranda was scandalized at the servant's appearance. "Ragstone, you ought not to be out in such weather," she gently scolded. "You will catch your death. Look at your greatcoat, it is soaked through. And where is your hat?"

Panting, he observed, "And so shall you catch your death, miss. And as to my greatcoat, your cloak is every bit as soaked, if not more." Ragstone had been too long a member of the household to stand on ceremony with its inmates, and when it came to handing a scold, he could give as good as he got.

Examining her cloak, Miranda found to her astonishment that Ragstone spoke the truth. She was drenched to her skin. "Well, then," she said firmly, "we must go inside."

He placed the umbrella over both their heads and, after she had taken one last dissatisfied look at the temple, they made their way back to the house in the silver rain.

Once she had made herself presentable, Miranda went into the cedar parlor to see her mother. At her entrance, Lady Troy stretched forth her arms. "My pet, your father and I were just speaking of you."

As Miranda permitted herself to be embraced, she inspected the room with an eye to tearing down walls, opening up views, and replacing the rigid circle of chairs with several cozy groupings.

"I have received a letter from Mrs. Hastings, inviting us to visit her in London," her ladyship announced.

It struck Miranda, as she seated herself in a dainty chair, that if looking glasses were hung strategically throughout the room, the effect would be to lend it spaciousness and air.

"Your father declines to go, though I think it cruel of him to send us to Town without his protection."

"Fanny, you are the last female to require protection," Sir Bascomb grumbled, "at least not the sort a gouty old man may provide."

"You are not old. You are merely perverse."

Miranda began to think better of the looking glasses. The six or seven she had pictured seemed a trifle excessive. Mr. Repton had a horror of ostentation. She must avoid it above all things. She wondered whether two looking glasses would serve.

"Fanny, you shall take Miranda to London if you must, but I shall not be a party to this scheme against her."

Her ladyship gasped. "Scheme against her! I do nothing but what is in her interest. Do you prefer that she remain a spinster the rest of her days?"

"Yes!"

Closing her eyes, Lady Troy shuddered. "I never thought I should hear such selfishness from her own father."

Another handsome addition to the parlor, Miranda thought, would be bookshelves, arched at the top in the Romanesque style and ornamented with the busts of sundry Caesars.

"Call me selfish, if you will," cried Sir Bascomb. "I do not care a fig. You have married off three of my daughters. Each has left me to go off with some nodcock of a husband to her own house. Only one child is left to me, and now you mean to send her away, too!"

"You think only of your own happiness!"

"If I do not think of it, who will?"

It occurred to Miranda that her esteemed parents were shouting at one another. She endeavored to catch the drift of the dispute.

"I have agreed to your going to London," Sir Bascomb snapped. "What more do you wish?"

"I wish you will come with us, for Miranda's sake."

Miranda was amazed to discover that the argument was about her.

"Is it not enough that you mean to take my child from me? Must you also insist that I witness the vile act and sanction it with my presence?"

"Who is taking me away, Papa?"

"Your mother. She wishes you to marry Charles Hastings."

"Who?"

"Charles Hastings, the son of Mrs. Hastings. Surely you have heard her mention Mrs. Hastings of London."

Miranda smiled. "Only a thousand times."

Lady Troy grew indignant. "If I have mentioned Tabitha once or twice, it is only because she is my oldest and dearest friend in all the world."

"And because you were at school in Devon together,"

Miranda said as though reciting a familiar litany, "and because you saved her from an imprudent marriage and because she came to nurse you when you lay dying with a putrid fever and because you were present at her son's birth and she was present at mine and so naturally you both thought it would be great fun if your children married one day. Have I forgotten anything, Mama?"

"You do not have to marry him if you do not like," her ladyship answered in a sulk. "Tabitha and I merely thought it would be a fine thing if you met."

"I have no wish to meet him."

Sir Bascomb beamed. "You are a good girl, Miranda." His smile faded as he absorbed the look his wife leveled at him. Taking a breath, he amended his statement. "That is to say, my pet, I suppose it can do no harm to have a look at the fellow. After that, you will have done your duty and may return home to your fath—, that is to say, your family."

"You are both so kind in always wishing to do what is best for me," Miranda said to her parents, "but in this instance, I am obliged to beg off. I cannot spare the time. You see, I must be here to see to the improvements."

Sir Bascomb and his lady stared at their daughter as though she had just announced that Bonaparte had come to drink tea.

"I was not aware that we were about to embark on improvements," the baronet said.

"That is because I have only just decided today. With your permission, Papa, we shall begin indoors—with this very room, in fact."

Sir Bascomb and his lady squinted at the room, endeavoring to find fault with it.

"When the spring rains have dried," Miranda said, "we may commence work on the gardens."

"Gardens?" Anxiously, the baronet tapped his chin. His daughter's plans hinted very strongly of inconvenience, noise, expense, and all manner of disruption.

"Yes, Papa. Perhaps we shall add a parterre, and we must do something about the topiary. What we shall do about the temple, however, I have not yet decided. I fear it may have to be destroyed."

Lady Troy threw up her hands. "It is that loathsome Humphrey Repton who has done this to you! He has addled your brain. You have not spoken a word of sense since you heard that odious name."

"His ideas interest me, Mama."

"He is a detestable creature. I have no opinion of him."

Sir Bascomb, who was still reeling from his daughter's announced plans, looked as though he suffered an attack of biliousness.

With an indulgent smile, Miranda tucked her hand in his. "Do not distress yourself, Papa. I shall not go to London and leave you. You would miss me shockingly, and I must make Arundel Abbey fit for living." Patting his cheek, she left him to go to her mother, take her hand, and caress it, too. "You must not distress yourself either, dear Mama. I do not go to market for a husband. If I can improve the abbey, both inside and out, I shall have nothing else to wish for."

Lady Troy, looking over her daughter's shoulder, and Sir Bascomb, tapping his chin, exchanged a look of despair.

Within minutes of Miranda's departure from the cedar parlor, Sir Bascomb and Lady Troy reached a compromise. For his part, said the baronet, the error of his former thinking was now apparent to him; he would never forgive himself if his daughter sacrificed a chance for marital happiness because she put his welfare above her own. Therefore, he agreed that Miranda ought to travel with her mother to London, as soon as it could be arranged, and though he could not go so far as to accompany them, he could send them with his blessing. Furthermore, he would give his wife carte blanche, so that she and Miranda might purchase all the gowns, bonnets, and ribbons required to capture the heart of a Town blade. No matter how much they spent, he declared, it could not possibly set him back as much as improvements.

On her side, Lady Troy pledged to do what she might to discourage Miranda's notion of improving the abbey.

"Once she has a husband to occupy her thoughts," her lady-ship assured Sir Bascomb, "she will not have time for non-sensical schemes."

Blissfully unaware of the plans being laid for her, Miranda waited until the weather cleared and then took herself off to the village. Though the lanes were muddy, she was determined to brave them in order to reach the circulating library. It was not much of a library. A few novels and volumes of sermons were the extent of its holdings. Still, Miranda thought it worth the trouble to go there on the chance that a book on landscape gardening might have been acquired since she had last visited. Had it not been so muddy, she would have taken her phaeton. As it was, she decided to walk. With her hopes high, she set out for Togbury, her head full of a design to change the course of a nearby stream so that it might run near her bedchamber and lull her to sleep with its pretty gurgling.

In Togbury, she found nothing at the circulating library that suited her. She did, however, meet Mr. Farris Lloyd, who lived on a prosperous estate adjoining Arundel Abbey. An unmarried gentleman of prodigious dignity, Mr. Lloyd was fourth in line to inherit a title from a dissipated old earl in Somerset. Indeed, if Lady Troy had not felt her first loyalty belonged to her old friend Tabitha Hastings and her son Charles, she would have put Mr. Lloyd forward to her daughter as a marital prospect.

Although Miranda was spared this constraint, she could not meet Mr. Lloyd without experiencing some awkwardness, for she had long felt that the gentleman's interest in her went beyond friendship. On two separate occasions, he had seemed to be on the point of declaring himself, and it had taken much determined chatter and pretended ignorance on her part to circumvent him. Each occasion had proved so exhausting that she feared the next time she would be obliged to give him a bald refusal, which she was loath to do, for she disliked giving pain to anybody.

He reported that he had found nothing in the library to suit his taste.

"I commiserate with you," she said. "Like you, I have failed to find my book. We both come away empty-handed."

"No doubt you wished to read another of Miss Burney's works. You are quite devoted to her, I believe."

"And you quite disapprove, I believe."

"I confess, I cannot read a book which sports a female name as its title."

"You ought not to judge a book on such a basis as that. You will deprive yourself of much amusement, I promise you."

"Novels do not interest me, but I suppose they are a harmless enough occupation for the gentler sex."

A dozen ripostes leaped to Miranda's mind, all of which might have disqualified her for membership in that docile circle to which the gentleman had alluded, but she knew it was no use expending her breath in argument with Mr. Lloyd. He had been too long a friend; his views were too thoroughly known and too thoroughly set in stone for argument. Miranda had taken a vow never to debate with the gentleman, unless keeping silent might suggest complicity and thus compromise her principles. In this instance, her thoughts did not tend toward principles so much as knowledge. She wished to learn what she could on the subject of landscape gardening so that she might set about improving her father's estate with all due haste.

"Although I love to read Miss Burney," she said, "I have another purpose today." She told him of her quest.

"Have you read Gilpin?" he inquired.

"I haven't."

"I believe I have a copy of *Lakes Tour* at Keycroft. Will you come?"

Miranda blushed. She was aching to have a look at the book. Though Gilpin was a trifle outmoded in the view of some, he was still the arbiter of taste on the picturesque. Miranda knew herself to be too ignorant on the subject to turn up her nose at Gilpin or anybody who might teach her. But a walk of some miles and an hour with Mr. Lloyd in his library were certain to bring on the gentleman's addresses, and thus she felt compelled to excuse herself. "Would you be so good as to send the book?" she asked.

"It shall be my pleasure to bring it to you in person."

Miranda contrived to smile, and they parted at the end of the High Street, he to scour his library, she to prepare herself for her lover's onslaught.

Miranda was at the window of her sitting room, deploring the monotony of the hedge maze beyond the lawn, when her mother scratched at the door and entered. From the expression Lady Troy wore, Miranda knew that they were about to have a tête-à-tête. Accordingly, she sat on a delicate mahogany chair, while her mother sat opposite her in its twin. At first she waited patiently. Then, when her ladyship could not seem to find words to begin, Miranda said, "Mama, something is troubling you. I hope you are not unhappy on my account."

Her ladyship endeavored to smile. "If I am unhappy, my pet, it is because I see you giving all your attention to improvements and none to your future."

Smiling, Miranda teased, "By *future*, you mean my marriage. Is that not so, Mama?"

There was no need to answer; Lady Troy's blush said it all.

"I wish you would not fret so, Mama. I am perfectly content."

"My pet, you know this is not the first time you have got a bee in your bonnet over some business or other. At one time, I recollect, you were consumed with sketching, and nothing would do but what your father and I must find you out a drawing tutor. From there, you went to painting screens, and though I do not wish to appear unkind by throwing it in your teeth, you must allow that we have upward of half a dozen unfinished screens standing idle. You then conceived an idea of writing a novel, and the entire household was put on notice to walk on tiptoe, for Miss Miranda was scribbling. However, you finished scarcely three chapters, and it all came to nothing. Forgive me, pet, but such a history compels me to doubt that embarking on im-

provements will give you any greater contentment than all
your other enterprises have done."

It was now Miranda's turn to blush. What her mother had
said was true, and though Lady Troy had spoken in all gen-
tleness, more to awaken her daughter's good sense than to
reproach her, Miranda reproached herself. She *did* have a
propensity to throw herself extravagantly into a project and
then abandon it before completion. Her enthusiasm burned
hot for a day and then cooled forever. Indeed, that was one
reason why she remained single, though she had been close
to marrying twice. In both cases, she had fallen in love,
fixed the gentleman's interest, and cried off. Obviously, she
told herself, she lacked steadiness of character.

"I did not say what I said to distress you," said her
mother. "If I believed that improvements would insure your
happiness, I should be altogether silent."

Miranda patted her mother's hands. "I do understand,
Mama. My performance has been such that one must doubt
my ability to stick with a thing. I suppose Papa will refuse
to give me a free hand with the estate, and it will be just as
well that he does, for I should very likely leave it half undone. However, I must confess, I do wish to see the abbey
made as beautiful as it ought to be."

Lady Troy stood. Dramatically she turned to face Miranda. "My pet," she said, taking a breath for courage, "if
you will agree to accompany me to London to meet Mr.
Hastings, I shall persuade your father to permit you to rip
out temples, plant flower gardens, and do anything else
with the estate that you may fancy."

Miranda's eyes sparkled, and she laughed. "Mama, you
are bribing me!"

"Yes, I am."

"And all for the sake of marrying me to Mr. Hastings!
But I fear you are putting yourself to the bother for nothing.
He is no doubt as reluctant to meet me as I am to meet him.
Who can be more tiresome than the child of one's mother's
bosom friend?"

"I must take my chances. Will you accept the bribe?"

"I do not see how it is possible. It is mortifying to be presented as a prospective bride to a gentleman one has never met."

"Oh, but you *have* met him. He accompanied Tabitha when she came to nurse me through my fever. He was six at the time; you were a year old. The two of you got on famously. You helped him win Ragstone's cap in a game of spillikins. He often held you in his lap, and one day your nurse looked up to find that he was present at your bath!"

Miranda shook her head and smiled, but this information did not make her any more desirous of meeting Mr. Hastings.

"Well, my pet, will you or will you not accept the bribe?"

Miranda considered for a moment. Then, on impulse, she kissed her mother, laughed, and replied, "Oh, very well! I shall go to London with you, but I shall not go on account of any bribe. I shall go merely to please you, and myself."

Her ladyship clapped her hands. "Oh, my dear, dear pet, I am very pleased!"

"I shall meet your Mr. Charles Hastings, Mama. We shall take each other in utter dislike, and you shall be persuaded to give over thinking of the match. Then I shall be at liberty to pursue some sensible course, such as educating myself in this matter of landscape gardening."

"Oh, I had hoped you might forget that dibble-dabble."

"I shall not forget. Although I have resolved not to tamper with Papa's grounds unless I can see the work well-done and finished within his lifetime, I am determined to glean every scrap of information I can unearth."

Resigned, Lady Troy wagged her head.

"In London, I shall visit all manner of public works, parks, and houses. Books and authorities shall be available to me that I should not find in Togbury. I shall have splendid interiors to study. Oh, Mama, thank you for taking me to London. I was blind not to see the good of it before!"

Lady Troy regarded her daughter in considerable perplexity. How was it possible, she wondered, for a sensible female to conceive more pleasure in rocks and trees than in a handsome gentleman worth twelve thousand a year?

* * *

Several days later, when the sun had ventured out timidly from behind the clouds, Mr. Farris Lloyd made good his promise. He brought Miranda *Lakes Tour* by Gilpin. If she had been permitted to, she would have commenced reading at once. Unfortunately, the gentleman remained standing in the parlor, giving no hint of any intention to leave.

"Miss Troy," he began, "will you sit a moment?"

Knowing what was coming, Miranda politely declined.

Mr. Lloyd augmented his considerable dignity by rubbing his palms together. "You must know that I have been wishing to speak with you on a matter of some particularity."

"I wish you would not."

"I ask you to hear me out."

Miranda saw that the time had come. She pressed her lips together and prayed for courage.

"Miss Troy, I come to propose marriage." A lengthy pause followed while he permitted her to calm her palpitating heart. "A union between us has everything to recommend it," he continued. "First and foremost, I believe it will add to my happiness. You are an attractive female, and I am partial to fair hair curled at the brow, such as yours. In addition, you are a lady of education and taste and would grace the table of any gentleman who was so fortunate as to win your hand."

Hoping he had said everything he had to say, Miranda glanced at him, prepared to answer, but she saw that his words had served merely as preface.

"All your sisters, both the eldest and the two younger, are married, and it behooves you now to seek a life's partner. That I should be that partner is manifestly clear when you think of the handiness of your father's lands to mine. As he has no sons, Sir Bascomb will wish to place Arundel Abbey in the care of one whom he can trust. Whom may he trust more than his own son-in-law?" He stopped to allow Miranda to agree with him.

Obligingly, she murmured, "Whom indeed?"

"And now I must broach a delicate topic, of which I should certainly say nothing except that I feel it my duty to employ all the logic at my command, and it is this, that you have now reached the age of twenty-six, at which time of life a woman may be thought to be a settled spinster. If you do not seize this opportunity to marry, you may, in all likelihood, never have another."

Had she been younger or less familiar with the gentleman's character, Miranda might have bristled at this observation. In this instance, she simply asked, "Are you finished, Mr. Lloyd?"

"Yes, except to add that I am aware of your interest in landscape gardening, and if you should wish to have a small shrubbery off the kitchen, I should allow it without reservation. My first wish would be to see you happy."

"May I speak now?"

"Please."

"Mr. Lloyd, I am flattered and touched by your wish to marry me. Although you have spoken in terms of reason and logic, I believe you also cherish certain sentiments toward me which you find difficult to express."

He colored and looked down. "That is true. I am not much in the sentimental line."

"I must tell you, I cherish those sentiments. Your friendship is a great treasure to me. And your reason and logic are irrefutable. However, I cannot accept you, and I hope that we shall be able to permit the matter to drop and not return to it again."

His brows knitted. "I suppose I ought to have spoken of love and romance. Then you might have accepted me."

"It would not have made any difference. You see, I cannot marry. My character is far too unsteady."

"That will change, once we are married."

"People do not change simply because they marry. An unsteady wife would make you very unhappy. And I think that I should also be unhappy. You see, unlike my sisters, I am an heiress."

"That ought not to prevent you from marrying. Indeed, it ought to enhance your prospects."

"Permit me to explain. My Aunt Miranda, after whom I am called, left me a great deal of money, the purpose of which, she declared, was to insure my independence. It was my aunt's opinion that a respectable young woman without money of her own had only three ways of getting her living. She must either become a governess, living obsequiously on the goodwill of her employers, remain a spinster, living obsequiously on the goodwill of her family, or embark on the career of wife, living obsequiously on the goodwill of her husband. Those, according to Aunt Miranda, were the only means by which a respectable woman could go on in the world."

"A rather cold view of the matter, I should say."

"Yes, but not entirely inaccurate, unfortunately. By bequeathing me her fortune, my aunt gave me freedom from all such constraints."

"I am not such a brute that I should constrain you."

"You might not mean to constrain me, but I should be obliged by law to turn over my fortune to you, thus relinquishing the independence Aunt Miranda wished me to have."

"Yes, but you would not find me ungenerous. I should grant you an excellent allowance."

"That is not the same as granting myself an excellent allowance."

"But a woman ought to wish to marry."

"Perhaps most women do. I do not. I am truly sorry, Mr. Lloyd. I cannot accept you."

He replied in some vexation, "Perhaps the rumors one hears in the village are true—you have set your cap at Mr. Charles Hastings and mean to go to London in order to capture his heart."

Miranda could not help laughing at this absurdity. "You must not credit gossip. Be assured, I have no interest whatever in Mr. Hastings. I only wish to please my mother by meeting him. Once I have performed that filial duty, I shall have done with the gentleman forever."

A pause followed, during which his expression went from manifest displeasure to something akin to contentment. Rubbing his palms, he answered in a manner calculated to make Miranda think that there was one advantage to being shackled to a husband, namely, that it precluded unwelcome proposals of marriage from all other gentlemen. "In that case," he said with a voice of satisfaction, "when next I see you, I shall ask you again."

THREE

Contra Dances

Hastings's Second Principle of Gaming: A gamester must be prepared to stake everything on his judgment. Though he be a man of genius in all other respects, if he suspends his own judgment in favor of the cautions and warnings of his acquaintances, he will never attain eminence. Had Adam not risked all on an apple, he would have languished in obscurity to this day.

Mr. Hastings entered the house in Queen Street and was immediately ushered into his mother's saloon. She looked up from a piece of work in her lap, arresting him with her expression. It was an expression of such luminous affection, such profound pleasure at the sight of him, that, though he was not a sentimental man by any means, it never failed to stop his pulse.

Mrs. Hastings had been widowed before her son and only child had uttered his first words. Her husband had been an excellent gentleman while he lived and was even more so in death, for he left his wife and heir handsomely situated. The most extravagant dandy could not have exhausted their combined incomes in three lifetimes. As young Charles grew to manhood, he and his mother became everything to each other, and even though he had long since reached the age where he maintained a residence of his own in Russell Square and led a life of which he made certain his mother did not know the details, still the attachment was strong. Whenever he saw that look on her face, he felt a rare tenderness. He acknowledged to himself that he would have turned out a thoroughgoing thatch-gallows if he had not had a mother who loved him out of all reason and proportion.

He went to her and kissed her cheek.

She smiled as she looked him over from top to toe, inspecting his cream breeches, hussars, dark blue coat, Valencia waistcoat, and immaculate cravat. "Charles," she said, "you are in splendid looks today."

"My tailor thanks you." Before seating himself by her, he poked the fire so that it might send an abundance of warmth her way.

"You are ready and eager for my soiree tonight, I collect."

"Soiree?"

Her expression of adoration changed to dread. "Oh, Charles, you have not forgotten!"

"I daresay, I have, but it cannot matter very much. We shall have our visit this very minute, and I shall dance such attention on you that you will not notice my absence tonight."

"Not notice! I expressly engaged you for tonight so that you might meet Lady Troy and her daughter. You took your oath you would come."

"Ah, I am very sorry. Truly, I am."

"What am I to say to them? They are expecting to see you at the soiree. They came up to Town yesterday, and I promised they would meet you. And you promised you would not fail me."

"I am afraid I am engaged elsewhere. You know I would not disappoint you if it were not important."

"Could you not put in an appearance, just for a quarter of an hour?"

"Perhaps I might meet the ladies now."

In her distress, Mrs. Hastings put her hands to her head and, though intending to arrange her cap, dislodged the hairpiece that curled under it. She now bore the appearance of a creature who looked in two directions at once. "You cannot meet them now," she mourned. "They have gone out. Miranda would not rest until she had gone to Hatchard's. The dear girl is on the hunt for books on landscape gardening. Gracious, she will be dreadfully let down when I tell her you are not to be here this evening."

Mr. Hastings straightened his mother's headdress, thinking that perhaps it would be just as well if Miss Troy were let down sooner rather than later, for she would have to learn at some point that Mr. Charles Hastings had no interest in making her his *cara esposa*. Unhappily, his mother would also be let down, and while he did not give a groat for Miss Troy's feelings, he was tender of his mother's. Therefore, he said, "I take my oath, I shall present myself to them tomorrow, and if I do not, I give you leave to scold me soundly. You don't scold me half enough, you know. It is a mother's duty to scold her children, and if you do not look to it, I shall accuse you of gross neglect."

"I wish you will be serious, Charles. I had my heart set on your coming tonight. Can you not break your engagement?"

"Impossible. I am to play piquet with Lord Everard."

"Gracious, I do not understand your devotion to such a difficult game. I have never been able to learn it. Surely he will oblige you if you request a postponement."

His jaw tightened. "Perhaps he will, but a postponement will not oblige me in the least. The only thing that will oblige me is having my revenge on the fellow."

Because he had spoken with uncharacteristic heat, Mrs. Hastings eyed him. Anxiety crept into her eyes. "Oh, Charles, you do not mean to duel, I hope."

"My dueling days are done. I have devised a much more interesting manner of giving the fellow his comeuppance."

Mrs. Hastings sighed in relief. Then, as she recollected that her efforts to bring her friend's daughter together with her son had all gone for nothing, she sighed again.

Those sighs were not lost on Mr. Hastings. Although he did not relish the prospect of meeting Miss Troy, he did not like to see his mother unhappy. Even more, he did not like to be the cause of her unhappiness. "Mother," he said, "I shall do what I may to dispatch my business with Everard by midnight. Then I shall present myself at your soiree and put myself entirely at your disposal."

Mrs. Hastings shook her head woefully. "You will become engrossed in your game and forget your promise."

"I'll wager anything you like that I shall not forget."

"Poof! You never do a thing but what you wager on it."

"Ah, frightened of me, are you? You are afraid I shall win, and I *shall* win. I always do."

She could not help laughing. "I'm not afraid of any such thing. If you win, then I shall win, for then you shall meet the dearest girl in all the world and she shall meet the darlingest boy in all the world."

"Do not attempt to disarm me with compliments, Mother. What is your bet?"

Mrs. Hastings gathered all her resolution and said, "I shall wager six buttons."

"Done! But I warn you, I mean to win all your buttons one day, and then, being button poor, you shall be compelled to play for ha'pence!"

She smiled fondly and rearranged one of his chestnut curls that had fallen onto his forehead. "You may take all my buttons, Charles dear, with my blessing."

As always, he could not find words to answer her loving look. Therefore, he raised her hand to his lips and kissed it.

No sooner did Mr. Hastings seat himself opposite Everard at the table than a parade of onlookers entered. They lounged here and there about the crimson parlor as though they had wandered in purely by chance. Indeed, if they had not seemed so bored and shambling, they might almost have been described as curious. The twenty or so gentlemen presented a lively spectrum of London manhood—ranging from the short and squinty to the tall and titled—and they all had one thing in common, namely, that they were members of either Brooks', Boodle's, or both. That fact was not lost on Everard, Mr. Hastings saw, for the man turned a trifle green. Mr. Hastings opened a new deck, shuffled, and repressed a smile.

Just as Everard reached for his deck, Felix DeWitt entered. On his arm, was Everard's mistress, Mrs. Buxleigh, who basked in the appreciative gazes of the gentlemen.

Felix brought her a cushioned chair so that she might sit between the two cardplayers. She arranged her skirts prettily and smiled at the gentlemen.

"What, has the whole world come to witness a paltry game of piquet?" Everard snapped. He directed his words principally at Mrs. Buxleigh, clearly with the intention of chasing her from the parlor, but she was oblivious to him. As the only female present, she was being accorded singular attention, and she had evidently made up her mind to enjoy it.

"I hope you do not mind these fellows, Everard," said Mr. Hastings. "Rumor has it that you mean to take everything from me that you failed to win last time we met. Having lost to me in the past, these good gentlemen all wish to see me go down to ignominious defeat at your hands. As to Mrs. Buxleigh, I had hoped she might bring me luck. To hold my own with you, I shall need all the luck I can muster."

With this explanation, Everard was forced to be content. He could not very well turn his brother club members out of the room, especially as their presence might signify that they had heard of his cheat and had come to see him exposed. Nor could he decline to have his mistress present without exciting suspicion. Mr. Hastings read the uneasiness on his lordship's face and felt that, thus far, his plan had been carried out to perfection.

To add spice to the stew, he rose, came behind Mrs. Buxleigh's chair, and leaned down to whisper something in her ear that impelled her to give out with a peal of laughter. Lord Everard endeavored to stare her into silence, if not absence, but he looked in vain. The lady raised her hand so that Mr. Hastings might kiss it. Mr. Hastings was only too happy to oblige.

He seated himself and invited Everard to cut the cards. Their eyes met for an instant, and Mr. Hastings could see that his lordship did not intend to surrender easily. He began to think he ought to have promised his mother to make his appearance at two o'clock instead of midnight.

The discarding complete, the declaring began, and it was

not long before Mr. Hastings began to see Everard's scheme. He would lose, lose seriously, and thus, nobody could accuse him of cheating. But Mr. Hastings had prepared for this eventuality. He took the rubber, took his lordship's money, and observed, "I vow, your luck is out tonight, Everard. It is too bad."

Mrs. Buxleigh favored his lordship with a pitying glance, then turned her smiles on Mr. Hastings.

He smiled back. Rising, he went to fetch a glass of wine from a waiter. Pausing en route, he leaned over the lady's shoulder so that his cheek came close to hers. He inquired silkily, "Do you care for wine?"

"Yes," she said, meeting his eyes. "I am parched."

Mr. Hastings gave her a look that said that if he had his way, she would never find even her most paltry desires of the flesh so abominably neglected. When he set the wine down in front of her, she raised her hand to him. Mr. Hastings kissed it and glanced up to gauge the effect of this flirtation on Everard. Seeing that his lordship was now yellow, Mr. Hastings concluded that his plan was going forward well, so well in fact that he would be able to purchase the new watch he had promised himself the very next day.

Felix took him aside to whisper in alarm, "Gad, Hastings, what do you mean by tweaking Everard? Do you wish to wake up tomorrow to find yourself shot through the head? You may have just signed your death warrant."

Mr. Hastings winked at him. "You fret too much. You will ruin your digestion."

"You don't know what Everard is capable of."

"He does not know what I am capable of." On that, Mr. Hastings took his seat.

After twenty minutes of play, Everard had lost seven hundred guineas. Mr. Hastings now pressed his advantage cruelly. His purpose was to tempt Everard to use his ring. Such a man could not endure to go on losing forever, he knew, not when winning was so easily within reach. After another quarter hour of play, his lordship doubled his losses.

Just as Mr. Hastings had calculated, Everard did at last

resort to the shiner. As soon as he did, his luck took a turn for the better. Foolishly, he gloated over his victory. Thus he did not notice how ominously still the room had grown. The spectators, who had conversed lightly among themselves when Mr. Hastings was winning, now comported themselves as though they oversaw a coffin. The air was thick and heavy.

Oblivious, Everard took all the tricks.

Mr. Hastings drawled his congratulations. "There now, gentlemen, you see how it stands. Lord Everard casts me quite in the shade with his skill."

His lordship laughed and took a long drink of wine. Nobody else laughed; nobody else drank.

Mr. Hastings offered the deck to Everard to cut. When he reached for the cards, Mr. Hastings stopped his hand, saying, "I vow, that is a devilishly handsome ring you are wearing."

Everard met his eyes. Judging by the whiteness of his color, his lordship knew his game was up. He glanced around the room and encountered severe looks in every corner.

"Yes, a devilishly handsome ring," Mr. Hastings said. "I believe I should like to have it."

"It is not for sale!" Everard said. He half rose from his chair.

"What a pity. May I see it?"

With so many eyes fixed on him, Everard did not dare refuse. Slowly, he removed the ring and handed it over.

Mr. Hastings slid it onto his finger. Holding out his hand for everybody to admire, he said, "I shall give you five hundred for it, Everard. That is twice what it is worth, I expect."

"It is not for sale!"

Mr. Hastings leaned across the table, coming close to his opponent's nose. "Then we shall play for it," he said, in a steel tone. Everard seemed on the point of refusing, but, after assessing the glow in Mr. Hastings's eye, he evidently thought better of it. Play resumed. The parlor was now so quiet that a delicate burp from Felix seemed to echo like a thunderclap.

To nobody's surprise, Mr. Hastings won the rubber and the ring. Everard stood stiffly. His face had lost all color. His lips pressed thin. He burned with such fury that Felix, in considerable anxiety, said to him, "Gad, Everard, let me fill you a glass and plate. Mrs. Stout has served up partridge tonight. Let us go and have a bite."

Everard ignored him. He stared at Mrs. Buxleigh, whose simperings were all for his opponent. Mr. Hastings went to her side and begged to be allowed to wait upon her at her lodgings the following day. She raised her hand so that he might kiss it as he had done so gallantly before. Though he took the graceful hand, he did not bring it to his lips this time. Instead, he pressed it to his heart. Then he leaned over and, in the bareness between the end of her glove and the beginning of her sleeve, he pressed his lips. The lady's skin grew rosy, and she trembled. Everard trembled as well, though not for the same reason.

Abruptly, Mr. Hastings stood upright and consulted his watch. It was nearly twelve, but if he made haste, he would arrive in Queen Street before the final stroke of midnight. Soon he would have a new watch, he thought, with figures of dancing maidens in place of numerals.

"I take my leave, dear lady, good gentlemen," he said expansively. He performed a smart bow and made for the door.

Everard grasped him by the coat. All the gentlemen moved forward. Seeing their readiness to come to Mr. Hastings's aid, his lordship let go. Restraining himself, he said, "Hastings, you cannot go until I have had an opportunity to win back my ring."

Unperturbed, Mr. Hastings smoothed his lapels. "I should like nothing better, old fellow, but I am promised to my mother. She has invited a young lady to her house expressly to meet and marry me. Truth to tell, I have no wish to do either, but one must not fail to keep an engagement with one's mater."

He kept his eye fixed on Everard until the man lowered

his glance and stood aside. After saying farewell to Mrs. Buxleigh in a voice of satin, Mr. Hastings took himself off, well pleased with his new ring and the prospect of collecting six buttons.

Mr. Hastings was able to slip inside the drawing room unnoticed. It was filled with the sound of a soprano accompanying herself on the harp. The listeners stood in uncharacteristic silence, genuinely enchanted by the performance. The singer's voice was so delicate that had they not given her their full attention, they would scarcely have heard a note. He peered between the heads of a pair of smart lieutenants and saw a young lady he did not recognize sitting at the harp between two tall, draped windows. The fireplace flickered behind, giving her white gown an ethereal air. As the illumination alternately shone and waned, the soft lines of her figure and the curve off her cheek were enhanced.

Because he recognized all the other guests, Mr. Hastings deduced that here before him was the young lady whose acquaintance he had so wished to avoid. *Well, at least she is not thin and pinched*, he said to himself once he had assessed her figure and carriage. After another moment, he allowed that though her voice was slight, she had a fair taste in music. After still another moment, during which he fancied he saw intelligence in the young lady's face, he considered that it might not be such dire punishment after all to make her acquaintance.

The instant she stopped playing and rose modestly to accept the applause that went up, Mr. Hastings was greeted by his mother. "You have won the bet, my dearest Charles," she said warmly. "You shall have your buttons before you leave us tonight. But first you shall have the pleasure of meeting the daughter of my dearest friend."

In another moment, he was kissing the hand of Lady Troy, who was clearly fretting. The poor creature looked from his face to her daughter's with much apprehension. Miss Troy, however, was cool as a cucumber. She said all that was required during the introduction without a hint of consciousness. Mr. Hastings liked her savoir faire.

"I was fortunate enough to arrive in time to hear you sing and play, Miss Troy," he said. "You are most accomplished, it seems."

"And you are most kind," she replied. "Had I practiced as I ought, I should have sung with more force. But I did not stick to my lessons, and you have heard the result."

She was sensible, too, he noted, refusing to let her head be turned by compliments. He begged to be allowed to show her the portrait of his father, which hung on the other side of the room. She put her hand on his arm, permitting him to lead her away from the two anxious mothers.

Miss Troy walked well, he noticed. She sang well, played well, spoke well, and looked well. He had expected—nay, he had hoped—she would prove dreadful in every way. Her failure to do so presented him with a difficulty. He did not wish to like her and thus raise the hopes of his mother and hers. The merest suggestion that he found her tolerable would bring down all sorts of tender coercion on both their heads. For Miss Troy's sake as well as his own, he must find her insupportable, and she must return the compliment.

They stood before the portrait in silence. He turned to observe her as she gazed up at the man whose elegant form graced the wall. Her profile was far from perfect, but it was fine. Her fair hair was too thick and frothy to be fashionable, but it was striking. Her bodice was too high, covering more of her bosom than was stylish, but it was more captivating than if it had been entirely bare. Despite her many imperfections, Miss Troy was—he searched for the word and found it at last—an *interesting* young woman.

"Your father was very amiable," she said.

"Was he? I do not recollect. He died before I was out of leading strings."

"Oh, yes, he was amiable. It is plainly written in his expression."

"You are a reader of expressions, I collect."

"There was a time, you see, when I studied physiognomy. I learned to read the character and temperament behind a face."

He smiled. "Indeed? And what do you read in that lady's face?" With the tilt of his head, he indicated a smartly turned out young woman who was engaged in conversation with several gentlemen.

Miranda looked for a time and then said, "Oh, dear!"

"I quite agree. Caro Lamb is certainly a lady to be exclaimed over. You have done well thus far. Perhaps you will venture to read my character."

She glanced at him sharply, then looked away. "I ought not to have boasted of my skill. I never applied myself when I studied physiognomy. I am certain I have forgotten my lessons."

"Must I die and hang on a wall before you will agree to look at me?" With a finger under her chin, he turned her to face him. "Hanging on the wall is such a bore," he said. "Will you do me the honor, of telling me what you see while I am still alive to hear it?"

She blushed. He had made her uneasy, he saw, and now he must press his advantage cruelly, just as he had done earlier that night with Everard. In this case, it was easier said than done, however, for he rather liked her. She was not flirting with him. She did not seem to regard him as an object to be won. And she was as fragrant as a breath of lavender.

The devil with her fragrance, he cautioned himself. He dared not like her. If he was to spare his mother disillusionment, and Miss Troy a broken heart, it was necessary that he detest her at the outset and that she detest him in equal measure.

"What do you see?" he said again, for she had studied him for a time without saying a word. "Say nothing of my handsome features, if you please. One grows weary of hearing oneself continually praised."

To his surprise, she laughed. She appeared to take his deliberate boast as a witticism. He must try again.

"Am I a devil or an angel? Come, come, Miss Troy, do not keep me in suspense."

She took a breath and said, "You have just won a victory and are wonderfully pleased with yourself."

Impressed, he said, "You have hit it exactly. Apparently you remember your lessons very well. What sort of victory have I won? Can you guess?"

When she paused to consider, he was struck by her thoughtfulness. She evidently cared less for banter than for an intelligent reply. He was not used to having his questions taken so seriously. What he was accustomed to was the titter and vapidness of ladies intent on snaring him. But Miss Troy was not just out of the schoolroom. She knew something of life. He was sure of it now—she was more interesting than any young lady he had met in some time.

"As I make it out," she said, "it was not a conquest in love."

"You have hit the mark again. No, it was far better than a conquest in love."

She studied him as though curious. Her head was slightly tilted. The eyes that searched his were richly brown. He made a mental wager that he would kiss those eyes before the week was out. Then he caught himself. That was precisely the sort of thinking he must avoid. If he was not careful, he would end by giving the appearance of admiring the lady, and although he did admire her, he must not allow anybody to guess it, especially not his mother, and more especially not *her* mother, and most especially of all, not Miss Troy herself.

Abruptly, he said, "I cannot tell you how delighted I was to hear that my mother meant to introduce us."

She smiled with a skepticism he could not help but find amusing. The lady evidently had no use for fustian.

"But I feel it my duty to apprise you at once, before you permit yourself to fall head over ears in love with me, that I do not intend to marry you. I know you and your mother will be disappointed and feel you have come all the way up to London to no purpose, but I trust you will bear up. If you like, I shall go and ask my acquaintance whether any of them will consider a match with you. As to myself, I have far too many engagements this Season to think of marriage."

To his gratification, her jaw fell. Her eyes blazed. If they had not stood in a drawing room with a blue-clouded ceiling, a brass chandelier, a scattering of rose-brocade sofas, and a horde of fashionable guests, she might well have hit him.

He grinned, so that in case she was wondering whether she had truly heard such an arrogant speech, she would be forced to believe it. Then he watched to see what she would do.

He honored the effort she made to collect herself and muster the words to answer him. Once again, her brown eyes inspired him to think of taking her cheeks in his hands and brushing his lips lightly against her brow.

"Mr. Hastings," she said, her voice shaking, "I thank you. If you had proved less impudent, less conceited, less detestable, I should have regretted the necessity of thwarting our mothers' plan. As it stands, you have made my way easy, and I may part from you not only without regret but with joy at the thought of never setting eyes on you again." On that, she turned her back on him and walked away.

He observed her with the concentration he generally reserved for piquet. She moved with an air. Her gauzy white gown clung to her legs. Her delectable shoulders were resolutely straight, and she did not look back.

Having succeeded in driving off the lady, Mr. Hastings ought now to have exulted. Instead he felt torn. Two choices lay before him: he might continue to stand where he was and watch her recede into the shadows until she disappeared from his view and his life, or he could follow his inclination and go after her.

FOUR

From Bad to Worse

Here I begin my notes on landscape gardening for the
purpose of devising a plan to improve the grounds of
Arundel Abbey. I shall also include anything of value
which will result in modernization of the interior of
the house. Mama and I went to Hatchard's today and
purchased sundry books relating to these subjects.
The authors appear to agree that lines, angles,
squares, and rectangles have no place in nature and
therefore are unnatural in the landscape. If so, then
the shrubbery at the abbey is formed with a far too
unyielding regularity. Not a hedge can be found that
has not been clipped and contorted instead of
encouraged to grow according to nature's dictates.
Curve and flow are wanting to add softness to the
views. I do not know what precisely is to be done to
alleviate this geometric rigidity, and I am not certain
that anything ought to be done. Can lines, angles, and
the rest really constitute such an evil as to require
total eradication? Surely there is room for variety on
an estate the size of Arundel Abbey. As I have not
yet tired of asking such questions, I expect I shall
persevere in my study. If only I were not obliged to
meet Mr. Hastings tonight and smile!

Miranda would have thrown politeness to the four winds
and quit the drawing room at once had not her mother intercepted her. She turned on the poor lady with an expression
of fury. "Odious man!" she said.

"Oh, you cannot mean Mr. Hastings! He is said to be all
that is charming."

"He is all that is horrid. He informed me, if you please,

that he was too occupied with engagements to think of marrying at present but would be happy to ask his acquaintance if any of them would be willing to have me, as though I required his charity!"

"Perhaps he only meant to be polite," said her ladyship lamely.

"As I anticipated, he had no more desire to meet me than I had to meet him."

"Oh, my pet, I am so sorry, but I beg you, do not mind his being odious. That is an excellent sign. It means he admires you."

"Surely if he admired me, he would not go out of his way to offend me."

"But that is where you are wrong. Gentlemen never take the trouble to offend a lady unless they admire her."

"I do not care a farthing whether he admires me or not. The fact is I do not admire him. I shall make my excuses to Mrs. Hastings and go to bed."

"You cannot retire so early! It will look very odd. Tabitha will be mortified."

At that moment, Mrs. Hastings came to them. The expression of distress she wore showed that she knew something was amiss. "Dear Miranda, what is the matter?"

Her mother answered for her, saying, "My poor dear pet is feeling a trifle down-pin."

"Gracious! Charles will be distraught. He is always so anxious whenever I am out of sorts."

Miranda remarked with considerable irony, "In my case, I daresay he will make a rapid recovery."

"Let us say nothing to him," said his mother in a conspiratorial voice. "There is no use troubling the dear boy."

"It will give me the greatest pleasure to say nothing to him," Miranda replied, but when she saw her mother reprimanding her with her eyes, she regretted her sarcasm. After all, it was the son who deserved punishment, not the mother. Mrs. Hastings had been all kindness. In a gentle voice, Miranda added, "I beg you to excuse me. I must say good night and thank you with all my heart for your concern."

Sympathetically, Mrs. Hastings said, "I expect you are feeling the effects of the heat and closeness in the room. If you rest a quarter hour, perhaps you shall feel well enough to rejoin us. The servant will light the way to your bed-chamber." Miranda was then led from the drawing room, along the carved staircase to the floor above.

Her bedchamber and dressing room were situated at the back of the house. When they entered, the servant lit a candelabrum and tiptoed from the room. Miranda opened the window. The night air was delightfully chill; the breeze cooled her neck. Nevertheless, her temper remained hot. She looked forward to forgetting the insupportable Mr. Hastings and losing herself in the books she had purchased that morning. Though Mrs. Hastings had encouraged her to return to the drawing room later, she had no intention of leaving her studies and risking another meeting with her son.

Taking up Walpole's *History of Modern Taste in Gardening* and her journal, she reclined on the chaise longue. She could not help admiring its scrolled and tassled top and scarlet-velvet cushion. Arundel Abbey boasted nothing so delightful as a chaise longue. Indeed, the abbey was as formal as a military review. Mrs. Hastings had done her house in the fashion that was called "informal." Furniture was not lined against the wall in rigid formation; rather it was arranged here and there in an easy manner. The style was neat, elegant, and comfortable. It was everything Mr. Repton called for. Miranda wrote the word *informal* in her journal and underlined it three times.

Then her eyes fell on what she had written earlier in the day, a sentence denoting her dread of meeting Mr. Hastings. "Oh, my prophetic soul!" she said aloud.

Their brief conversation had turned out more disastrous than anybody could have imagined. How was it possible for a man with such a charming, boyish face, such an innocent, sweet expression, to turn out such a popinjay? His complexion must be the envy of every female in London. Rarely had such long and luxurious lashes been seen on a man. His smile, when it was not a vile smirk, was enchanting. And yet he was so conceited as to efface these manifold attractions altogether. He might as well have been a gargoyle. With such thoughts swimming in her head, she fell asleep.

After a time, a series of shouts startled her awake. Perhaps, she thought, she had dreamt them. They had been rough, angry, violent, like voices out of a nightmare. She yawned and shook herself. Suddenly, she froze as she heard the shouts again.

Instantly she knelt on the chaise longue and looked out the window. She saw three men moving among the shadows in the mews below. There was only enough moonlight to see them in silhouette, but one thing was clearly visible—they were beating a fourth, beating him mercilessly. She gasped as they hammered him with their fists. She gasped again as she saw him rise and give battle, despite his being outnumbered, outweighed, and outpummeled. By rights, he ought to have been lying senseless on the ground, but he was so wiry, so agile, so determined, that he waged a splendid fight. In defiance of all logic, he contrived to fling one of his attackers onto his back, howling. Miranda wondered that the noise they made did not rouse everybody in the house. Then she recollected the party going forward in the drawing room. The guests made far too much noise to allow any other sound to penetrate. The servants of the guests and Mrs. Hastings's stable hands ought to have been close enough to hear, but perhaps they could not distinguish the cries and grunts of the four men from the usual sounds of the city. In any case, nobody came to the poor gentleman's aid.

The aforesaid poor gentleman, meanwhile, continued to elude his attackers and deal them sound blows at every opportunity. The one who had fallen stood and, after some searching, located a hefty stick. Miranda went rigid with fear as he came behind his quarry and poised to strike. He brought the stick down on the man's head in what appeared to Miranda to be a crushing blow. It sounded with a crack. Miranda saw him fall to his knees, dazed, and the attackers gathered round him to finish their work.

To her surprise, she heard herself cry out. The three men turned and looked up at the window. "Stop that at once!" she commanded. "You are behaving like a collection of schoolboys!"

The men looked at one another. She could scarcely make out their expressions in the dim light. It did seem, however, as though they were confused. In another moment, they recovered their wits and, at the sound of a grunt from one of them, took themselves off at a run, disappearing into the night.

The fourth gentleman remained, still kneeling. Slowly, unsteadily, he got to his feet, gingerly touching his head wound. He looked up, then performed a graceful bow. "I thank you, Miss Troy," he said grandly. "If I had not lost my hat, I should not hesitate to tip it to you." On that, he collapsed in a dead heap.

It took Miranda several minutes to locate a door that exited onto the mews, time in which she feared, the gentleman had very likely breathed his last. She had flown from her bedchamber so quickly that she had not taken her shawl. Thus, when she opened the door that led up from the kitchen to the back entrance, she was greeted with a blast of cold night air. Stopped momentarily, she remembered something she had been too anxious to absorb earlier—the gentleman had addressed her by name. She would have chewed over this mystery if she had not felt obliged to put all chewing aside and tend to the dying gentleman, who lay on his side, his arm thrown over his face. So still was he that she felt certain he was done for.

She knelt and felt for his heartbeat. Either he had none or it was so weak as to seem nonexistent. Gently, she rolled him onto his back and placed her ear against his chest. Still she could not tell whether he was alive or dead. She sat up and decided to inspect his head. As soon as she removed the arm that still covered it, she gave out with a cry. The face was smudged with dirt, streaked with blood, and swollen with bruises, but it was unmistakably the face of Mr. Charles Hastings. It shone in the moonlight with eerie serenity, the serenity of the dead. She put her fist to her lips, trying to comprehend the fact that the gentleman who had not an hour ago affronted her beyond speaking had now received his punishment a hundredfold.

But this was not the time for philosophizing on the nature of divine justice. The blow she had witnessed must have wounded him dreadfully. Moving a little closer, she inspected his head. The moonlight did not permit her to see all that she suspected was there, but she saw enough to cringe. The gentleman rested in a small pool of blood that streamed from a large, matted clump of hair. Without pausing, she tore a length from the hem of her shift with the intention of winding it around his head. She wished she knew whether it was good or bad that he remained unconscious. When she had torn enough cloth to serve as a bandage, Miranda contemplated the gentleman's face. It was still handsome, she noted, despite the blows it had been dealt, despite the despicable manners of the man who wore it. She started when she felt him grasp her hand.

"I liked it when you put your hand on my heart," he said with an effort. "Would you be so kind as to do it again?"

With an exclamation, she snapped, "If you stop my hand, sir, I cannot wrap your wound."

Slowly, he pulled his hand away. His eyes caught the moonlight, and he smiled.

"I thought you were dead," she said.

"You mean you *wished* I were dead."

"You are not only arrogant and rude, Mr. Hastings, you are deceitful as well. You merely pretended to be senseless."

"Yes, yes, I'm a bounder and all that. I should like nothing better than to lie here all night and review with you the myriad defects of my character. At the moment, however, I have the devil of a headache."

"One of your adversaries hit you with a stick. No doubt you offered to match him up with one of your acquaintance, and he took offense!"

"I never saw the fellow before in my life. I never saw

any of them before." Though his tone was cavalier, his voice was unsteady.

Miranda suspected that he was in very great pain. He could not have sustained such a blow without feeling severe effects. Unable to help herself, she scolded gently, "You ought to have given them your purse and let them go. It was very foolish of you to fight them for the sake of a few crowns." She wondered whether wrapping the bandage around his head would cause him insupportable discomfort.

He tried to raise his head a little but failed. Closing his eyes, he said, "They were not attempting to rob me. They meant to beat me within an inch of my life, and they appear to have succeeded."

"Why would they beat you if they did not mean to rob you?"

He looked up into her eyes. "They were hired to take revenge."

She returned his steady gaze. "I did not hire them, if that is what you are thinking."

He laughed. "I absolve you entirely of blame, Miss Troy. I am well aware that somebody got to me before you did."

"Who?"

"It is a long tale, and I expect I shall faint before it can be told."

Alarmed, Miranda replied, "Please do not try to explain, Mr. Hastings. And do not faint if you can help it. I shall go and fetch the surgeon. I have stayed too long as it is." She would have risen, but he grasped her hand.

"No," he said. "Do not fetch the surgeon."

Responding to his urgency, she knelt again. "You are seriously wounded."

"If you fetch the surgeon, my mother will learn of my mishap. It will give her palpitations, fidgets, and all manner of flutter. I beg you, spare my poor mother."

"But you may well die if you are not properly attended to."

"Exactly so, and then you shall have your revenge. On my side, I shall be happy to be able at last to gratify you."

"A pretty opinion you have of me to think I would wish

to see you dead, no matter how much you might deserve it. I shall fetch the surgeon. Let go of my hand, if you please."

"No."

"You are an obstinate man, Mr. Hastings."

"There is no end to my depravity. But, Miss Troy, hear me out. You have a mother. Do you protect her from evil tidings, or do you confide everything to her?"

"Of course I do not confide everything to her. She would fret day and night if I did. But this case is different. Your life is at stake."

"My life is at stake if you tell. If you keep mum, I shall be safe."

"I do not understand."

"It is quite simple. If no word is heard of me, the gentleman who hired the attackers will think he has driven me into hiding or to my grave. I daresay, either one would satisfy him sufficiently to wash his hands of me and go his merry way. If, on the other hand, he learns that a surgeon has patched me up, he will send his henchman after me once more, this time to send me packing for good. I should like some time to recover from my present wounds before I meet with those three jolly fellows again, at which time I shall have the pleasure of thwacking each one soundly and sending them off to their employer with black eyes and bloody noses and a polite message to the effect that I mean to come after him."

Angry that he devoted more thought to his revenge than his injuries, Miranda said, "I do believe you find this all vastly entertaining."

He glanced at her with a gleam. "Not half so entertaining as being nursed by a charming young lady who would like to rip my heart out. Reach into my pocket, if you please."

Reluctant to touch him any more than she was absolutely obliged to, she said, "I hope you do not carry a pistol."

"Not a pistol, a flask."

"Oh." In a breast pocket of his coat, she located a small, flat silver flask and opened it. He took a drink, then instructed, "Pour it on the wound."

"It will smart," she said.

"But not as much as you would like."

Indignant that he should think her so lacking in compassion, she poured. If he winced, she could not detect it, but it did seem to her, even in the dark, that he grew even more pale than before.

He took the flask from her and drank again. "You may put it away, if you please."

"You may put it away yourself."

He smiled and complied, saying, "It is ever so much more pleasant when you do it."

Unwilling to banter further, Miranda said, "If you will keep still a moment, I shall wrap this bandage around your head."

"You are a remarkable young lady," he said. "You go about with bandages on your person, in case you should come upon a victim of attack. Such foresight, Miss Troy."

"It was my shift, my new linen shift," she answered and wound the cloth roughly, half hoping he would be induced by the pain to keep still.

Keep still he did, gazing at her all the while. When the bandage was wrapped and tied, she helped him to his feet. He swayed a little, and rested against her, putting his arm around her waist to steady himself. The suspicious look she gave him went unanswered. A spell of vertigo seemed to have genuinely gripped him. He was pale. From his expression, she judged he was nauseated.

"How do you expect to walk to your house in this condition?" she asked. "I suppose I shall have to summon you a hack."

He rested the side of his head against the wall of the house. "My dear Miss Troy, if I was unwilling to have the surgeon fetched, you cannot actually think I shall permit you to hire a hack. Apart from my unwillingness to bleed all over the driver's livelihood, it would be foolish of me to return to Russell Square. My enemy—or his henchmen—will be lying in wait for me. Indeed, I suspect they will be lurking about every place I am known to frequent."

"But where will you go? Suppose your wound festers?

Suppose it kills you?" Looking up into his face, she bit her lip. She was certain he was in great pain.

His eyes closed, he smiled. "I assure you, Miss Troy, I am not going to die on your hands. That would not only prove me ungrateful in the extreme, but it would give you far too much gratification."

Miranda, who scarcely knew what to do with the man, ignored this sally and, taking him around the waist, encouraged him to walk a few paces. His step was tentative, and he continued to suffer dizziness. She held his arm. No smirk appeared on his lips, no gleam in his eye. The struggle to walk was sincere, she saw, and again she mentioned the surgeon. This roused him to a more energetic pace.

"You are dreadfully unsteady, Mr. Hastings. I do not see how you can possibly get yourself to safety under these circumstances."

"I shall do very well, thank you."

"I am relieved to hear it. I expect you have an acquaintance nearby who will assist you."

"Yes, in a manner of speaking."

"If you will give me the direction, I shall send a note without delay."

"That will not be necessary."

"How will your acquaintance come to your rescue if you do not inform him of your circumstances?"

"You are my rescuer, Miss Troy."

"Be serious, Mr. Hastings. We cannot stand in this mews all night. It is cold, and you must have that wound dressed as soon as possible."

"It appears we agree on something."

"Excellent. Then let us go at once."

"Yes, indeed, let us go at once."

She steered him toward the street, but he resisted.

"What is the matter, Mr. Hastings?"

"We are going in the wrong direction."

"Why, what do you mean?"

"Unless I am more gravely wounded than I thought, this is not the way to your bedchamber."

Her start was so violent that he nearly fell. Luckily, he

had the wit to put his arms about her and steady himself. She extricated herself from his hold. Glaring at him, she said, "That is a vile trick, Mr. Hastings. Have you no scruples?"

"It was not a trick. I merely thought to spend the night in your bedchamber, just long enough to recover my equilibrium, you see, and then I should be on my way and trouble you no more."

"Whatever gave you the delusion that I should invite you to my bedchamber?"

He raised his finger, opened his mouth to reply, and could not. She saw him sway precariously. He seemed on the point of collapsing at her feet. She knew he was not above pretending to be dizzy merely in order to bamboozle her, but she could not help herself. It was her moral obligation to assist someone in distress, even someone as provoking as Mr. Hastings. She steadied him with her arms.

After swallowing hard, he said, "You are quite right, of course, Miss Troy. Permitting a gentleman to enter your bedchamber, though he be on the brink of death and without any other recourse, might kick up a scandal. Your first thought must be to protect your reputation."

On that, he nodded his head in an approximation of a bow and began to walk toward the entrance to the mews. She watched in horror. His gait was uneven. Each step seemed as if it would be his last.

When his knees gave way momentarily, she could bear it no more. Running to his side, she took hold of him before he fell.

"Very well, Mr. Hastings," she said, breathlessly, "you may spend the night in my bedchamber. But in the morning, you must be gone."

"Yes, of course." He scarcely seemed to know what he was agreeing to.

"I shall attend to your wound. You may sleep in my dressing room."

He was silent. She could not tell whether he comprehended. However, it did not matter whether he did or not. She had made up her mind, and now she must contrive to get him into the house, up the stairs, and along the corridor to her chamber—and she must accomplish it all without being seen.

Taking a deep breath, she directed him toward the door. They walked slowly. Once they had got inside the house, he said to her, in a rasp, "Do not be afraid. I shall not faint. If I bloodied my mother's rugs, I should never forgive myself."

"Do be still. We shall rouse the servants." Seeing that the back stairs were empty, she helped him make the climb.

"I must talk, Miss Troy. If I do not keep myself awake with the sound of my own foolery, I shall in all likelihood faint on the spot."

"Then by all means talk, sir. But please to do it quietly."

They attained the first landing. The sounds of animated voices drifted toward them from the drawing room. Miranda steered him along the stairs to the second landing, which they attained with considerable effort. She opened the door and peeked into the corridor. It was as empty as a newly dug grave. With a bracing tug on his arm, she indicated that they must now run, or rather *limp*, the final gauntlet.

"If we should happen upon a servant," he said, "you shall explain that I got very drunk and made amorous advances, whereupon you hit me over the head, as I well deserved." Though he spoke lightly, his voice was hoarse.

He must not faint now, she thought, *not when we have come so close*. To keep him talking, Miranda asked, "What did I hit you with?"

"A vase."

"Was it Sevres?"

"It was a piece of crockery from Mr. Wedgwood's warehouse. It cost eight shillings, which you have promised to repay." It was now so difficult for him to walk that he leaned on her heavily.

They approached the door of her bedchamber. "It appears," she said, adopting his line of nonsense, "that I am in your debt for eight shillings."

He looked at her solemnly with a clouded gaze. "Indeed, you are in my debt. I have permitted you to save my skin. I have given you the opportunity to behave in a manner that is noble, courageous, and good. I do not know how you can ever repay me."

She opened the door, and they went in. "I shall be well paid when you are well and gone."

The candles had burned low. The room flickered with shadows and dancing flame. A cold breeze blew through the still open window. In the center of the room stood the bed, with its shapely posts, draped canopy, and soft counterpane. She looked at it; then, confounded, she looked away.

Collecting her wits, Miranda led him to a chair and eased him into it. She heard him suppress a moan and, in spite of herself, whispered to him kindly, "I shall just ready the dressing room for you. Then you shall be able to rest." It amazed her to feel such sympathy for a man she so thoroughly disliked.

Hurrying, she closed the window, then lit a candle and went into the dressing room. There she folded down the sheets on the small cot that stood against the wall, and poured water from the pitcher into the basin. She brought the basin into the bedchamber, prepared to dress Mr. Hastings's wound, but when she looked at the chair in which she had placed him not an instant before, she found it empty. He had gone.

A confusion of feelings gripped her. She was relieved and disappointed at the same time, relieved that she was no longer answerable for his well-being, disappointed that he had not said good-bye or told her where he meant to go. Perhaps he had taken her concerns about her reputation to heart and, to spare her, had stolen away into the night.

With a sigh, she set down the basin and sank into the chair he had vacated. In the quiet of the next half minute, she acknowledged that she was more than a little troubled. She imagined taking up the *Morning Chronicle* in the next day or two and reading that Mr. Charles Hastings had been waylaid by unknown assailants and found dead on The Strand, and she knew how she would feel. She would feel responsible. She would feel that she ought to have shown more willingness to assist him. She ought to have given over all thoughts of her reputation and devoted herself to saving another human creature from harm. If Mr. Hastings came to a bad end, she thought, it would be her fault.

Sighing again, she rose and rang for the maid so that she might undress. When the girl did not appear, she assumed she had fallen asleep belowstairs. Daisy was only sixteen and had not been a lady's maid very long. Miranda pitied her and took care to inconvenience her as little as possible. Unwilling to waken her, Miranda endeavored to undress herself. She spent considerable time tussling with shoulder pins and back buttons and several times changed her mind as to waking Daisy. But when at last she stepped out of her gown and inspected the remnants of her shredded shift, she was glad she had not called the girl. What would poor Daisy have thought of the wreckage of her undergarments?

She went to the wardrobe to put away the gown when something struck her as not quite right. For a moment, she stood with her head to one side, trying to make out what it was that had caught her eye. Then, as a feeling of ominousness overcame her, she turned slowly to the bed.

Lying across it was Mr. Hastings, with his feet stretching over the side. He had removed his coat and spread it under his head, as though he meant to protect the counterpane from bloodstains. His legs sprawled wide. His arms were spread almost the entire length of the bed. His face was turned, so that she could only see his handsome profile. Chestnut curls had fallen onto his forehead.

He might be pretending, she thought. If anybody was capable of perpetrating an abominable hoax, it was Mr. Hastings. But her instinct told her that he was sleeping. His position was so vulnerable that he must be sleeping. He would not have left himself so defenseless unless he could not help it. Her only fear was that he was sleeping the sleep of the dead.

FIVE

Oh, What a Tangled Web!

Hastings's Third Principle of Gaming: In gaming, as
in life, one must never lose sight of one's object.
While at the tables, the seasoned gamester thinks of
nothing but the play. Though he is unfailingly
agreeable in his manner toward other gamesters, he
does not become immersed in their badinage. In a
private contest, he never permits conversation to
distract him. Whatever the game, even if it be E.O. or
speculation, he directs his entire store of skill to the
odds and probabilities before him. Most particularly,
he does not succumb to the temptation to divert
himself with a female. For the duration of the game,
he does not so much as deign to notice her, be she
ever so interesting, soft, and desirable.

There was no moving the man. When Miranda endeavored
to wake him, he flailed his arms as though reliving the attack in the mews. He quieted long enough to open his eyes,
smile at her, and rest his cheek against her hand. Apart
from that brief episode, he remained unconscious.

It was futile, Miranda saw, to try moving him to the
dressing room. He had availed himself of her bed, and that
was that. The first order of business was to see to his
wound. Consequently, she ripped the remainder of her shift
hem into lengths and fetched the basin. Then she knelt on
the floor by the bed and unwrapped the bandage so that she
might inspect the cut on his head.

Immediately she felt sickened. Nothing had occurred in
her twenty-six years to teach her how to nurse an injured
pate. Indeed, her worst difficulty in life up to now had been

how to improve the grounds at Arundel Abbey. A few hours ago, she had thought of nothing but how to follow the principles of Humphrey Repton. Now she had a dying man on her hands.

The thought crossed her mind to disregard the promise she had made and send for the surgeon, but she was stopped by a glance at Mr. Hastings's boyish, innocent face. He appeared so vulnerable that she could not find it in her heart to betray him. He was utterly in her power. She had never held in her two hands such power over another human creature. She was determined to use it honorably.

Dipping the cloth in the basin, she wrung it out and placed it on the wound. Mr. Hastings moaned. It was a sensual sound, almost as though he took pleasure in the sensation of the cool water. She did not know whether to be glad that her touch did not cause him pain or to suspect that he was actually enjoying himself. Because the question was unanswerable, she focused her sights on the matted hair and brutal gash.

In time, she became used to the sight and was able to cleanse it without wincing. The bleeding had stopped, but there had been some loss. His coat was covered with bloodstains. Happily, she recollected that bleeding was reputed to be salubrious. Indeed, when she had fallen from her pony at the age of nine and the doctor had been brought in to attend her, her parents had questioned him narrowly on the question of leeching. It was, the doctor had said, a good thing to bleed a patient no matter what the complaint, and so they had set about the task. She had grown so horrified at the sight of the leeches that she had fainted, but she had awakened feeling greatly refreshed, either because of the bleeding or because of the sleep. Mr. Hastings had undoubtedly been bled—and without recourse to leeches. He was now in the process of sleeping. With any luck, she told herself, he would wake refreshed. And then, if Heaven was merciful, he would go away and leave her in peace.

She removed the flask and poured the remaining contents over the wound. Knowing it must sting, she expected that he would wake. However, he remained still. Having cleansed the cut as best she could, she twined a length of fresh cloth around his head. Then to help him breathe more easily, she loosened his cravat and opened his shirt. Accidentally, her hand brushed his cheek, and she felt the bristled growth of new beard. It cast a shadow on his face that eradicated the earlier impression he had given of boyishness. Indeed, if he had not slept so peacefully, he would have put her in mind of a dashing pirate, though she had never in her life set eyes on one, except in imagination.

She wondered if she had the strength to turn him so that his head might lie on the pillows. As it was, it lolled dangerously near the edge of the bed. Surely, he would recover more rapidly if he could rest properly. Coming around to the other side, she faced him. She was obliged to confess that he was charming in sleep. It was difficult to believe that when awake he was as irritating as a hornet.

Leaning over, she took his hands in hers and gently pulled. He made a sound that she could not interpret. Afraid of worsening his wound, she held still, then tried again, a little more gently. This time he moved a bit. She pulled again, coaxing him in the direction she wished him to go. Moaning again, he moved. She saw a flash of pain cross his bruised face as he lifted his head. She stopped. He remained asleep, breathing with perfect evenness. Even more gently this time, she pulled his arms again. To her surprise, he resisted. She pulled with greater firmness. In his turn, he pulled with such force that she tumbled onto the bed by his side.

Incensed, she was poised to strike him across his cheek when she saw that he lay perfectly still. He made no attempt to touch her or offend her in any way. To all appearances, he was completely unconscious. Looking at him, Miranda shook her head. "You are the most provoking creature," she told him.

He seemed to have heard her. Though his eyes remained closed, he turned his head toward her. He opened his dry lips and murmured something she could not make out. Coming closer, she listened. Soon she heard the sound again but it was no more distinct than before. She would have given up, but he said a tender voice, "Jane, dear Jane."

Propping her cheek on her hand, she regarded him through slitted eyes. "This Jane of yours," she said, "I expect it is her husband who hired those ruffians to attack you. And I expect you deserved every blow they delivered."

"Ah, don't scold me, Jane."

"I *shall* scold you if I have a mind to. It is my bedchamber, after all, even though you have stolen it from me for the moment, along with my bed. I daresay, you have the worst manners of any gentleman who ever plagued a lady."

"Dear Jane," he whispered and putting his arms around her waist, he held her close and nestled his head on her breast.

At first, she was so stunned that she did not know what to do. She looked down to see a mass of chestnut curls under a bandage and a black-and-blue cheek snuggling close to her with perfect contentment. It struck her that if her mother were to come in just then, or Mrs. Hastings or the maid, she would be ruined for all eternity. How absurd she would look. How absurd they would look! The image nearly made her laugh.

But another thought struck her—that Mr. Hastings had deliberately taken advantage of her. Instantly, her face grew hot, and she extricated herself from his arms. His head fell to the side in such an awkward position that she knew at once he could not possibly have been pretending. No, she concluded, as she adjusted his head more comfortably, he had really thought she was his "dear Jane." And if dear Jane was put to half as much bother on his behalf as she was, the lady was greatly to be pitied.

She stood, picked up his coat from where it had fallen on the floor, and assessed the situation. Mr. Hastings was as well positioned on the bed as one could hope. There was nothing to do except to dispose of the coat, cover its owner with a blanket, and lock the door. Once she had taken these precautions, she went to the dressing room, removed her shift and stockings, pulled her nightdress over her head, and retired to the cot, where she spent what little was left of the night in restless, dream-filled sleep.

A timid scratching at the door woke her. She stretched luxuriously and was on the point of calling out for the maid to enter, when she recollected that she was not in her bed, that Mr. Hastings was, and she must find a way to fob off the girl at her door.

Daisy scratched again and called, "Why is the door locked, miss? Don't you want me now?"

Miranda sat bolt upright and said, "No, Daisy, I do not want you now."

"Are you well, miss?"

She threw off the quilt and got out of the bed. "Yes, perfectly well," she said, in a voice that rang false in her ears. "I shall sleep a bit more."

The welcome sound of the maid's assent floated through the door as the girl took herself off. Sighing with relief, Miranda tiptoed into the bedchamber and inspected her guest. He appeared not to have moved an iota. His bosom rose and fell in peaceful slumber. It was insupportable, she thought. He insinuated himself into her bed, called her by another woman's name, nestled his head in her bosom, obliged her to behave deceitfully to her lady's maid, and all the while, he lay there sleeping, as though none of these enormities had anything to do with him.

However, it was useless to rail against the man. She had best get herself dressed. It would not do to have him wake and find her in a state of dishabille.

Though it took considerable time and trouble, she at last contrived to button her buttons. Just as she was appraising herself in the glass, she heard a gentle knock at her door. Alarmed, she glanced at Mr. Hastings. He continued to sleep, oblivious to all danger.

"Yes?" she called.

"It is I, my pet. Are you quite well?"

"Oh, yes, Mama, quite well." She shuddered. Miranda had never before told her mother a bold-faced lie. But then she had never before concealed a man in her bed.

"Daisy said she thought you were not quite awake, my pet. It is not like you to sleep so late."

"Yes, I am quite well. I read until early morning and did not wish to rise at my usual hour."

"Do you wish to have your breakfast?"

Miranda was very hungry. She would have liked to indulge in her usual buttered toast and a cup of chocolate on a tray. But the last thing she wished was for the maid to come into her bedchamber. "I shall come down to the breakfast parlor today," she said.

There was a heavy pause and then Lady Troy inquired in a fretful tone, "Are you quite *sure* you are well, my pet?"

Rolling her eyes, Miranda wondered why her mother had chosen this moment to cosset her. "Yes, I am quite well, I assure you."

"But you never breakfast in the breakfast parlor."

"Well then, I expect it is time I did."

"Perhaps you wish to look it over. I vow, your Mr. Repton would think it a handsome room."

"Yes, I am hoping it will inspire me as I contemplate improvements at the abbey." Miranda was amazed at the lies that issued from her lips.

Lady Troy sighed, saying, "I expect your disappointment in Mr. Hastings has strengthened your devotion to improvements."

"Yes, indeed, Mother. I long to do nothing but occupy my thoughts with improvements day and night. I shall see you in the breakfast parlor momentarily."

To Miranda's infinite joy, Lady Troy went away.

She went to Mr. Hastings's side and undid his bandage. For a time, she studied the head wound. It looked something like a leg gash she had once seen on a horse. The groom had cleaned it with a vile-smelling mixture, causing the animal to whinny and stomp his feet. When she had questioned the groom, he had explained that he wished to prevent infection. She had asked, what did infection look like? Well, it was white and yellow and green and all manner of disgusting shades, especially to a twelve-year-old girl.

Mr. Hastings's wound was red and brown but devoid of any other colors. That was probably an excellent sign. Still, he ought to be looked at by a physician, if not a surgeon. Indeed, she thought, if he did not waken within a reasonable time, she would send for one, regardless of what she had promised.

He stirred. His arms rose above his head, and he yawned. Opening his eyes, he saw her and smiled. Closing his eyes, he let out a breath. Then, as though suddenly startled, he opened his eyes and looked at her again, this time with indignation. "What the devil are you doing here?" he demanded.

"This is my bedchamber, Mr. Hastings!"

He frowned in disbelief. When he glanced around the room, his skepticism faded and puzzlement took its place. "Permit me to amend my question, Miss Troy. What the devil am *I* doing here?"

"You do not recollect?"

"I recollect that you did not like me well enough to invite me to your bedchamber. What persuaded you otherwise?"

"You were beaten very badly."

He grimaced as the memory of the previous night's events came flooding back. His fingers touched a tender spot on his chin, then raked through his curls, stopping at the wound. "They dropped an anvil on my head, if I recall. At any rate, it feels as though they did."

"I dressed your head as best I could, but I think the surgeon ought to be sent for."

"No!"

"I have no experience in this sort of thing, Mr. Hastings. You may die of an infection, and I shall be to blame."

"I promise not to return from the grave to reproach you."

"Will you be serious?"

"I am serious. Think of what will be said of you if the surgeon is brought to me now. It will raise a scandal. None of my acquaintance will agree to marry you then."

She grew livid. All her concern for his head wound vanished. If he did not wish to send for the surgeon, she would not press him. Why should she sacrifice her reputation for a gentleman she so heartily despised?

For half a minute, she indulged such resentful thoughts. Reason, however, soon quieted her emotion. One did have certain moral obligations to one's fellow creatures, she reflected, no matter how impudent and offensive they were. "The surgeon ought to be sent for," she said firmly.

"I believe I explained last night that my enemy will profit from such a visit. However, I shall make you this promise. If you will permit me to stay here long enough to recover my strength, I shall go to the surgeon myself. It shall not be necessary for him to come to me."

"How soon do you mean to recover?"

"As soon as I may."

"You promised you would leave this morning."

"I have overstayed my welcome, I see."

The manner in which he looked at her was so pathetic that she knew he was deliberately playing upon her sympathies. "I shall help you to the door," she said, half smiling.

He grinned. "I do not fool you, do I, Miss Troy? Very well, off I go."

As he struggled to sit up, a knock was heard at the door, freezing them both. She looked at him, stricken. He gestured to her to answer. She gestured back. He mouthed the word *answer*. Frantically, she turned to the door and said as lightly as she could, "What is it?"

"Daisy, miss. Her ladyship wishes to know if you are meaning to come to the breakfast parlor as you said."

"Tell her I have changed my mind, Daisy. I shall have toast and chocolate on a tray, if you please."

"And sausage and kidney," Mr. Hastings whispered.

"I beg pardon, miss?"

"And sausage and kidney!" Miranda said between her teeth.

"Why, miss, are you certain you are well?"

"Yes, Daisy, so well in fact that I have a yearning for sausage and kidney." She glared at Mr. Hastings, who smiled and licked his lips in anticipation of breakfast.

"Very well, miss," said Daisy, and then there was blissful silence.

"Well," Miranda said with a challenge in her eyes, "what do we do when she returns with the breakfast?"

The sausage and kidney had been an impulse of the moment. In fact, Mr. Hastings did not know whether he could eat it, or if he did, whether he could stomach it. Whenever he moved, he felt nauseated and light-headed. He could not see clearly. Miss Troy appeared to him in duplicate, and while he would ordinarily have relished the sight of so much loveliness, he was not up to it at the moment. In fact, he felt deucedly sick.

"What shall we do?" Miranda repeated. She stood with her hands on her hips, a defiant glow in her eyes. There were two Mirandas at the moment, and the unreality of her appearance gave him pause. How was it, he asked himself, that he could feel so miserable and yet notice that a lady's neck was soft and inviting? How could he feel his cheeks and brow so sore and yet wish to bury them in her breast? How had he ended up in the bedchamber of the very woman he had set out to avoid?

Then he remembered. Everard. The ring. The mews. The attack. Miss Troy's miraculous appearance at the window. Her miraculous appearance at his side. His aching head. Her steadying arms. She had assisted him up the stairs, down the corridor, and into her chamber. He had sat in a chair. After that, it had all gone black.

With a jolt, he saw that Miss Troy had come closer to him and now peered at his face with concern. "Are you going to faint?" she asked. Her voice had lost all of its previous sharpness.

Loftily, he replied, "Are you implying that I am in the habit of fainting?"

"I imply nothing, but you have not answered me, and you look very odd."

"To quote you, I am perfectly well, so well, in fact, that I have a yearning for sausage and kidney." One glance at her well-formed face told him that she did not quite believe him. Determined to prove himself hale and hearty, he moved to get out of the bed, but was seized with a spell of dizziness. It was so severe that he put his hands to his head. When he recovered, he looked up to see her watching him. "If you say one word about the surgeon, Miss Troy, I shall never leave this chamber. You shall have me as a permanent guest. I shall haunt and plague you all your days. I shall—" and here he stopped as a wave of nausea overcame him.

He felt her hands on his shoulders. "Perhaps you ought to lie down again, Mr. Hastings," she said. Her voice was musical, almost as though she were accompanying herself on the harp. Its soothing quality nearly convinced him to lie back. He caught himself, however. "I cannot," he said. "I must hide in your dressing room before the maid returns."

"I doubt you will be able to walk."

"Then I shall dance!" he snapped.

When she did not reply, he looked at her. Her lips—and there were a great many of them at the moment—were deathly grave.

"If you mean to dance," she said at last in a gentle voice, "perhaps you will allow me to be your partner."

He looked down at his hands. He did not like her sudden softness. It suggested compassion. While he was feeling the excruciating discomfort of her nearness, she was feeling sorry for him. He ought to quit the room at once and take his chances with Everard's men, he thought. He would rather be dead than pitied.

"Mr. Hastings, please let me help you," she said.

"Why do you wish to help me?"

"Because the sooner you get well again, the sooner I shall be rid of you."

This answer pleased him. Clearly, she was not pitying him. Her pointed dislike was reassuring. He was free to admire the curve of her neck and the plumpness of her arms. Smiling, he said, "In that case, Miss Troy, you may have the honor of assisting me."

Getting to the dressing room proved difficult. He found he needed to rest heavily against her, which went sorely against the grain with him. He did not like to rely on anybody, let alone a woman who smelled of lavender, and whose soft halo of hair brushed his ear, and whose murmured encouragements aroused sensations in him that he had gone to some lengths to keep hidden from all the world. If he had felt alive to Miss Troy's charms the night before, he was even more so now. It irritated him to think that he could be bludgeoned, bruised, and beaten, and still not be indifferent to the attractions of a Miss Troy.

At last they attained the dressing room. Guided by Miranda, he fell onto the cot. Although his eyes were closed, he was aware that she kept by his side. Her nearness disturbed him. He could not think while he was inhaling her scent. Instead of Everard, he was thinking of her. At this rate, he would never discover the means of disposing of Everard once and for all.

A knock at the door announced Daisy's return. He heard the swish of skirts, the opening of a door, and the sound of Miranda's voice. Vaguely he made out that she was urging Daisy to tend to things in the bedchamber but to leave the dressing room for later. The girl asked repeatedly if miss was feeling quite well. Evidently, Miss Troy's routine was so different this day that it caused remark. Finally, he heard a door open and close, and deduced that Daisy had gone out. In another moment, Miranda returned.

"Your sausage and kidney have arrived," she announced.

The thought of eating sickened him.

He was aware that her face was close to his. Opening his eyes, he saw that hers were brown with flecks of gold. His head swam, and he could not keep his eyes open.

"You must eat your sausage and kidney," she said. "Daisy heard me ask for it expressly. If it is not eaten, she will suspect something is wrong."

"You eat it," he said.

"Oh, you are an odious man!" she cried, startling him into opening his eyes again. "I detest sausage and kidney."

Her fury was splendid, so splendid that he had to warn himself not to admire her overmuch. "My condolences," he said, and drifted off to sleep.

* * *

He could not tell how long he had slept. He blinked and regarded the blue flowers on the wallpaper. It seemed to him that he saw them clearly, one at a time, but he could not be sure. Gingerly, he sat up and put his legs over the side of the bed. Now that it was gone, he realized that up to now he had felt a steady throbbing in his head. Blinking again, he looked at his hands. There were only two of them.

Pleased, he attempted to stand, and after two tries, he found himself on his feet. He waited for a wave of light-headedness to seize him but none did. Heartened, he took a few steps. The success of this effort led him to the water closet. His mother, ever in the forefront of fashion, had caused one to be installed in the bedchambers. After availing himself of its amenities, he inspected himself in a looking glass. He noted that he wore no coat and vaguely recalled that it had cost considerable effort to remove it. His cravat and collar had been loosened, but he could not recall having loosened them. He imagined what it must have been like to have Miss Troy untie and unbutton him, and wished he had been awake to enjoy it.

Walking into the bedchamber, he looked about and saw that it was empty. Miss Troy had gone out.

It was a good thing, he thought. Her staying confined to her chamber the entire day would have aroused suspicion. Her going out prevented her mother and his from visiting her there.

Cautiously, he moved to her dressing table and inspected her belongings. He admired a pretty gold locket and a miniature of a gentleman who, he hoped, was her father. He took up a book and opened to a page, thinking that if he could read it, he would know for certain that he was recovering from the blow he had sustained. It was a ponderous volume by Horace Walpole, and the words appeared clear and singly on the page. He read from a paragraph she had marked:

The contiguous ground of the park without the sunk fence was to be harmonized with the lawn within; and

the garden in its turn was to be set free from its prim
regularity, that it might assort with the wilder country
without.

He noted that Miss Troy had underlined the words "set
free from its prim regularity" and "the wilder country." He
smiled. It intrigued him that these were the words she had
chosen to distinguish. Obviously, the young lady was even
more interesting than he had estimated.

Setting down the Walpole, he took up a pretty, cloth-
bound book that, upon inspection, proved to be a journal.
He paused, knowing that he ought not to read it, not merely
because it was private, but also because he had always held
it as a maxim that one who reads another's diary is certain
to come upon something to distress and dismay.

On the other hand, what could distress and dismay him
more than the events of the previous night? There were
only a few entries in the journal. Reading them would help
him make out the character of his hostess. Why he should
wish to make it out, he did not ask. It was sufficient that he
was curious.

He read the first entry, and because he agreed with her
estimate of Blaise estate and its folly, he concluded that she
was a prodigiously sensible young woman. Soon he came
to the final entry, and found himself mentioned in the last
sentence: "If only I were not obliged to meet Mr. Hastings
and smile!" He dwelled on those words for a considerable
time. They demonstrated, much to his vexation, that she
had dreaded meeting him as much as he had dreaded meeting her.

He had assumed that she was eager to snare him, just as
their respective mothers were eager to see him snared.
From the entries in her journal, however, he gleaned that
she was a great deal more fascinated with tree-lined av-
enues and moss-grown terraces than with Mr. Charles Hastings. He drummed his fingers on the book, thinking that he
had just proved the truth of his maxim: He *was* distressed
and dismayed.

What was worse, it appeared that at his mother's soiree

he had gone to all the trouble of offending Miss Troy for nothing. She could not have been less interested in him if he were a pimple on the nose of a flea.

At that moment, the door opened and she came inside. He turned and did what he customarily did when he was caught in an awkward situation—he smiled his charming smile. She did not return it, however. She merely glared at him and at the book in his hand.

SIX

Dear Jane

If Mr. Hastings is correct, and one's avocation
represents one's general philosophy, then I suppose
my philosophy is founded on a belief in partnership.
In the matter of landscape gardening, for example, I
take a middle road, regarding the world as a place
where beauty is not the exclusive province either of
nature or of humankind. It is the partnership between
nature and humankind which establishes the
harmony we think of as beauty. According to Mr.
Hastings's theory, I ought to apply this same
philosophy to life. I ought to view partnership—in
marriage, for example—as an ideal to be pursued.
However, I am better able to see art and nature
wedded in a landscape than to imagine real harmony
subsisting between myself and a husband. I am more
convinced than ever that I am unfit for matrimony,
and never have I felt this to be so true as now, when I
defy propriety and sense by harboring a gentleman in
my bedchamber and utter so many falsehoods as to
be taken for a minister of state.

Miranda burned with anger at the violation of her privacy.
This is my reward, she told herself, *for risking my reputation for the sake of such a man*. But she had only herself to
blame, she reflected. She had known from the first what he
was. His poking his nose into her journal was of a piece
with his general conduct. It would not surprise her in the
least if he had peeked into her wardrobe to take an account-
ing of her stockings, shifts, and stays.

On his side, he was struck with Miss Troy's gentle dignity. Even seething, glaring at him with fire, repressing her

temper, she was admirable. Her strength drew him; it enhanced her allure. It was not often he felt sorry, and he could not be sorry he had peeked at her journal, but he was sorry he had distressed her.

She approached and snatched the journal from his hand. "You are quite recovered, I collect," she said in an unsteady voice. Walking to the chaise longue, she did not sit but merely gazed out the window. "I trust you are now well enough to leave," she said.

He saw that whereas the night before he had merely offended her, this time he had given her real pain. "I cannot leave," he said, "until I have explained."

She flared. "Do not put yourself to the bother. There can be no excuse for snooping into another's private writings."

"I do not mean to excuse, merely to explain."

"I do not require your explanations, only your absence."

His chin hardened. Coming to her, he fixed her with his gray eyes while, to her horror, he whipped off his cravat. Then, taking the journal from her, he tied it up with the cravat in several large, bulky knots. "Your journal is quite safe from me for the rest of all eternity," he declared.

Indignantly, she turned from him, but he caught her arm and compelled her to face him. "The blow to my head caused my vision to be faulty. When I awoke, I wished to test it. I thought I ought to try to read something; it scarcely mattered what."

"I see, and you just happened upon my journal, by accident. That is your explanation."

"Not entirely. That is only the first part of it. Once I saw that I could indeed read and comprehend a page, I noticed your journal, and wishing to learn more of you, I read it."

"You read it knowingly!"

"I did, but you will be happy to learn that I immediately regretted it. You mentioned me in a most insulting manner."

"I scarcely mentioned you at all!"

"Which added injury to the insult."

"I cannot imagine what you could have misconstrued as an insult."

"You said that you wished you were not obliged to meet

me and smile." He was gratified to see her grow pale. "I wonder if you can imagine how vexing it was to learn that you cherished the same sentiments toward me that I cherished toward you. I had flattered myself that you not only wished to meet me, but to marry me. Reading your journal, I discovered, to my chagrin, that I was mistaken."

She eyed him, somewhat mollified by this admission and the directness with which it was delivered but unwilling to let him see it.

"Though I read nothing at all to my credit," he went on, "I did learn much to yours."

"I do not see how. The journal contains little except my observations on landscape gardening."

"Your observations confirmed what I had already come to believe of you, to wit, that you are not likely to be swayed by what others have to say. You have your own notions and the courage to act upon them."

She vowed not to be softened by flattery. "Nonsense," she said.

"Miss Troy, it is not nonsense, not to me at any rate. You came to my rescue. It requires a certain character to risk scandal for the sake of aiding another human creature."

Though he seemed sincere, she remained skeptical. "How is it possible to read all that in my journal?"

"One's avocations reveal one's philosophy. Naturally, having read your words on the subject of landscape gardening, I have discovered your philosophy."

Skeptically, she shook her head. "Do not mistake my avocations for philosophy. I pursue new interests in the same manner that I buy new hats, changing them with the season and the fashion. Indeed, I should not be surprised if my passion for landscape gardening did not outlast the month."

"You mean to portray yourself as fickle."

"If you doubt me, you need only ask my mother. She can attest to my successive passions for painting screens, writing novels, playing the harp, studying physiognomy, and all manner of folly."

"That is not fickleness. Your range of interests demonstrates that your philosophy has breadth and depth. You dislike confines, Miss Troy. You like to roam among the many riches of the world and not limit yourself to any one of them, just as you prefer a landscape in which nature is permitted to grow wild and free. That is why, I suspect, you remain unmarried."

She flushed. "I beg your pardon!"

"There is no need to apologize. I merely state the truth as I see it, and the truth is, Miss Troy, that you are quite right to eschew matrimony, which is too confining for a mind such as yours, unless, of course, you should find a husband whose philosophy is compatible with your own."

Mortified by this analysis, Miranda looked to turn the subject. "You appear to know a great deal about avocations, sir. What, if I may ask, is yours?"

He smiled. "Gaming."

"A gamester!" She stated the word with satisfaction, for she had expected something of the sort.

He bowed magnificently. "Indeed, I am."

"Tell me, Mr. Hastings, what does a gamester do precisely—when he isn't matching up young ladies with his acquaintance, that is?"

"Well, for one thing, he plays cards."

"Oh, how very dull."

His smile faded. He regarded her as though she had just sprouted another head. "You do not like cards?"

"I have never learned to play. There are those who have attempted to teach me, but I could not learn."

"Impossible to believe. Anybody can play cards. Even my mother plays."

"Perhaps I could learn, if I had the interest, but I find cards—indeed, I find games of every variety—tiresome."

Now it was his turn to be offended. "*Tiresome!*"

"Well, what is the point of a game? Merely to win. It does not interest me."

He stepped back, fully taking in the sight of such a heretic. "What is the point of a game, you ask? Why civilization is founded on games, for gaming is nothing more nor less than the willingness to stake everything, or a great deal at any rate, on one's own judgment. The object is not mere winning; it is *risking*. Risking is as old as humankind and as venerable as the Bible, which mentions it many times over. Recollect, if you will, that the ancients used sticks of varying lengths and headless arrows to elect kings, select armies, and settle disputes. We see risking in our own day—in the game of politics, for example, and the game of courtship. Only think what you have risked in agreeing to save my skin."

"These are serious matters, Mr. Hastings, not games."

"But you will acknowledge that each contains an essential element of play, not to mention absurdity."

After a moment's pause, she said, "I see you have given extensive thought to the subject."

"As extensive as Mr. Walpole has given to the subject of landscape gardening."

She tossed her head. "Perhaps you will imitate his example and write a book."

He saw the challenge in her expression and smiled. "Perhaps I shall." He was as willing to call a bluff in a bedchamber as in Mrs. Stout's gaming house and had done so on more than one occasion. "Yes, I believe I *shall* write a book. I shall set down all my principles of play. They shall constitute not merely rules for winning but an entire philosophy."

Ironically, she inquired, "Shall I go and fetch you pen and paper?"

Her defiance appealed to him. She was so much more interesting than the pliable, simpering misses he was accustomed to. None of them would have concealed him in her bedchamber.

He approached. "Do not fetch the pen and paper yet, if you please. Just now I mean to teach you to play cards." It was not an offer so much as a command.

She shook her head. She was not so easily diverted from her purpose as that. "Your time will be much better employed in seeking out another bedchamber to invade."

"I shall lay you a wager, Miss Troy."

"I am not accustomed to laying wagers."

He ignored that. "These shall be the stakes: if I succeed

in teaching you a game of cards in the space of an hour, you shall permit me to stay another night under your generous protection. If I fail, I shall take myself off and torment you no more."

Miranda stared, then quickly glanced away. The man's impertinence was insufferable. Added to that was the force of his eyes. They glowed starkly against the bruises on his forehead. But what stunned her most was the fact that he had just paid her an immense compliment. He had put it in her power to cheat, if she so chose. She could spend the next hour resisting his lessons, pretending not to learn, and thus be rid of him for good. A seasoned gamester, he knew the full import of what he was offering, and yet he offered it anyway. That could mean one thing only—he was betting that she would not cheat.

She was flattered beyond measure. He could have waxed poetic for a month on the subject of her beauty and charm and not have flattered her as much as this testimony to her honesty. She was not certain she deserved such a compliment.

He interrupted her meditation by saying, "If you will be so good as to locate my coat, we shall proceed with the game."

That recalled her to the present. "I hid it away before Daisy came in. It is quite bloody, I'm afraid."

"Bloody or not, it contains a deck of cards in the pocket. I cannot teach you, Miss Troy, without the proper tools."

She led him to her wardrobe, where she opened the door and located the coat at the back, behind her boots. It amazed her that he did not seem the least concerned about the wrinkled filthy condition of the fine garment. He was intent only on finding the deck. Coming up with it, he held it aloft and smiled. The coat was carelessly thrown across a chair. He took the journal from her hand and set it on top of the coat.

With glances in every direction, he endeavored to decide where they might play. The bed, he declared when he had tested its firmness, was too soft. "The chaise longue, I think," he said, seating himself on the left side. He set the deck down in the center and gestured for her to sit on the right.

With a brief glance at him, she sat. The game appeared to her in the light of a test: Would she or would she not cheat, as he had given her the opportunity to do? It was tempting, she acknowledged. After all, she would infinitely prefer to restore her life to its former serene condition than to go on harboring a rascal in her private sanctum. At the same time, to cheat for the sake of convenience did not suit her. It was better, in her view, to risk scandal and to endure another night of Mr. Hastings's impudence than to stoop so low. She braced herself and turned her attention to the game.

Mr. Hastings had dealt each of them four cards facedown and had set another four between them faceup. He was explaining the meaning of court cards. "For a knave, score 11," he said, "for a queen, 12, and for a king, 13." All the while, she was remarking the gracefulness of his hands, and although she was more attuned to the ardor in his voice than the meaning of his words, she nodded when he asked whether she understood.

Pleased, he proceeded to demonstrate how one went about capturing cards from the table, or, rather, the chaise longue, in this instance. Carefully, he placed a red card on a black and placed them at his side, explaining as he did so that had his card been the ten of diamonds, he would have been entitled to another two points. Had it been the two of spades, he would have earned a single additional point. "You see," he said, dazzling her with his smile, "it is beautiful in its simplicity."

At this juncture, Miranda remembered having seen her nephews and nieces playing at a similar game. They had endeavored to include her but she had grown restless and inattentive, and they had scolded and laughed at her. Like Mr. Hastings, they had played with fervor. Like his, their cheeks had colored and their eyes had glowed with animation.

Mr. Hastings, she noted, instructed with passion, so much so that she glanced at his face more often than at the cards, which led inevitably to her losing the train of thought. Soon she was entirely lost. She stared at the four cards in her hand, unable to think what use she was to put them to, and unable to care.

Sighing, she confessed, "Mr. Hastings, I am afraid I do not understand." It gave her comfort to know that she had failed to learn the game without having to cheat; however, she felt it did not redound much to her credit to be incapable of learning a game favored by six- and seven-year-old children.

He blinked at her. "I cannot credit it. A young lady who studies physiognomy, screen painting, and landscape gardening can have no difficulty learning casino."

"I find my mind wandering to other things. It does not hold my interest."

"What other things?"

As she recollected what her thoughts had been, and that they had been centered on him, she blushed. "It is difficult to say," she answered truthfully.

"Permit me to ask, Miss Troy, do you know how one catches a fish?"

Surprised at the abrupt change of subject, she replied, "My father fishes. I have accompanied him on many occasions. What has that to say to card playing?"

"Only that casino is a fishing game. That is to say, it is a game which contains a pool. In the pool, tantalizing fish swim about." Here he pointed to the cards lying faceup between them.

She nodded. The analogy made sense to her, for she pictured her father about to cast his fly into Arundel Lake.

"In your hand," he said, "you hold the bait to catch the fish." Here he reached across the "pool" and squeezed the hand in which she held her cards. Their eyes met. His were inquiring. Clearly, he was determined to make her understand. She became conscious of the press of his hand, the intimacy of the setting, the nearness of the bed, the impropriety of his being there at all, and the absurdity of their playing cards in such a setting.

Remarking her confusion, Mr. Hastings went to her side and leaned over her shoulder so that he might inspect her

hand. His cheek was close to hers. She inhaled a discon-
certing smell of maleness.

"Now here you have a six," he said. "You will note that
there is a six in the pool. Your six is bait with which to
catch the six in the pool. Do you see?"

To her amazement, she did see. Smiling, she turned to
face him, and their noses nearly touched.

All the amusement he had felt now dissolved. The game
forgotten, he became suddenly aware of his surroundings—
the chaise longue, the bed, the lusciousness of Miss Troy's
earlobe. He was in the bedchamber of a woman who was
becoming every minute more attractive to him. If he stayed
longer, he knew, he might offend her in earnest. It was a
first principle with him never to offend a lady unless he
stood to gain by it. In this instance, he could only lose.

Consequently, he returned her smile as best he could and
stood up straight. The swiftness of the movement caused
him to experience an episode of vertigo. If he did not move,
he told himself, it would go away, but it continued to grip
him.

"What is it, Mr. Hastings?" he heard her ask.

"Nothing, I am perfectly well. I shall just be on my way
now. My coat, if you please."

Her sudden touch on his arm came as a jolt. It would
have been the work of a moment to turn and hold her to
him. On the other hand, though he was dizzy, he told himself, he was not altogether daft. The instant he gave a hint
of his feelings, it would all be up with him. He would soon
find himself in love; worse, he would soon find himself
married, and his bride would find herself a widow. Perhaps
if he kept still long enough, she would take her hand away,
and while he would regret that loss, at least he would be
able to breathe again.

"You are not well enough to go," she said.

He closed his eyes. "It might go worse with me if I stay."

"You ought to have thought of that when you insinuated
yourself into my bedchamber last night. You have made
your bed, sir. Now you must lie in it."

"An infelicitous turn of phrase, Miss Troy." A wave of nausea made him throw his head back.

"Perhaps I ought to have compelled you to eat your breakfast. You have not taken any food for nearly a day."

"I shall be obliged to you if you will not mention food."

"I understand. You shall just lie down on the chaise longue until you have recovered."

He vowed he would not lose his senses, either literally or amorously. "I shall take my leave of you now," he insisted. "I wish you good day and beg you to know that I am entirely at your service."

When he swayed, he found her at his side, steadying him. Though her fingers burned him, he could not break away. Against his will, he allowed her to lead him to the bed.

"Mr. Hastings," she said, "you have won the bet. I understand the game. Consequently, you may stay the night."

"The devil with the bet!"

"Please lie down."

"That is a most unseemly suggestion, Miss Troy." In spite of himself, however, he sank onto the bed.

"I shall just have a look at your head wound. I shall do my best not to cause you any additional pain, but I warn you, if it is any worse, I intend to send for the surgeon, regardless of what your enemy might discover.

He found he could not reply. Something—and it was not merely the dizziness he felt—gripped him. Aware that her gentle hands unwrapped his bandage, he endeavored to stay awake. "The concussion does not appear any worse," he heard her say from far off. And then he heard nothing.

When Miranda joined the others at dinner, she was showered with questions. Mrs. Hastings wished to know whether she had caught a cold. Was that the reason she kept to her room? Before Miranda could leap upon that convenient excuse for her odd behavior, Mrs. Hastings offered to send up to her bedchamber all manner of doctors, physics, potents, servants, and palliative broths.

"Do not trouble yourself. I shall be perfectly well in a

day or two," said Miranda. "Indeed, I fully intend to send
my malady packing as soon as possible."

"Are you truly ill, my pet?" her mother inquired solicitously. "Or has some matter overset you?"

"What matter?" Miranda asked, eating a great deal of
partridge and pudding for one who purported to be so un-
well.

"You know very well what matter," said Lady Troy sig-
nificantly.

"No, Mama, I do not know."

"I refer, my pet, to the gentleman who offended you at
the soiree. I vow, you were quite distraught when you
parted from him."

Mrs. Hastings cried out, "What gentleman is this who
has offended one of my guests?"

Lady Troy blanched. With her eyes, she begged Miranda
not to name him.

"I have not given him another thought," Miranda said.
"Indeed, I have quite forgotten his name." The lie made her
cheeks flame.

Mrs. Hastings grew concerned. "I am mortified, my dear
Miranda," she said, "to think that a guest of mine should be
offended in my house."

"He has paid for it ten times over, I assure you."

"You must not make light of the matter," Mrs. Hastings
said. "When one catches cold, one is sensitive to all manner
of slights." Then, as an inspiration seized her, she cried, "I
have it! I shall make it up to you. I shall come and sit with
you in your chamber tonight. I shall read to you. I shall
even read that dreadful Mr. Walpole, if it will comfort you."

Miranda wished the two mothers were more neglectful
and less kind. "I believe I shall recover quickest if I have
complete quiet," she said. Her distaste for lying was growing in leaps and bounds. Mr. Hastings would leave at dawn,
no matter how weak he was, she resolved. She could not
endure this deception another day.

Mrs. Hastings sighed. "As you wish, child. Only let us
say nothing to Charles. He is so healthy himself that it quite

oversets him to hear of anybody else's affliction. I daresay, the dear boy has never been ill in his life."

"I daresay, his time will come," Miranda observed dryly.

Lady Troy sighed. "It is true. One cannot live a life and not encounter some complaint or other. I myself have an excellent constitution; yet I have recently suffered from palpitations. Let us hope that Mr. Hastings does not encounter anything so grave."

"I have been hoping as much myself," said Mrs. Hastings with a heavy sigh. "However, I fear he is very ill and does not wish me to know it. He ought to have called today, you know. Charles never fails to wait upon me the day after a party. When I sent to Russell Square to see whether he was well, I was informed that he had not returned to the house at all. Naturally, as a mother, I cannot help but fret at such news."

Miranda felt her cheeks grow hot. She longed to soothe the mother's anxiety but did not dare to so much as hint at the truth. Though it was a poor substitute, she offered to play on the harp after dinner. This revived Mrs. Hastings's spirits somewhat, and within fifteen minutes, the three women were gathered in the drawing room around the instrument.

Miranda sang a song that she had learned during her years as an enthusiast for things Italian. Though her audience understood not a word, they were charmed by the melody and her delicate soprano. Their pleasure was interrupted, however, when a footman entered to announce a visitor. Then Lord Everard was ushered into the drawing room.

The instant she set eyes on him, Miranda disliked him. He oozed compliments during the introduction, bowed far too low over her mother's hand, and spoke in a voice that she found far too silky. Unlike Mr. Hastings, who merely made her furious, Everard made her flesh crawl.

"Mrs. Hastings," he said, "I have come to Queen Street in order to pay what I owe to your son. Unfortunately, I do not find him at home. Perhaps he is here?"

"Oh, no, I only wish he were!"

"I thought perhaps he might have fallen ill or some such thing and had decided to recover under your tender care."

"How kind of you to concern yourself with Charles's health. But I am afraid I do not know where he has gone to."

It appeared to Miranda that his lordship was vexed. She suspected that he cherished a lively hatred for Mr. Hastings and found herself wishing to protect Mr. Hastings from him. Her knowledge of physiognomy told her that Lord Everard was vain, sly, and cruel—in short, the sort of man from whom she would enjoy withholding not only the truth but all manner of communication whatsoever.

At last he went away, no wiser than when he came, and after another song, Miranda bade the two ladies good night, kissing them each on the brow.

When she reentered her bedchamber, she lit the candelabrum and turned to observe her guest. He was sitting in her bed, propped against the pillows. Smiling, he said, "I have repaid your hospitality most ungratefully. However, I promise never again to put such an abrupt period to our card game. Will you accept my sincerest apologies?"

"Who is Lord Everard?" she asked.

He pursed his lips. "How do you know Everard?"

"He was here, inquiring after you."

Inhaling, he nodded. "He is the one," he said.

"I am not surprised."

"What did you tell him?"

"Merely that you were even now to be found in my bedchamber, in my bed."

He laughed. "He would not have believed you, even if you had told him. He would have thought you were gammoning him. You are too proper a damsel ever to be guilty of such an enormity. Why just looking at you, one knows you are the very model of probity."

She leveled at him a look of steel. His insouciance roused her indignation. "I do not mind lying to Lord Everard. In fact, it gives me great pleasure to thwart the schemes of such a fellow. But I detest lying to my mother and to yours. They are the best creatures in the world. They

think I am, as you say, a very model of probity, and I am
obliged to deceive them with every word I utter." Shaken,
she turned and glared at the dressing table. Only a lunatic,
she told herself, would have permitted Mr. Hastings to
enter her chamber. What had she been thinking of?

Suddenly, she was alarmed to find him standing by her
side, speaking softly to her.

"I shall go at once," he said.

She stepped away. Irritably, she answered, "We agreed
that you might stay the night. You shall go in the morning,
before light."

"I am quite recovered. It may be best that I go now."

Distressed, she cried, "I shall not have your blood on my
hands!"

Gravely, he nodded. "You are quite right. There is no use
in your taking the trouble to deceive our mothers and Lord
Everard if I am to end my days in the street, tragically dead
and my coat a perfect fright."

Near tears, she said, "I wish you would not joke." His
closeness disquieted her. She had the most maddening impulse to put her hand to his bruised forehead.

After a pause, he asked, "What do you wish me to do?
Name it, and it shall be done."

She avoided looking at him. What did she wish him to
do? A hundred notions flashed in her brain, none of them
very clear or very rational. "Go to sleep," she said at last,
and made quickly for the dressing room.

When the maid knocked ten minutes later to assist Miss
Troy into her night shift, Miranda sent her away. After considerable time spent in wriggling out of her dress, she
crawled into the cot, tucked the blanket around her waist,
and unwrapping her journal, which was still tied with Mr.
Hastings's cravat, made a brief entry. She then slid under
the covers, in preparation for sleep. For a time, she observed the shadows that the candlelight cast on the ceiling,
then sighed.

"You sighed," Mr. Hastings said from the adjoining
room.

"I thought you were asleep."

"I cannot sleep when I hear a lady sighing."

"My sighs are none of your affair."

"I am obliged to contradict you. They are my affair. I have caused them. Before you met me, I'll wager, you never sighed in your life."

"What is Everard's grievance?"

"I caught him cheating at cards."

"He means to call you out?"

"He would like nothing better than to call me out and shoot my head off, but I have foresworn dueling. I arranged for his mistress and our mutual acquaintance to witness a game of piquet between us. In due course, his lordship succumbed to the temptation to cheat, as such fellows always do. I contrived to mortify him in such a way as to prevent his ever cheating again, and apparently, I succeeded. He is so engrossed in wreaking revenge on me that I doubt he has time for cheating."

"What do you think he means to do?"

He was silent.

"Tell me," she said.

"I expect he means to do serious harm. He will arrange it so that it appears I have been set upon by robbers. The end result, however, will be that I shall lie in my grave exactly as I lie here in your bed, except that I shall clasp a lily to my bosom."

"What do you mean to do?"

"I haven't decided. My thoughts have been elsewhere of late."

There was a long pause, after which she wondered whether he had fallen asleep. "Mr. Hastings?" she whispered.

"Yes?"

"Who is Jane?"

SEVEN

Disguise

Hastings's Fourth Principle of Gaming: Only a poor
player sticks in the game because he has lost nearly
all his pot and is determined to recoup. A wise player
knows it is in the nature of things to lose on occasion
and that he will do best if he loses small. He will do
well to wait till a later date and win large. Likewise
in life. It is the wise player who knows when to
withdraw.

The unexpectedness of the question prompted Mr. Hastings
to smile. "Did you say *Jane*?"

"Yes. *Dear* Jane, you called her."

"I called her *dear Jane*?" He sat up, throwing off the
blanket, intrigued by this report of his conduct and even
more intrigued by her curiosity. He saw from the flickering
shadows that she had not yet doused her candle.

"Indeed, you did. You had lost consciousness, or so I
thought, and mistook me for your *dear Jane*. I assumed she
was the lady for whose sake you had been thrashed so violently, but when I met Lord Everard, I was obliged to revise
my conclusion."

"If I was not attacked by Jane's husband, you are thinking, then who can the lady be?" He rubbed the back of his
neck, hoping he might somehow turn her curiosity to account.

"Yes, that was my thinking."

"And why do you wish to know, Miss Troy? I did not
think my concerns affected you in the least, apart from the
loss of reputation I might cause."

"Mr. Hastings, you behaved in such a manner toward me

when you thought I was your *dear Jane* that I believe I
have a right to know."

"Exactly how did I behave?" He hoped her reply would
betray a more personal interest in him than she had yet
shown.

"Suffice it to say, you behaved most improperly."

He regretted that he had been too unconscious to enjoy
the moment. On the other hand, she sounded a trifle indignant, which, he thought with satisfaction, might indicate a
tinge of jealousy. "Impossible," he assured her. "I would
never behave improperly where Jane was concerned."

"Mr. Hastings, though I have grown accustomed to lying
of late, I do not lie about such matters."

After a brief inward debate, he acknowledged he could
not reveal dear Jane's identity without having the pleasure
of seeing Miss Troy's reaction. Thus, he rose from the bed
and, wearing no shirt, only his pantaloons, began to approach the dressing room. To his gratification, he walked
steadily, without the least hint of vertigo. When he reached
the doorway, he saw Miranda in a white nightcap and
chemise, lying in her cot, with her eyes fixed on the ceiling.
The candlelight feathered across her form under the blanket. Her eyelashes cast a shadow on her cheeks. Taking a
step inside, he said softly, "Jane was my nurse, you see, and
I would not have dared to offend her. I was very little at the
time, while she was exceedingly large."

When she saw him, she neither gasped at his impudence
nor got on her high ropes. Her eyes enlarged; all she said
was, "Your nurse?"

It was tempting to take another step inside, too tempting
to resist. "Yes. You may inquire about her of my mother, if
you doubt my veracity."

"Why should I doubt your veracity?"

"You should not," he said, noting that she pulled the
blanket tightly to her neck. "Apart from the occasion of our
delightful first meeting, I have told you nothing but the
truth."

"You did not tell the truth at our first meeting?"

Though he half expected her to lower her lashes, indicat-

ing a consciousness of their situation, she looked at him
forthrightly. She was not afraid. Indeed, she was making it
a point not to acknowledge the nature of their situation.
One would have thought it was the most natural thing in the
world for a gentleman to appear unannounced at her bed-
side, half undressed.

"I did not lie, precisely," he said, "but I did give a false
impression. I am not entirely the arrogant puppy you
thought me. In truth, if we had the opportunity to further
our acquaintance, you would find me an excellent fellow."
Unable to help himself, he drew nearer the cot.

"That may well be, Mr. Hastings," she said pleasantly,
"but as you leave tomorrow at dawn, I shall never have that
opportunity. And so good night." She raised herself on one
elbow so that the coverlet hugged the outline of her hips
and legs. Briskly, she blew out the candle, and then, turning
her back to him, left him standing in the pitch-dark.

Her gesture, subtle and cool, brought him to his senses.
He let out a breath, relieved that she had not screamed,
amused that she had not succumbed. For the first time in
his experience, a young woman had not dissolved into a
mass of palpitations at his approach. The aplomb she had
displayed confirmed his impression that Miss Miranda Troy
was a sublimely interesting young woman.

Gingerly, he made his way back to the bedchamber in the
night, thinking that it was not a great many hours till dawn
and that the thing he wished most was that she would prove
as reluctant to see him go as he was to leave.

Before daylight, Miranda was awake and dressed, no difficult task as she had not slept for more than a few moments during the night. The recollection of Mr. Hastings's
appearance in her dressing room the night before had made
sleep impossible. He had stood barely a yard from her cot,
without a stitch to cover his chest. She ought to have repri-
manded him soundly, but she had been unable to catch her
breath, let alone think clearly enough to hand the man a
scold.

She wondered how she would look him in the eye this

morning, so awkward did she feel, but when she knocked at
the entrance to the bedchamber, and he called out that it
was quite safe to enter, she saw with gratitude that he now
wore his shirt. Casually, he held up his coat for inspection
and frowned. "This will never do," he announced. His preoccupation with his attire took the wind out of her sails.
She wondered what she had expected—that he would be
awaiting her appearance in a state of high suspense? That
he would pant after her like a hound after a fox? That he
would moon and pine and sigh for her? The suspicion
crossed her mind that he had come to her room the night
before for no other reason than to explain the matter of
dear Jane. Any thought that there had been another motive
might well have emanated from her mind, not his.

This realization gave her pause. She warned herself not
to rate her attractions too highly. Mr. Hastings was the sort
who preferred women of the world to young ladies from the
rural regions. His good looks, even under his bruises and
swollen cheek, guaranteed his success among the fair sex.
He had a manly energy and youthful mischievousness that
could not fail to enchant any woman who permitted herself
to be susceptible. As a result, he had no doubt amused himself with a great many women, all of them a thousand times
more attractive than the spinster daughter of his mother's
dearest friend. No, if she held any charms for Mr. Hastings,
they consisted solely of her usefulness in saving his skin.

Vowing not to indulge further in romantic notions, she
brought in the basin and pitcher and set them down on a
table so that he might perform his morning ablutions. It fascinated her to watch a man wash. He did it quickly and
roughly, as an afterthought. Oblivious to his bruises, he
rubbed his chin and cheeks, which sported a stubble. He inquired whether she might have a razor lying about.

"Of course, I do not have one," she said.

"It scarcely matters," he replied cheerfully, "for I know
where you may get one."

Her heart sank as she realized that if he meant to shave,
there would be another delay.

"Earlier, Miss Troy, you offered to fetch me pen and

paper. If you will be so kind as to do so now, I shall set about obtaining a razor and fresh clothes."

Uneasily, she said, "Mr. Hastings, you said you would leave at dawn. It is well past dawn now."

"You do not expect me to leave unshaved and wearing a wrinkled shirt?"

"I do not care how you leave, just so long as you leave."

He regarded her in surprise, then consternation. With a humility she knew was assumed, he bowed his head, sighed in the tone of a martyr, and put on his coat. "It appears you no longer fear having my blood on your hands, Miss Troy. I thought you wished to assist me to safety, to help me avoid certain death. However, I have been mistaken before and, if I live, I daresay, I shall be mistaken again. I have thought of an excellent plan to effect my escape from this house. I did not sleep a wink last night thinking of it. It would inconvenience you scarcely at all. But as you insist I leave you now, before so much as confiding the plan to you, I shall not protest. Nay, you shall not hear another sentence pass my lips, not a word, not a syllable, not a breath." As though marching to his doom, he went slowly to the door.

His parody of pathos was too amusing for her to hide her laughter. "What is your plan, Mr. Hastings?" she said.

Animated, he came to her and drew her to the chaise longue. Inviting her to sit, he said, "I must assume a disguise."

"What sort of disguise?"

"You shall see."

"Why is it necessary for you to disguise yourself?"

"Principally for the adventure of it, but also because I wish to exit this house without causing a stir and without catching the notice of anybody who may be watching the house."

"Oh, do you think they are watching the house?"

"I think it very likely. Moreover, I do not wish my mother to know anything of this business. If my plan is successful, I shall be able to quit London without encountering Everard or any of his henchmen."

Only one part of this speech affected Miranda. "You mean to quit London?"

He smiled. "Oh, I am well aware that you will miss me dreadfully when I go. I have been such an amusing guest, have I not? Nevertheless, it is best that I find a venue where I may recover from my head wound without fear of discovery. In the few days it will take me to recover, I shall devise a plan to deal with Everard."

With a trace of a pout, she replied, "I do not see that you must leave Town in order to recover."

Taking her hand, he looked at it a moment, then put it to his lips. "Conceited as I am, I take that to mean you do not wish to see me go."

His warmth evidently alarmed her. She pulled her hand away and stood. "You are mistaken. There is nothing I wish for more ardently. Simply tell me what I must do to expedite this plan of yours."

Folding his arms, he sat back and took the measure of her. If she did like him, he saw, she was not going to confess it. So intently did he study her that she blushed.

It was just as well, he thought, that she professed eagerness to see the last of him. If she had given the least suggestion of regretting his departure, he would have had the devil of a time tearing himself away.

At the first opportunity, Miranda put a note and a coin in the hands of a footman. The note was addressed to Felix DeWitt, and the coin insured the servant's discretion. It was Felix who would supply the costume and bring the carriage that would take Mr. Hastings into the country. Until he answered the letter, they could do nothing further.

To pass the time, Mr. Hastings applied himself to drafting the initial pages of his book, which, he informed Miranda, was to be entitled *Hastings's Principles of Gaming*. While he was so occupied, Miranda was employed in obtaining some breakfast for him. It had now been a day and a half since he had eaten. She feared that he would faint from hunger before he could leave, and she was determined there should be no further obstacles to that end. She persuaded

Daisy to bring her a chop, smoked fish, fried egg, biscuit, muffin, and coffee, and to say nothing to her Mama, who would fret herself into a frenzy at this unaccountable display of voraciousness in her daughter. Miranda explained her appetite to the girl by saying that she had read Dr. Bearhaves's prescriptions for overcoming a cold, the first of which was to eat a hearty breakfast. When the maid accepted this lie without a murmur, Miranda sighed, not merely at her duplicity, but at its success. Lies rolled off her tongue so often and so easily that she might, if she wished, find employment with a London newspaper.

After receiving Mr. Hastings's instructions regarding his escape, she left him to his meal while she went to sit with their mothers in a sunny parlor overlooking Queen Street. Although she was reluctant to face their anxious questions regarding her health, she wished even more to forestall a visit from one of them to her bedchamber. Mr. Hastings had had no difficulty hiding from Daisy when she came in to bring the breakfast tray or air the feather bed or wash down the tapered bedposts, for she was a trusting young girl who never noticed anything out of the way, whether it was toes sticking out from under a bed or unexplained noises in the wardrobe. But a mother always noticed something out of the way, however minuscule. Her mother had an uncanny knack for being on the alert for oddities, especially when her daughter went to great lengths to hide them.

Entering the parlor, Miranda found the ladies with their heads bent over a pretty patchwork. They worked in silence; an air of gloom appeared to oppress them.

"Good morning," Miranda greeted them, causing them to glance up. To their inquiries, she answered that she was on the mend, a report that did not produce the joyful smiles on their faces she had expected. Each congratulated her on her recovery and cautioned her not to exert herself overmuch lest she suffer a relapse. They invited her to take up a corner of the patchwork and apply her stitching to the flower pattern. These inquiries and invitations were delivered with such an air of sorrow that Miranda was obliged to ask, "What is the matter?"

Mrs. Hastings put her linen to the corner of her eye. "It is Charles," she said. "I've had no word from him."

Miranda's heart went out to the poor woman. She longed to tell her that her son was safe under her own roof.

"Perhaps," Lady Troy ventured, "he wrote to you, Tabitha, and the letter was lost."

Mrs. Hastings shook her head. "I have sent the servants several times now to inquire at his house. He never returned after the soiree. I am convinced something has happened to him."

Again, Lady Troy endeavored to allay her friend's fears. "Perhaps he has gone off with an acquaintance and will write you when he returns to Town."

"No, no, it is not like him to neglect me so. Even when he takes a lady to the country, he never forgets to send word."

"I am convinced you need not put yourself in such a stew, Tabitha. All will be well, as long as you do not fret yourself. I have it! We shall go out today, and you shall occupy yourself with shopping, and by the time we sit down to supper, you shall laugh at yourself, and you shall receive word of Mr. Hastings and be ashamed that you were such a ninnyhammer."

"Do you mean to be gone long?" Miranda asked, hoping they would not return until she had got rid of Mr. Hastings.

"We shall be gone a very long time," her mother replied, "for I fear it will take many shops and many purchases to cure dear Tabitha of her blue devils."

Biting back tears, Mrs. Hastings replied, "Surely he would have taken a few belongings with him if he had gone away, but Dimpson says not a single item of clothing has been taken, and not one of his valises." Here she dropped her section of the patchwork and wrung her hands.

Unable to restrain herself, Miranda reached out and covered the lady's hands with her own. "It would not surprise me," she said softly, "if Mr. Hastings had got himself in a game of piquet and was lost to all sense of time."

"Oh," said Mrs. Hastings, as she was struck with the strong likelihood that Miss Troy had hit on the very thing.

Lady Troy frowned. "You did not tell me, Miranda, that Mr. Hastings was fond of cards. I did not think you had spent sufficient time in his company to discover a liking for piquet, or for anything else."

Miranda kept silent rather than utter another falsehood.

Her mother fixed her with an expression of concern. Miranda blushed but was spared the necessity of replying by her mother's asking, "Is that why you quarreled with Mr. Hastings, because he is fond of cards and you are not?"

The relief that flushed over her nearly provoked a smile, but she caught herself in time. Bowing her head meekly, she said, "It is true, Mama, that Mr. Hastings and I do not agree in the matter of cards. But perhaps I have been a trifle strict in my views. At any rate, I believe I can promise not to dislike the gentleman merely on account of his fondness for piquet."

Her mother would have inquired further but the butler entered with a note, which he handed to Miranda. Quickly she read it. Then, aware that the two mothers observed her closely, she said, "It seems a gentleman has come to call." She did her utmost to appear tranquil as she spoke.

"I was not aware," said her mother, "that you had any acquaintance in London."

"Oh, I do not!"

"Then who is calling?"

Miranda bit her lip, unwilling to speak a lie if she could help it. Abruptly she stood and said, "I shall go and see my visitor, and then I shall be able to tell you all."

On that, she left the two ladies to their puzzlement and went directly to the library, where a gentleman she had never seen awaited her. He was a round-faced, pleasant-looking, sumptuously dressed fellow about the same age as Mr. Hastings, but very different from him in form and figure. While Mr. Hastings was lean and energetic, the stranger was plump and slow. While Mr. Hastings exuded a boyish appeal, which bordered on the dangerous, the visitor put one immediately at ease with his ruddy cheeks and pale eyes. At the moment, those eyes were full of anxiety.

"Do you know where Hastings is?" he asked.

"Are you Mr. DeWitt?"

Felix nodded impatiently. "Is he well?"

"I am pleased to be able to assure you that Mr. Hastings is quite well, except for a head wound, and as to that, I believe he is recovering rapidly."

Putting his linen to his brow, Felix mopped up beads of perspiration. Miranda detected tears of relief in his eye. "I thought he might be dead. From Everard's hints and smirks at Mrs. Stout's, I was certain Hastings had met him and had got himself killed."

"There was no duel. Three men, whom I believe to have been hired by Lord Everard, set upon Mr. Hastings."

"Gad, there were three rapscallions lurking near the door as I came to call just now. Very burly they were, and not at all agreeable."

At this news, Miranda grew alarmed. The thought of three attackers hovering so near the house made her forget what an inconvenience it was to have Mr. Hastings underfoot. She realized how perilous it was for him to leave. Thank Heaven, she thought, he meant to disguise his appearance.

"I did not intend to frighten you," Felix said. "I beg your pardon."

In some agitation, she confessed, "I fear they mean to do Mr. Hastings great harm. Indeed, they would have made short work of him earlier if they had not been prevented."

"What prevented them?"

In heightened color, Miranda replied, "Mr. Hastings will tell you everything in good time. Meanwhile, have you brought the things he sent for?"

Felix nodded and reached to his feet for a package tied in paper and bound with string. He handed it to her. "What the devil Charles wants with such frippery is more than I can fathom. Instead of pranking, he should look for a way out of this pickle. His being alive is good news, but Everard will certainly look to remedy that condition."

"This frippery *is* his means of escape. Mr. Hastings wishes to disguise himself."

Felix's jaw dropped. "Disguise himself?"

"Yes, and given what you have said of the danger he may yet be in, I think he is wise to take such a precaution."

After a time, Felix's grimace faded. With a shrug, he said, "Well, if Hastings does not mind looking a fool, I suppose I ought not to mind either."

"If you will come to the mews at three o'clock today, when everybody will be gone from the house, Mr. Hastings will meet you there. You must instruct your coachman to wait at some distance, so that it will appear you walked to Queen Street. You will both be seen knocking at the front door, and then leaving again a minute later. Those watching will report that Mr. DeWitt and a companion called on Mrs. Hastings while she was out. And as nothing exceptionable will be observed, you and Mr. Hastings may walk to where the carriage waits and immediately drive into the country. That is what Mr. Hastings desired me to say to you."

"Oh, I may drive with him to the country, may I? Did it never occur to him that I might be engaged this evening? Did it never occur to him that I have no wish to quit London? Did it never occur to him that Lady Ponsenby, who has the best chef in Europe, has invited me to dine? Did it never occur to him that her ladyship means to serve haricot of lamb and sweet sour venison?"

The thought struck Miranda that the excellence of Lady Ponsenby's menu might well delay Mr. Hastings's departure for twenty-four hours. And though she would have given much to see him safe, she could not endure another night with him. The man's presence was more than a nuisance, more than a threat to her reputation. It was intolerable. Every time they conversed or disputed or played cards, he smiled at her very particularly, as though he guessed at some secret she kept in her heart. Some sign of him was always about the chamber—a coat stained with blood, a cravat he had tied around her journal so that he would not read it by accident, a shirt carelessly tossed onto a chair, a linen that smelled starkly of its owner. She lived in fear every moment that somebody would enter and spy one of his belongings.

When some item of his was not underfoot, he was. It

seemed they were always passing one another in the tiniest
spaces. They lived so intimately that it was often difficult
to breathe. And then there had been the episode of the previous evening. It had made her almost feverish to look up
and find him watching her as she lay in her cot, the candlelight alternately throwing shade and light on his chest. Although she had assumed an unruffled manner in snuffing
the candle and turning her back, she had felt anything but
cool. She had remained awake the rest of the night, electri-
cally alive to the fact of his presence in the next room. Consequently, she had awakened the next morning looking
positively owlish. It would not do to spend another night—
nay, another moment—in such proximity to the man.

"I am certain," she said carefully, "that Mr. Hastings has
no intention of being high-handed in this matter. He merely
wishes to get to a place of safety where he may permit his
wound to heal and think of a plan to deal with Lord Everard."

"Could it not wait until tomorrow?"

His plea was most pathetic, but she remained adamant.
"If it were not a matter of life and death, Mr. Hastings
would not hesitate to oblige you, I feel certain. In this instance, however, I'm afraid it must be today."

All at once Felix looked at her with curiosity. "Who are
you, Miss Troy? Why do you take such an interest in Hastings? Why do you speak for him? Are you the one who is
hiding him?"

These pointed questions raised color in her cheeks. She
forced herself to say, "May I tell Mr. Hastings that you will
come at three? Or do you mean to disappoint him?"

Sighing for the lamb and the venison, Felix said, "Oh,
very well, I shall come. But I shall expect him to make it up
to me. And you may tell him so."

Miranda smiled. "It shall be my pleasure."

"Be sure and tell him that if we stop at an inn which
boasts an inferior bill of fare, I shall never again borrow a
shilling from him. Tell him that!"

Demurely, Miranda promised.

* * *

At the door to her chamber, Miranda was intercepted. "Who was your caller, my pet?" her mother inquired.

"Mr. DeWitt." Miranda endeavored unsuccessfully to mask the fact that she carried a large package tied with string.

"I am aware of that. The butler gave me his name. Who is he?"

"Who is he?"

"Yes, how did you make his acquaintance?"

"I never met him before, Mama."

"Why does he call on you then?"

"Why?"

"Yes, why? Are you acquainted with a relation of his? Or an acquaintance?"

"Yes, that is it."

"Oh, I see. Somebody you were at school with, I expect."

Miranda did not answer.

"DeWitt? I cannot recollect that you were at school with anybody by that name."

In despair, Miranda considered divulging the entire truth. If she uttered one more lie, she felt, she would choke on it.

"At the same time," Lady Troy said, "I cannot be expected to remember every girl you were at school with, can I, my pet?"

Miserably, Miranda answered, "No, of course not."

"Well, as you were at school with her, you must invite her to drink tea with us. I am certain Tabitha would enjoy the company of a young person. The poor creature is in such fidgets over Mr. Hastings's neglect that I daresay she would welcome a distraction."

Miranda hoped that the conversation was now at an end. Unfortunately, her mother did not betray any intention of leaving.

"My pet," said her ladyship sorrowfully, "I wish you could have liked Mr. Hastings a little. He really is awfully eligible, and handsome, too. I do not understand how you can be impervious to his attractions. But," she added with a profound sigh, "I expect a daughter is not likely to admire the same gentleman her mother admires. Shall I help you inside with your books?"

Paralyzed, Miranda repeated, "My books?"

Lady Troy indicated the package Miranda half shielded behind her skirt.

She stammered. "I believe I shall manage very well."

"My pet," her mother said gently, "I must warn you."

Closing her eyes, Miranda waited for what was to come.

"You must promise me you will not ruin yourself."

Aghast that her mother should hit so close to the truth, she opened her eyes wide.

"If you do nothing but pore over books day and night, you shall be ruined, you know. It is all very well to have a hobbyhorse and to apply yourself diligently to the study of landscape gardening, but you must not let it keep you indoors every minute of the day or you will make yourself ill with too much study."

Near tears, Miranda kissed her mother. "You are very kind," she said hoarsely.

"Promise me, my pet."

What she promised she could not have said, but she did promise something. Giving her mother an apologetic smile, she slipped inside the bedchamber, closed the door, and leaned against it. Mr. Hastings came to her at once. But before he could greet her in his usual hearty manner, she put a silencing finger to his lips.

EIGHT

Cousin Charlotte

Today I have studied groves, coppices, lime walks, dovecotes, stew ponds, succession houses, prospects, vistas, yew arbors, bowers, gravel walks, sweeps, paddocks, and ha-ha's, but I do not think I recollect a syllable of what I have read. Mr. Hastings has gone, and under such circumstances, that I cannot stop the pounding of my pulse, let alone absorb a chapter on landscape gardening.

The stricken look on her face had brought him to her side. Taking the package from her, he would have expressed his concern, but she stopped him, and in such a manner as to tempt him to kiss her fingertip. She shook her head, indicating he must not speak. "My mother," she whispered.

Together, their foreheads almost touching, they listened at the door. After a considerable time, they were sufficiently reassured by the silence to open it a fraction of an inch. At Mr. Hastings's silent invitation, Miranda peeked outside. Her head reemerged a second later. She reported, with infinite relief, "She is gone." Coming inside again, she pressed the door closed, paused, and put her head in her hands.

It struck him that the deception she was maintaining for his sake was taking a very great toll on her. Though she was courageous, she did not lie easily or well, and as that constituted one of her most admirable qualities, he could not help wishing to ease her mind. The best means of easing it, he acknowledged, was to give her the gift of his absence, and though he had become increasingly disinclined to do that, he was ready to put her welfare before his own, not only because he liked her but because he was in danger of liking her too well. He was not accustomed to liking ladies who did not like him in return. If he did not take care, the wound on his head would fester in his heart.

Lifting the package she had brought, he carted it to the bed, untied and unwrapped it, and examined the contents. "Damn!" he said. He glanced at Miranda to see whether she had heard. She appeared oblivious. She had not moved, except that her hands now rested at her sides.

It was up to him, he saw, to shake her out of her distress. He fell back on the device that had always succeeded in stirring her in the past, namely, goading her.

"Damn!" he said, a great deal louder this time.

She stared at him and, it seemed to him that after a time, she was recalled to the present.

"Felix forgot the hair."

Perplexed, she approached.

He paced, as though irritated. "How does he expect me to disguise myself without hair? What can he have been thinking of? I cannot possibly make my escape in my own hair."

Miranda staggered to a chair and sat. "I suppose, Mr. Hastings," she said numbly, "that the want of hair will necessitate your remaining another night."

Her forlornness pierced something in him. He did not like to see her unhappy. More particularly, he did not like to see her unhappy on his account. He came near and, standing behind her chair, resisted the impulse to put a hand on her shoulder. "I shall not torment your another night—not another hour, if I can help it," he said with feeling.

Skeptically, she shook her head.

"Do not despair, Miss Troy. Though Felix neglected to send the hair, I know where some may be found."

A tear glimmered; she turned her face to wipe it away.

"It will take scarcely a moment for you to get it."

She turned and looked up at him, aghast. "You expect *me* to get it?"

"Well, *I* cannot very well steal into my mother's bedchamber, can I? Suppose somebody should see me?"

She shot from the chair. "Your mother's bedchamber? You have forced me to lie and deceive at every turn, and now you expect me to rob the kindest hostess in the world?"

He noted with satisfaction that she was too furious with him now to be melancholy. "Not *rob*, Miss Troy. Merely *borrow*. She is my mother, after all. I am certain if I asked her for the loan of one of her hairpieces, she would not hesitate. She quite dotes on me, you know."

It pleased him to see her roll her eyes and throw up her hands. Indignation had roused her. She was animated, alive, adorable. "Very well, Miss Troy," he said in his martyr's voice, "if you are too craven to fetch me a bit of my mother's hair so that I might get out of yours once and for all, I shall just have to do it myself." On that, he went to the door. He took grave steps, as though he were marching to the chopping block.

As he reached for the knob, he felt her hand on his arm, stopping him.

"I shall do it!" she said between her teeth.

"You are very good." As he gazed into her large brown eyes, he was obliged to warn himself not to go too far. He discerned in her face a vulnerability that coexisted with her strength. It gave him the impulse to take her in his arms and not let go. If he was not careful, he told himself with rueful irony, he would end by gratifying their mothers' fondest wish.

"I would do anything, short of murder, to see the last of you," she hissed, and in an instant, was gone, leaving him with the knowledge that once again he had gained his object with Miss Troy and once again success tasted like ashes on the tongue.

As soon as she found herself at the door of Mrs. Hastings's bedchamber, Miranda regretted her credulousness. She had permitted Mr. Hastings to maneuver her into stealing his mother's hair. As usual, he had found the means of compelling her to do what offended her principles. And instead of seeing through the transparent device, she had allowed herself to be taken in. There was no end to her naïveté, just as there was no end to the man's odiousness. At her age, she ought to have known better. Indeed, she was so easily taken in, one would think she was besotted with love.

The door opened suddenly, and Mrs. Hastings, wearing a bonnet and a matching sable-trimmed barouche coat came out. She stopped when she saw Miranda. "My dear," she said in as much surprise as concern, "is something the matter?"

As Miranda could truthfully say there was, she nodded vigorously.

Taking her by the hand, Mrs. Hastings drew her into her bedchamber. "You must tell me all about it," she said.

Devoutly, Miranda wished she could.

Mrs. Hastings led her to a chaise longue upholstered in a silvery green satin. She sat and induced Miranda to sit by her side. "You need not be afraid of telling me, Miranda. Your mama and I have been more than sisters these many years. We conceal nothing from each other. Will you do me the honor of allowing me to extend such a rare, valuable, and cherished friendship to yourself?"

This generosity nearly undid Miranda. She dared not speak for fear of weeping.

Seeing her distress, Mrs. Hastings squeezed her hand. "Is it Charles?" she whispered.

Jolted, Miranda stared at her.

"There, there," her hostess said soothingly. "I have hit on the very thing, have I not? I am well aware the two of you did not get on when you were introduced at the soiree. Let me assure you, I do not blame you. Nor do I blame Charles. If anybody is at fault it is your mother and I. We ought never to have insisted upon your meeting. With two mothers poking and prodding at you, you were bound to take one another in dislike."

Before she knew what she was saying, Miranda protested, "We do not dislike each other!"

Mrs. Hastings blinked at her. "Oh, I felt certain you did."

Reddening, Miranda said, "I scarcely know him. It is difficult to dislike a creature one scarcely knows."

"Very true, but I promise you, if you are to know each other better in future, it shall not be a result of any stratagems on my part. No, dear girl, fate will have to bring you and Charles together, or you shall have to do it yourselves. I wash my hands of the business. I have said as much to your mother, and she quite agrees. And so you must give me your word that you will not distress yourself any longer with regard to my son."

Miranda wondered how to bring the conversation around to the subject of hair.

"I fear I have overset you, my dear."

Should she pretend to admire her hostess's coif? Should she complain that her own hair lacked fullness and required a supplement? Mrs. Hastings's collection of hairpieces had not escaped her notice. Indeed, the lady wore so many different shades and styles and so often knocked them askew that it would have been impossible not to notice. Should she feign a desire to purchase a hairpiece and solicit Mrs. Hastings's advice?

Mrs. Hastings rose. "I can see," she said tenderly, "that you require a few moments alone. Perhaps I ought never to have mentioned Charles. I perceive the subject makes you uneasy, and I quite understand. I fret a good deal on his account, as you do, but your mama says I am a goose for doing so, and one goose living in Queen Street is sufficient, I think. I shall take myself off now. Lady Troy has been waiting for me these several minutes, and I shall leave you to collect yourself." On that, the kind lady kissed her forehead. Then she tiptoed away, closing the door behind her.

When she had gone, Miranda looked about the room. Not five feet away, stood Mrs. Hastings's dressing table. On it sat a head. And on the head sat a wig of bright yellow curls.

In Miranda's absence, Mr. Hastings had donned the costume Felix had sent, a bottle-green morning dress, a matching tippet, and a cottage bonnet. Peering at himself in the glass, he turned his head from side to side to see whether the bruises on his cheeks were well hidden by the narrowness of his hat and his skillfully applied rouge and powder. For the most part, they were. His boyish good looks and newly shaved chin could easily be mistaken for a female complexion, if one did not look too closely. Nevertheless, he would not feel quite the thing until he had hair curling fetchingly from his bonnet. He wished Miss Troy would hurry.

Felix had had no difficulty, he trusted, in acquiring the ensemble. Mr. Charles Hastings was almost as well-known in various elegant houses of pleasure as he was in Mrs. Stout's gaming establishment. Any one of a dozen ladies would have leaped at the opportunity to trust him with one of her best dresses and finest hats. Moreover, the ladies would have refrained from asking Felix any questions. Their morals might not bear up against close scrutiny, but their discretion was unimpeachable.

His only difficulty had been squirming into the blasted dress. Luckily, he had had considerable experience in pinning and unpinning, buttoning and unbuttoning, tying and untying ladies' garments, and thus he had schooled himself to be patient. Even more important, he had discovered the efficacy of shawls, tippets, and capuchins in hiding what could not be fastened or tied. In the time Miss Troy had been gone, he had contrived to clothe himself, and even though the back of his dress remained unbuttoned and he could not seem to get his bosoms to match, he did think he made rather a creditable female.

At the sound of the handle in the door, he turned. Before he could invite Miss Troy's approval of his disguise, she glanced his way and said in a weary voice, "Oh, Daisy, you needn't bother with the feather bed today. Tomorrow will do as well." Then she stopped. Clearly, she suspected that she was not addressing Daisy. After all, Daisy would not don a bonnet and a tippet in order to shake out the feather bed. As Mr. Hastings watched this logic penetrate, he could not help admiring her. Intelligence lit her expression like a star shower. He smiled to see her studying him.

"Daisy?" she said uncertainly.

"I see you have brought my hair," he said, taking the wig from her. Untying the bonnet, he set it on the dressing table, then peered into the glass to adjust the fair curls on his head. "This is not one of my mother's best pieces, Miss Troy. I do wish you had contrived to find me out something a trifle less gaudy."

Disbelieving, she said, "You do not mean to disguise yourself as a female!"

"You do not like my raiment, I collect. I confess, the color is not as flattering to my complexion as apricot or biscuit, but I think it will serve."

"Do be serious, Mr. Hastings. There are three men watching the house even now. Mr. DeWitt told me so. I fear they may be Everard's men. You must not risk exposure."

"I quite agree, which is why I have adopted this ingenious disguise. His lordship's henchmen will be on the lookout for a gentleman, not a gentle*woman*. I shall steal away right under their noses." He laughed as he fitted the bonnet over the wig.

In the glass, he could see Miranda's expression. Her anxiety seemed to increase with every jest he made, and he found himself in an interesting pickle. He was gratified by her disquiet; it demonstrated a real concern for his wellbeing, one which he flattered himself went beyond the concern she would feel for any ordinary human creature in danger of losing his life. At the same time, he could not witness her troubled expression without wishing to soothe and soften it.

"But what if they do not see a gentlewoman issue from this house?" she cried. "What if they should recognize you?"

Smiling, he faced her. "Miss Troy, do you mean to impugn the excellence of my ensemble? I assure you, this dress was stitched by the finest modiste in Bond Street."

She shook her fists. "You delude yourself, Mr. Hastings. Nobody will ever take you for a female."

Approaching her, he put his hands on his hips. "And why not, if I may inquire? I have shaved. My figure is passable, especially if I cover it with a cape. My gloves, reticule, and slippers are in the highest kick of fashion."

He was aware that as her eyes swept over his figure, she blushed profoundly. He asked, "My dear Miss Troy, what is wanting?"

She looked at the window curtain, not at him. It seemed that as a female he made her even more uneasy than as a male.

"For one thing, you do not walk like a female," she said.

"If you mean I do not take small mincing steps, you are right. That would constitute mockery. The females I observe walk in the manner of rational people, and I intend to follow their inspiring example."

"Then you must walk, not stride!" She sounded almost fierce.

Suddenly, their eyes locked. It occurred to him that having been a female for nearly thirty years, Miss Troy had greater experience in the feminine line than he and that her advice might be worth heeding. Besides, sparring with her entertained him as well as piquet, better in some aspects, and he meant to keep it up as long as she would permit. "Very well," he said magnificently. "Bowing to your superior knowledge in this matter, I shall endeavor not to stride." Thereupon, he proceeded to walk, adjusting the size and manner of his steps. "Thank you," he said, for as his walk improved, he began to enjoy himself. It was possible, he discovered, to walk gracefully without an excess of daintiness. "That will do splendidly, I think," he announced.

She shook her head. "It will not do at all. There is the matter of your voice, Mr. Hastings. How will you disguise your voice?"

"I shall not disguise it. I shall not need to. Everard's men will not engage me in conversation. In the carriage, if I speak at all to Felix, I shall whisper, so that neither the coachman nor the footman shall hear me."

She shook her head, still unable to allow her eyes to rest on him for more than three seconds together. "You may argue and cajole all you like," she said, "but I cannot be persuaded. Nor, do I think, will you persuade anybody else that you are female, especially not the men who so brutally attacked you. They will know you for a man in an instant."

"I beg leave to disagree. You are not convinced because you know that I am a man disguised as a woman. But anybody who does not know will trust that what he sees is in fact what is. He will have no reason to doubt it."

Her arms folded tightly across her chest, she insisted, "You do not understand. It has nothing to do with your disguise. If it were merely a question of clothing, you would succeed. But you carry yourself with an air which nobody could mistake. There is about you a resonance, an aura, which is decidedly masculine. Nobody will believe you to be female."

Intrigued by this analysis, he came close to her, so close that she was compelled to look up at him. In her expression, he read consternation. He smiled, but she did not return the smile. It seemed to him that she really was in great trepidation over his safety and that he did not merely imagine it. He took pleasure in her concern.

"What are you willing to wager?" he asked.

Appalled, she grew pale. "You wish to place a bet on such a matter? Mr. Hastings, you might be killed!"

"Do not overset yourself on that point. I shall leave explicit instructions to my executors to pay you your winnings after my demise."

She stamped her foot. "I do not give a groat for collecting my winnings. My aim is to persuade you to reconsider this foolish course you are set on."

"And my aim is to persuade you that my course is not foolish in the least. In fact, I am so convinced my disguise is brilliant that I am willing to lay a bet on it. And you, Miss Troy—are you willing to stand behind your conviction, too?"

"Do you expect me to wager on your life?"

"Yes."

She put her hand to her forehead. "I do not understand you. How can you disregard the risk you take for the sake of a bet?"

"There is risk in everything we do. Your standing here with me now in your bedchamber is a risk. Suppose Daisy should come in, neglecting to knock? Suppose a fire should break out and the two of us were to be seen issuing from your chamber? Suppose I should forget myself in a moment of violent passion and do insult to your person? These are all risks, and yet you stand here, chatting with me, as though I were no more than a eunuch and not at all the gentleman your mother and mine wished you to marry."

He could see that his speech staggered her. The images he had painted were affecting. By turns, dismay, pain, and horror flashed across her face. The word "eunuch" provoked a crimson blush. The reference to their mother's wish replaced the crimson with the palest of whites.

She let out a breath and gestured helplessly. "I do not know what to say."

"Say what you will wager."

When she answered with a pained look, he took her hand. He forgot that he was attired in a morning dress, wig, and bonnet, and put the hand to his lips. "Will you cruelly refuse to indulge the last wish of a doomed man?" he said.

"I do not know what to wager," she said unhappily.

"I have it. I shall leave you my book—*Hastings's Principles of Gaming*. After all, you were my Muse, so to speak. You ought to have it. If you win, you have my permission to have it privately published and distributed to all my acquaintance, including Everard."

She half turned away. "Please do not speak of my winning. I do not wish to win."

"Ordinarily, I should feel obliged to hand you a lecture on gamesmanship, Miss Troy. I should expound all the reasons why winning is in every way necessary and noble. In this instance, however, I shall forego that duty. I do not wish you to win any more than you do."

"Then we are agreed on one point, at any rate."

"And if I win, what shall be my prize?"

"Other than your life, what could you possibly wish to have?"

A dozen thoughts came to his mind, among them, a lock

of her hair, a dance, a kiss. But he only said, "What you say is true. One would think that one's life would constitute enough of a prize, but it does not. I must collect my winnings, even if they are merely buttons. It is a prime principle of gaming that the winner must come away with something tangible, however minuscule."

With a tinge of bitterness, she said, "Perhaps you would like to have a painted screen. We have at least half a dozen at liberty at Arundel Abbey."

"I should much prefer a game of piquet."

She blanched. "If you succeed in eluding Everard's men, I shall have to learn to play piquet?"

"Do we have a wager, Miss Troy?"

For a moment, he thought she would refuse. The conflict in her breast played itself out on her lovely face. After a time, she sighed and appeared to relent. Reluctantly, she extended her hand. He took it, and they shook on the bet. Then, inhaling with bracing vigor, he turned his back to her and permitted her to fasten his buttons.

Miranda led him down the back stairs that exited on the mews. At the door, she wished him well and made as if to go.

"Miss Troy," he said, preventing her from leaving, "before you leave me, you must allow me to thank you."

Inexplicably, his sincerity confounded her. Whenever he said anything to her of a kind, friendly nature, she experienced an excruciating uneasiness. He was easier to deal with when he was odious. She put up her hand, saying, "Please say nothing more on the subject. I shall go inside and wait for your appearance at the front door."

He grasped her hand. The intent look he wore made her catch her breath. "I do not believe," he said, "that I have ever met a woman of such courage, integrity, and generosity as you."

This was too much for her. It would have been easier if he had engaged her in a dispute. Earnestness undid her altogether. "Please," she said, trying to stop him from continuing.

He inspected her palm, then smiled at her. "I must also thank you for not saying that I look ridiculous in my costume, which I no doubt do."

At this reference, she stared at him, aware as though for the first time that he was dressed in the garb of a woman. So conscious was she of his manliness that his disguise seemed irrelevant. This recognition brought heat to her cheeks. Luckily, at that instant, she heard Felix's footfall. "Mr. DeWitt has come," she said, withdrawing her hand. When he turned to meet his friend, she dashed up the stairs and made her way to the saloon at the front of the house, thankful to have escaped. The farewell had left her breathless, and it required several moments of quiet reflection to collect her wits.

As she made her way to the sitting room in anticipation of receiving visitors, she wondered if she would ever learn to be easy in Mr. Hastings's company. Then it occurred to her that she would never know. In ten minutes, perhaps five, he would set forth from Queen Street, and she would never see him again.

If that fact inspired any emotion, she had no time to examine it. She heard the butler answer the door, then heard him say that the ladies had gone out but Miss Troy was at home. A moment later, Mr. Hastings and Mr. DeWitt were ushered into her presence. Mr. DeWitt glanced at Mr. Hastings a thousand times with ill-concealed hilarity. Mr. Hastings did not deign to notice but comported himself with serene dignity. Miranda observed that he did not play his role by using exaggerated gestures or silly mannerisms. Nevertheless, she could not look at him without seeing the gentleman who had appeared in her dressing room without his shirt, candlelight dancing on his generously furred chest. He could spend the rest of his life wearing flounces and feathers, she thought; she would never forget that he was a man.

"Mrs. Hastings and my mother have gone out," she said for the benefit of the butler. "Perhaps you will be so good as to call another time."

"Alas," said Felix, playing his role grandly, "my cousin

must return to the country, and I with her. Please present my compliments to Mrs. Hastings and say that I shall present them to her myself when I return to Town." Having carried off this little speech with gratifying effect, he stepped past the butler and went outside.

Miranda and Mr. Hastings followed. They looked up and down the street and, though Miranda could not tell what Mr. Hastings saw, she herself was unsettled to see across the way the figure of a man who bore a striking resemblance to Lord Everard. Her eyes sought out Mr. Hastings's, and they might have exchanged a furtive word when, at that moment, a hack drove up in front of the house, blocking their view of the figure.

To Miranda's horror, when the driver opened the door, he handed out Mrs. Hastings and Lady Troy, both of whom caught sight at the same time of the visitors standing on the step. Mrs. Hastings, dabbing at her eyes with a linen, hurried past them and disappeared inside. Mr. Hastings started and would have gone after her if Miranda had not clutched his hand and prevented him. His concern for his mother was evident, but he must be prevented from committing any action that would give him away.

It was left to Miranda to supply the greetings. She contrived to present Mr. DeWitt and his cousin to Lady Troy with a tolerable semblance of tranquility and to add that they were engaged elsewhere and must be on their road without delay. She then bade them farewell and turned to take her mother indoors.

"I shall not hear of their going away," Lady Troy said, slipping her arm through Mr. Hastings's. "They must come in and drink a glass of ratafia." Before Miranda could object, Mr. Hastings nodded his acceptance of the invitation. In another moment, her mother had led him inside.

NINE

Downish

Hastings's Fifth Principle of Gaming: There are as many different species of gamesters as there are of birds or flowers, and I have gone to the trouble of naming them, just as Adam named the creatures he consorted with in Paradise. First is the fellow one too often meets whom I like to call The Smart, that is, the gentleman who has no real love for games of chance but indulges because he wishes to be seen doing whatever he imagines to be the current fashion. Another type is The Gambler, whose practice it is to seduce innocents into playing for high stakes. The Merchant regards gaming not as a sport but as a means of getting his living, while The Birdwit is consumed with gaming and cannot forgo a bet, no matter how done up he is or how little pleasure he derives from it. The fellow who asks to be duped is The Gull, and the one who asks anybody and everybody to lend him money so that he may squander it at the tables is The Dunster. Finally, there is The Stallion. He is the gamester who is so clever and cunning that he gains a reputation for being unconquerable. Indeed, the frequency and degree of his triumphs make it appear that no man born of woman can beat him. But the truth is that he can easily be undone, and by no other gamester than himself. He is his own undoing. Too confident by half, he forgets to keep his sights on the game. He permits his thoughts to deviate and his heart to cleave to a mistress other than Lady Luck. He falls in love, and before he knows it, his pot is gone and no amount of diligence will help him recoup what he has lost.

* * *

Hurrying after them Miranda came inside, with Felix following close behind. One glance at his blanched face informed her that she could not look for assistance in that quarter. He was speechless with terror. Mr. Hastings's hand was still tucked irrevocably in Lady Troy's arm.

Outside the saloon, her ladyship stopped, released Mr. Hastings, and whispered so that all three might hear, "My poor dear Tabitha. She is quite distraught, I fear."

"Is she ill?" Miranda inquired. She glanced momentarily at Mr. Hastings to see how he had borne this observation on his mother's condition. As far as she could discern, he had not borne it well. It was not anything she saw in his face, for the bonnet scarcely permitted one to see his face. She knew it instinctively. She was able to see in his posture and his manner of turning his head an irrepressible impatience.

"No, not ill," Lady Troy replied, "just downish." Darkly, she added, "It is her son."

Miranda saw Mr. Hastings stiffen.

Felix cleared his throat nervously. "Her son?" he repeated with assumed lightness. "Why Hastings is the best fellow in the world."

Lady Troy confided, "Yes, indeed, but she has not heard any word of him for some days now. It appears he has disappeared, and she is most anxious on his behalf. We were obliged to interrupt our shopping, for she burst into tears in the middle of Grafton House."

Miranda grew alarmed at Mr. Hastings's demeanor. He appeared agitated. Determined that he should not give himself away, she slipped her arm around his waist, in the manner of girlish intimates, saying, "I am sorry to hear it, Mama. I shall just bid Mr. and Miss DeWitt good-bye, and then I shall sit with Mrs. Hastings as long as she requires company."

"Yes," said Felix with false heartiness, "and please do extend my compliments to the lady. We must be off now."

Mr. Hastings glanced in surprise at Miranda's hand on his waist. Instantly, he put his hand around hers, and pulled her close. The glare she shot him only tightened his hold or her.

"No, no, I insist that you come inside," Lady Troy protested, "if not for the sake of the ratafia then for the sake of Mrs. Hastings. The company of young people is precisely what she needs to set her to rights again."

"Oh, but Mama, you must excuse them. They are engaged elsewhere." She endeavored to extricate herself from Mr. Hastings's firm grip, but could not without calling her squirming to her mother's attention.

"Engaged elsewhere. That is precisely what we are," Felix chimed in. "In any other circumstances, we should be only too happy to spend a quarter hour cheering Mrs. Hastings and drinking her punch and perhaps tasting a bit of lemon cake and that splendid plum tart her cook prepares but it is quite impossible."

"A pity," Lady Troy said sighing, and would have seen them out had not Mr. Hastings intervened. "Our engagement shall wait," he said. "I should very much like to meet Mrs. Hastings."

The sound of his voice, if it could be described as "his voice," shocked Miranda into momentary silence. For an instant, she did not believe that the voice had come from him. It was gentle, soft, endearing.

"You are a sensible girl," Lady Troy told him. Slipping her hand through his arm once more, she wrested him from Miranda's side and led him into the saloon.

Miranda and Felix exchanged a desperate look.

"He's as queer as Dick's hatband," Felix mourned.

"He is distressed on his mother's account. We must help him," MIranda said. Taking Felix by the arm, she pulled him after them.

In the saloon, they found only Mr. Hastings and Lady Troy. Mrs. Hastings was not to be seen. Lady Troy instructed the servant to bring the young people some refreshment. She then took herself off to locate the mistress of the house.

As soon as she was gone, Felix upbraided Mr. Hastings "Is the midsummer moon with you?" he cried. "Far be i from me to decline a glass of wine and a bit of cake, but we cannot stay, Hastings. You know very well we cannot. You saw that fellow lurking about, did you not? If it wasn't Everard, then my eyes deceive me. You are in danger. We cannot delay our departure another instant."

Calmly, Mr. Hastings shook his head. "I must speak with my mother."

Felix rolled his eyes. "You are dicked in the nob."

Miranda would have added her arguments to Felix's, but there was no opportunity. Lady Troy led Mrs. Hastings into the salon, coaxing her along with soothing invitations. "Come and meet these charming young people," she cooed.

It was no difficult thing to present Mr. DeWitt, for he was already known to Mrs. Hastings. But Felix stumbled over his words as he attempted to introduce Mr. Hastings as his cousin. At last, Mr. Hastings came to his rescue, saying, "Poor Felix is so accustomed to calling me *Charlotte* that he scarcely knows how to introduce me properly." He spoke in that peculiar voice he had contrived. To Miranda, it was recognizable as Mr. Hastings's voice, but so sweet and pleasing that she heard it with astonishment. She had not thought it possible that he could disguise his voice; indeed, she had told him as much, but Mrs. Hastings and Lady Troy apparently found it unexceptionable, for they invited the young lady to refresh herself with a sip of ratafia.

What does he mean to do now? Miranda silently asked Heaven.

"I fear I cannot stay long," Mr. Hastings said. "My dear cousin Felix has consented to take me into the country, where I may rest myself and recover from a slight malady. Is that not so, Felix dear?"

Miserably, Felix replied, "Yes, Charlotte."

"He is the dearest cousin in all the world. I am completely devoted to him." He went to Felix and planted a kiss on his ruddy cheek.

Felix's mouth flapped in confusion.

In spite of herself, Miranda could not keep from smiling. Mr. Hastings clearly intended to derive some entertainment from his absurd situation, and Miranda was obliged to confess that his amusement was infectious.

Lady Troy invited Miss DeWitt to sit on the sofa next to Mrs. Hastings, who remained in gloomy silence, oblivious to the polite conversation going forward around her. When they were both settled, Lady Troy said to him, "So you are Charlotte DeWitt? I do not recollect hearing your name mentioned at Mrs. Wortle's school."

He regarded her as though she had just addressed him in the language of the Hottentots.

Miranda rushed to say, "Oh, Charlotte was one of the senior girls, Mama. They seemed so far superior that I did not have the temerity to claim a friendship with any of them."

"Ah, that explains it." Lady Troy beamed at the young people. "Well, then, if Miss DeWitt was so far above you, my pet, how was it that you met at all?"

This question, innocently asked, froze Miranda. The inventiveness that had earlier been born of desperation now deserted her. She cast a helpless look at Felix, who shrugged.

"Oh, it is a vastly amusing story, is it not, Miranda?" Mr. Hastings said softly in his Charlotte voice.

Having no choice, Miranda nodded her agreement. She waited for Mr. Hastings to continue, but he remained silent.

"I should like to hear the story," Lady Troy said. "And so would Tabitha, would you not, dear?"

Too occupied with blinking back tears, Mrs. Hastings could not answer.

"Dear Miranda must tell you the story," Mr. Hastings said.

"I wish *you* would tell them, dear Charlotte," she answered, baring her teeth in a sugary smile. "You are so much more adept at telling tales than I."

"Oh, but your manner of telling a story is quite rare," he persisted. "Do oblige us, dear, dear Miranda." He then turned to his mother, whom he addressed in a tone so quiet that nobody else could hear.

It was clear to Miranda that he meant to seize the opportunity to put his mother's mind at rest. It was up to her, she saw, to keep the others distracted until he had attained his object. Consequently, she inhaled deeply and began:

"I first encountered Charlotte at Mrs. Wortle's school when I chanced to find her lying senseless in the enclosure behind the kitchen."

"Gracious Heaven!" Lady Troy exclaimed. "Was she ill?"

Felix, who had moved to the edge of his chair, said helpfully, "No doubt she had fainted."

"It would have been better if she had fainted from illness," Miranda said. "The truth, I learned, was much more hideous."

"Mercy be upon us!" her mother cried. "What was the truth?"

"The truth was"—and here she paused to inhale—"she had been beaten dreadfully and might have breathed her last if I had not happened along at just that moment."

"Aha!" said Felix. "I had been wondering what precisely had brought you into it."

"My poor dear pet," Lady Troy said with a sigh. "How frightened you must have been!"

"There was not time to think of fright, Mama. She had received such an ugly head wound that it was imperative I forget everything save her condition."

"And so you fetched the surgeon," Lady Troy said.

"No, no. I could not, though I very much wished to. Charlotte would not hear of it."

"But why?" Lady Troy asked. Her agitation was increasing in leaps and bounds.

Miranda looked at Mr. Hastings, who was now engaged in earnest conversation with his mother. As far as she could tell, he was not ready to make his adieus. He evidently meant to torment her as long as he conceivably could.

"You may well ask 'why,' " she said. "But my dear friend Charlotte is a willful, obstinate, contrary care-for-no-body, and one's behavior tends always to conform to one's character."

Felix nodded. "And she cannot tell a fricassee from a ragout, more's the pity."

Mystified, Lady Troy glanced at Miss DeWitt, who seemed a very model of tenderness and charm as she whispered softly to Mrs. Hastings. "She appears pleasant enough," her ladyship observed.

Realizing she had wandered from her tale, Miranda said, "Well, she improves upon acquaintance. In point of fact, she does have one or two qualities to recommend her."

"Indeed!" Felix seconded. "She is entirely open and free with a purse, and never asks a fellow for collateral or duns him for the interest."

"An odd quality in a young lady," her ladyship remarked, "but you never told us, Miranda, why she had been so abominably beaten."

"Oh," said Miranda, swallowing with difficulty, "I did not mention that?"

"No, my pet. I wish you would tell us."

"Yes," said Felix. "I cannot wait to hear it myself."

"I fear you will be greatly shocked, Mama."

"I am already greatly shocked."

Miranda found that despite her uneasiness, a part of her enjoyed weaving the tale. It gave her an opportunity to tell the truth in a manner that would do no harm to anybody. More important, the situation was laughable. Mr. Hastings had been on the mark when he had observed that there were aspects of life that much resembled games and that risking boldly added spice to the game. "Well, as you insist upon hearing it," she said, "I shall tell you the truth, to wit, that poor Charlotte had been set upon by ruffians."

Lady Troy fanned herself rapidly. "It is well you never wrote to me about it, my pet. I should have pulled you out of the school at once."

"These were not ordinary ruffians, Mama, but three Amazons hired by one of our schoolmates to give Charlotte the drubbing of her life. It seems that she had caught the girl cheating at her examinations and had threatened to expose her unless she mended her behavior. Her reward was a cudgeling."

Because Lady Troy had never before known anybody who had been involved personally in such wicked doings, she sank back in her chair and breathed deeply. "Please do go on, my pet," she said between gasps.

"She begged me not to send for the doctor," Miranda said, "saying that if I did so, her enemy would have her set upon again. Her only hope, she said, was myself. She begged me to hide her in my chamber."

"Gad, what a clever ruse!" Felix cried. "And so that is where the sly fox hid—in your bedchamber!"

Blushing, Miranda acknowledged that it was so. "For nearly three days, I concealed her from all the world."

"You are quizzing me, I think," said Lady Troy. "You cannot possibly have kept such a secret. For one thing, the housemaids, Mrs. Wortle, and your schoolmates who shared the chamber would have found her out. For another, you are not an accomplished liar, Miranda. You never could have pulled it off."

With her head bowed, Miranda said, "You are too partial, Mama. I wish I were as virtuous as you make me out. All I can tell you is that we succeeded."

"And what happened then? How did she mend her quarrel with that loathsome little girl who hired the ruffians? Surely, she did not leave the school. That would have been cowardly."

"Do tell us how it all ended, Miss Troy," Felix said. "I should very much like to know how the difficulty was solved."

The color left Miranda's cheeks. To this point, she had been able to follow actual events in the telling of her tale. Now she found herself wholly in the realm of fiction.

She was spared the necessity of telling yet another lie, however. Mr. Hastings rose from the sofa. Mrs. Hastings rose with him. They held hands warmly, and then he turned to Felix to say in his Charlotte voice, "And now, Cousin, I think we must be on our road. We have stayed too long, I fear, and shall be late."

As the others rose, Lady Troy exclaimed, "Oh, Miss De-Witt, Miranda has told us your history. How brave you have been. I am prodigiously proud of both of you."

Miranda discerned his intent look. His gray eyes seemed suddenly serious.

"Yes," he said, "Miranda has been extraordinarily brave. I shall forever be in her debt." On that, he came to her, folded his arms around her, and kissed her cheek, in what to her mother must have seemed a charmingly affectionate display but what struck Miranda as a shockingly warm embrace. She was still endeavoring to quell her emotions when he left the house.

After passing a restless night in her own bed, the same bed which had lately rested and comforted Mr. Hastings, Miranda appeared in the breakfast parlor to announce her complete and miraculous recovery from the malady that had lately confined her. Mrs. Hastings regarded her with exultation, tinged with such a twinkling affection, that Miranda knew the lady no longer suffered spasms of weeping for her wayward son. Clearly she had been reassured as to his safety—and something else besides. The lady squeezed her hand as she might a daughter's, with fervid fondness, a fact which made Miranda uneasy in the extreme. She recollected the farewell embrace Mr. Hastings had given her in full view of his mother. Only Lady Troy, who as far as she could tell did not suspect Miss Charlotte DeWitt's true identity, had seen nothing to wonder at in that tender squeeze. All the others, though, including Mrs. Hastings, must have known precisely what it had constituted. Miranda feared that her hostess would allude to the incident, but to her infinite relief, whatever the lady knew or thought she knew, she kept to herself.

Lady Troy addressed her daughter with her usual endearments and expressed the hope that now her pet was quite well again, they might see something of the Town. This suggestion was most welcome. Miranda had felt sufficiently choked with airlessness in recent days to long to be anywhere but Queen Street. It seemed that only by dedicating herself to the pursuit of knowledge in the parks, palaces, and pleasure gardens of London could she forget the mortifications she had lately borne and the troublesome man who had inflicted them.

Thus, the three ladies embarked on a tour of the Town. Miranda endured visits to the Museum, the Tower, and the Waxworks so that she might, with a clear conscience, spend an inordinate amount of time inspecting the meandering lake Nash had shaped in St. James's Park, the Capability Brown gardens at Harrow-on-the-Hill, and the maze at Hampton Court. Because Mrs. Hastings procured invitations to dinner parties, card parties, tea parties, dancing parties, walking parties, and theater parties, Miranda retired very late each evening, too exhausted by the rigors of gaiety to dwell overmuch on the lingering scent of Mr. Hastings's hair on her pillow or the cravat that remained tied about her journal and that she continually forgot to destroy.

When sightseeing wearied Lady Troy, and she begged to be allowed to rest in Queen Street with her lady's magazine and a glass of negus, Miranda and Mrs. Hastings went about the Town visiting china shops and picture galleries, always contriving to dawdle long enough at a bookstall to allow Miranda to supplement her tower of volumes on landscape gardening with a copy of Whately or Price or *Observations on the Theory and Practice of Landscape Gardening,* penned by the master himself. It was during one of these excursions that Mrs. Hastings, in a burst of feeling that would not be contained, seized Miranda's hand and whispered, "My dear child, I promised Charles I would never breathe a word, but how can I obey when you and you alone have been the instrument of his salvation and have restored my peace of mind?"

Pained, Miranda looked up from the book she had been perusing in a corner of the shop. She was well aware that Mr. Hastings had conveyed to his mother something of the circumstances that had resulted in his aforesaid "salvation," but she had hoped that the lady would never humiliate her by alluding to them. She experienced a fiery shame at the suspicion that Mrs. Hastings knew of all the improprieties she had committed for her son's sake. Her mortification only increased when it became evident that far from condemning, Mrs. Hastings seemed to have conceived an excessive fondness for her.

Worse than the lady's gratitude, though, was her expectant glow. It seemed to reflect the renewal of hopes for a marriage between herself and Mr. Hastings, as though being miscreants who flirted with scandal had united them in a bond that prefigured permanent union. She would have gladly told Mrs. Hastings that she had no desire to marry anybody, least of all a man who made wagers on his life, risked his life for the sake of his amusement, and made himself generally detestable on principle; however, she could not speak a word, for at no time did Mrs. Hastings mention matrimony. The idea was there between them, as large, visible, unavoidable, and insurmountable as the Great Wall of China, but because Mrs. Hastings did not utter it, neither could she. It would have been the height of presumption, not to say conceit, for her to allude to it.

Mrs. Hastings was quick to soothe Miranda's alarms by saying, "Charles has told me nothing of the manner in which you came to his aid, and I shall not ask you to tell me, for knowing will only give me a dreadful case of the fidgets, but I cannot forbear thanking you. I should be a heartless creature indeed if I went about pretending I did not know you had acted a heroine's part."

Miranda made every effort to persuade the lady that no thanks were due, that any human creature would have done as much for any other human creature in difficulty, and that thanks instead of gratifying her, only put her to the blush, but Mrs. Hastings would not be silenced. "I shall say nothing to your mother, of course," she went on. "Have no fear on that head. However, I shall avail myself of the opportunity to thank you in a manner you shall not soon forget!" Her eyes shone with affection as she made this declaration, and Miranda could not but think with dread of what the lady meant to do.

The mystery was solved one evening—a full week after Mr. Hastings had quitted Queen Street—when Miranda entered an elegant eggshell drawing room furnished in ivory, pale gold, and lawn green, to find herself introduced to Sir

Humphrey Repton. As soon as she had gasped her gratitude to Mrs. Hastings, the lady bustled off, leaving her to sit beside the great man on a regal sofa and to ransack her brain for something intelligent to say. After a period, during which the eminent landscape gardener smiled at her and made her welcome, she gathered the courage to study his countenance at close range and thereby snatch this singular opportunity to contemplate the face of genius.

Though he was a little beyond his sixtieth year, Sir Humphrey had a youthful, unlined face. Bald on top, he wore his white hair puffed at the sides so that it hid his ears. His nose was angular and strong and his eyes were large, with the aspect of a man who had the ability to see far. His thin lips pressed together in a line that seemed to mark approval. The fingers that spread on his breast stretched fine and long. His dress was plain—a black coat, high-starched collar, and flat cravat. Miranda liked his looks well enough to determine that instead of bolting, as she was tempted to do, she would stay to hear any pearls that dropped from his lips.

With an appreciative glance at her, he said, "You are a vast deal more pleasant to look at than my last companion, Mr. Cox. You are, if I may say so, a welcome improvement. And you must know that I am a great believer in improvements. I am also excessively fond of pleasant prospects, and must thank you for providing me with the best one in this drawing room."

Miranda thanked him for the compliments and summoned the courage to return them. "I admire your work greatly," she said. "I beg you will forgive my repeating what you are no doubt weary of hearing and hope I will not bore or seem to flatter you with my encomiums, but I cannot help being much taken with your philosophy."

"I assure you, my dear, nobody tires of hearing himself praised. Only one thing is better, namely, hearing oneself quoted. One of the advantages of making something of a mark in the world is attracting the admiration of beautiful young ladies. Though I tire easily, it is not from boredom, I assure you. Last January, I suffered an accident. My carriage overturned as I made my way home from Sir Thomas Lennard's house in Essex. The foolish incident has left me a semi-invalid. The doctors, in their infinite wisdom, have prescribed remedies for me which induce me to grow sleepy and yawn at the most awkward moments. You must promise me that if I nap in the middle of a compliment or quotation, you will save the rest until I wake again. I should not like to miss a word of anything good said of me. I strive to sleep only when I am bring ridiculed, scorned, and raked over the coals, which is a good deal of the time."

"Sir Humphrey, do you regard it as ridiculous for a female to take up landscape gardening?"

"I do not see that a female is any less capable of scarring and damaging the estates of our nation than a male. I believe the sexes to be equally competent in their capacity for destruction."

"Oh, dear, if that is your view, then I expect you think poorly of the amateur improver, of whom I would count myself one if I could aspire to even so lowly a title as that."

"I do not speak of you particularly, my dear, for I do not know you. I speak of the general decline of my profession. I lay the fault at the door of our Parliament, which taxes us beyond mercy whenever we attempt to enhance our lands. It is also the fault of the new sort of owner we see nowadays, a mushroom of a fellow who is more solicitous to increase his property than to enjoy it, and who is more anxious to increase its value than its beauty."

"What of the creature like myself, Sir Humphrey, who thinks as you do, of enjoyment and utility, but has no substantial education or experience?"

"As to that, I had very little myself when I began. I was a ramshackle sort of fellow until I attained the age of forty. It was during a restless night, when sleep would not come, that I conceived the idea of taking up the profession of landscape gardening. I coined the name *landscape gardener* merely in order that I might have a respectable handle with which to introduce myself to anybody with money enough to hire me. I sent letters to all my acquaintance, informing them that I was available for consultation, and with the perversity for which my countrymen are renowned, they chose to believe that I was as able and gifted as I said I was."

"I do not know whether I have any gift for designing a landscape. I know I do not have the face to improve an estate without any notion of what I am doing."

"You are more scrupulous than I. Well, I suppose you must begin by educating yourself. Read everything and everybody, and not merely my *Sketches* and red books. You must read those imbeciles Knight and Price, for without their hen-witted notions, you might lean too heavily on one side or the other, and that is a thing you must avoid at all costs. Some modern improvers have gone so far as to call any crooked line a beautiful line simply because it is crooked. They mistake slovenly carelessness for natural ease and call every species of regularity 'formal,' merely because they have heard somebody, very likely me, assert that nature abhors a straight line. You will not be guilty of such extremes of nonsense, I hope."

Miranda did not immediately reply, for her mind raced with ideas. She suddenly realized how confused, eclectic, and aimless her study of landscape gardening had been. Perhaps she had been foolish to begin it at all.

Sir Humphrey inquired gently, "Shall I advise you?"

"Oh, I wish you would. I have been so scattered that I fear I must give up all notions of putting my hand to any improvements."

"My dear, you cannot have been more scattered than I myself was as a youth. I was intended for a mercantile career. Over the years, I dabbed in watercolor painting, farming, writing poetry and essays, architecture, investment, and bankruptcy. And then my idea came to me, as though in a dream, and I have not wavered from the path since. Not even my accident has separated me from my life's work. I am at Sheringham at present, and mean to keep on until the Almighty summons me to formulate a plan to improve the heavenly estates."

Miranda, who had been liking the man more with every sentence he uttered, was grateful to learn that his youthful dilettantism very much resembled her own. "I wonder," she mused, "whether I shall ever find a thing that I shall love so well as you love your profession, and to stick to it for all the years of my life. I have never yet stuck to a thing, and I fear that if I were to undertake to improve my father's estate, I should soon tire of the project and leave it in disarray."

"There is a solution to that, my dear."

Feeling a stirring of hope, she listened.

"My advice is simply this: Do not bite off more than you can chew. In short, do not attempt to address the entire estate. Begin with a flower garden or a shrubbery or a walk."

Miranda clapped her hands. Like all brilliant formulas, this one was simple and obvious. No wonder she had left half a dozen fire screens unpainted; her object had been to provide one for every room in the house. No wonder she had left off writing after the third chapter; instead of trying her hand at a poem, a story, a sketch, an essay, or a page of thoughts, she had set about authoring a novel. No wonder she had given up Italian, physiognomy, and music lessons; her notions of what she was obliged to accomplish were so rigorous, so vast, so unreasonable as to be wholly discouraging. She exhaled fully, as though at last she breathed the air of freedom.

Warmly, she thanked Sir Humphrey. Before she could wax effusive, however, his son came to collect him. The great man had grown tired, as shown by the drawn look he wore. He must be taken home and made to rest, said the younger Repton. Miranda watched him depart with a heart full of gratitude and a head full of ideas.

That night, as Daisy undressed her, she felt a surge of energy that rendered her too restless to stand still. Life was replete with possibility, she saw, very much akin to the grounds of an estate. One could make something of it, practically anything one wished to in fact, for there was nothing that could not be accomplished once one found the method of accomplishing it. One could roam through life as one roamed among hills and hollows, narrows and expanses, fountains and woods, learning to know them intimately, absorbing what they had to teach, all the while savoring their loveliness and potentiality. None of these fancies was very specific; nor would she have been able to explain them to any other living creature. However, they buoyed her spirits and nearly set her to dancing.

Abruptly, she was recalled to earth by Daisy, who burst into tears and wept as though her heart would break.

Astonished, Miranda begged to know the cause of this explosion.

Through sniffs and hiccups, Daisy explained, "I made sure you wuz cross with me, miss."

"Not at all, Daisy. I have no cause to be cross with you."

"Oh, but you must have!" came the reply. Enormous tears glimmered in her enormous eyes. "Why these past several days, miss, you hant so much as let me in your door so as to do your buttons and your ties. If I made so bold as to wish to bring your morning chocolate, you said you wuz fixed in your mind to breakfast in the parlor, and then you never did so. When I knocked so as to shake the feather bed, which was only my duty which Mrs. Blunt the housekeeper instructed me to do of a Thursday, you sent me away. I must be in your black books for you to use me so, though what I have done is more than I can conceive, for I never meant anything but to please you, miss, and I hope you do not mean to see me dismissed, for if I lose my place, I do not know how I shall eat or where I shall go."

Miranda heard this speech with considerable emotion. Profoundly, she regretted having been the unwitting instrument of hurting an innocent girl. Daisy had been a victim just as surely as if she had known of Mr. Hastings's presence and conspired to keep his secret. The injustice boiled in Miranda's breast. She blamed Mr. Hastings. She blamed herself.

Taking Daisy in her arms, she patted her back until the sobs subsided, and then she led the girl to her dressing table, where she picked out a locket and tucked it in her hand.

"You must keep this, Daisy," she said earnestly, "and may it reassure you that I do value you. Your service has been loyal and proper. If I have kept you from your duties, I do apologize. Please believe I could not help it."

Daisy wiped her nose with her pinafore. "Perhaps miss thought I might be in danger of catching her cold and did not wish to expose me to it."

Miranda sighed. "You have hit very close to the mark. I should never have forgiven myself if you had caught any taint of my indisposition."

At last, having reached a good understanding, the two parted. Miranda was now at liberty to resume the happy ruminations Daisy's tears had interrupted. Her anger at herself and Mr. Hastings was soon swallowed up in thoughts of a shrubbery—one with lilac, privet, and syringa. She then imagined a walk, a covered walk for exercising in winter, with clematis and honeysuckle twining through the pillars. Next, her thoughts conjured up a flower garden. Gardens devoted to some particular interest were all the rage just now. She might have pansies and daffodils and pinks. Imagining these delights, she fell into a sweet sleep and dreamed.

In the dream, she saw a lady enter a long, narrow garden, walled on either side by beeches, larches, and oaks. She walked slowly. Every few feet, she encountered three graceful marble steps set in the neatly clipped grass as though they had grown there naturally. At the top of each set of steps was another garden, first a blue one, followed by magenta, yellow, violet, and white, each in succession, and as she went, she climbed higher and higher toward the sky, until, at the end of the white garden, she reached a latticed bower. Inside was a carved iron bench, where she sat and gazed at the path she had just traveled, gorgeous with clumps of color, shade, and gently swaying tree branches. The lady seemed familiar to her.

A movement to her left caught the lady's eye. When she looked, she saw a man appear. At first she thought he had stepped from behind the chestnut that protected the bower. Then she was aware that he had emerged from the depths of the tree itself, as though it had given birth to him. Seeing her, he began to approach, and as he did, she leaned back languorously against the bench with her hand outstretched, inviting him to sit by her. Her lips parted as he firmly grasped her hand and when she spoke to him, in an alluring song, tiny, starlike flowers spilled from her lips.

At that instant, Miranda awoke, drenched to her skin. The dream that had begun so prettily had ended by horrifying her. Remembering the woman in the dream, she blushed and scolded herself for permitting such nonsense to disturb her rest. Then, remembering the man, she shivered. Though his face had been indistinct, he had been naked to the waist.

TEN

An Unexpected Visitor

My dear Miss Troy,

That you are reading this at all suggests you have
thought my manuscript worthy of perusal to this
point, despite your abhorrence of the subject. I
address you here simply to acknowledge that a cravat
is poor recompense for your remarkable generosity to
me. I ask you not to burn the thing, much as you may
despise its owner, not because it is made of the finest
China silk, but because i propose someday to collect
it from your hand and present you with a more fitting
memento of my gratitude. I beg one more favor
besides, Miss Troy, and that is, if you are able, to
remember me from time to time, and not unkindly. I
shall certainly not forget you.

Believe me to be your most devoted,

C.H.

Mr. Hastings braved a snow-threatening day to walk along
the beach toward the Cobb. The quality that had attracted
him to the seaside village was the very quality that had driven him in desperation to turn up the collar of his greatcoat
and march headlong into the chill wind: namely, that it was
a place nobody frequented in December and he was as little
likely to stumble upon a game of piquet there as he was to
stumble upon the Lost Tomb of the Pharaohs.

He had been at Lyme Regis upwards of three weeks now,
following a rough carriage ride for some miles in the opposite direction. For several days after quitting London, Felix
and his cousin Charlotte had shown themselves at Mar-

cross, Felix's house in Kent. During that time, Mr. Hastings suffered a recurrence of vertigo and nausea so intense that, over his protests, Felix sent for a physician. Dr. Meecham shrugged when it was explained to him that Miss Charlotte was, in fact, a gentleman. The doctor had seen a great many peculiar patients in his time and neither judged nor gossiped. However, he had rarely seen a head wound as ugly as the one that Mr. Hastings sported. The gentleman was very lucky it had not got infected, he scolded. Whoever had cleaned and tended it had done a thorough job, but Mr. Hastings ought to have been advised not to travel. It was a wonder he was conscious at all.

Though a lengthy regimen of medicine, rest, and fresh air was prescribed, five days was as long as Mr. Hastings could bear to follow it. On the sixth, he declared it was time for Felix to return to London to see how the land lay with Everard, and it was time for him to find a place where he might conceal himself without resorting to a disguise.

As soon as his own clothes were sent to him—packed neatly and lovingly by his discreet butler Dimpson—he shed his feminine costume. If any of the servants at Marcross thought anything odd in the fact that Miss DeWitt went into the best bedchamber and Mr. Hastings came out, they said nothing. Indeed, they had been given so many sovereigns as to make them entirely blind, deaf, and mute.

Alone, Mr. Hastings had set out for Lyme Regis, to which his mother had once brought him as a boy, and there he had stayed, under an assumed name, in a house Felix's agent had let for him. He was thankful to have settled on a location that was so deserted as to permit him to discard his woman's disguise. The bones of his stays, the buttons, hooks, pins, and ties that kept him together, and the bulkiness of his shifts and skirts had irritated him beyond endurance. He wondered why women, who, for the most part, were intelligent, sensible creatures in his estimation, submitted to such tortures. He marveled that a female could wear what was fashionable and still keep a civil tongue in her head.

Thoughts of the female species brought him inevitably to

the subject of Miss Troy, whose image obtruded on his musings so often that Everard seemed to fade. Although he could see her face distinctly, could conjure the arch of her neck, the regal line of her nose, the succulence of her ear-lobe, the curve of her bosom, it was not solely the recollection of her appearance which operated on him powerfully. It was also the memory of her voice. Even now, as the waves roared onto the shore, he could hear her asking "Who is Jane?" He heard the sound of her concern as she bathed his wound. Her voice was as musical as the harp she played. Against the soft rhythms of the sea, he heard her say his name over and over again, "Mr. Hastings." He vowed that one day she would address him as *Charles.*

Along the Cobb, he saw the dark gray waves crash high on the stone, spraying the air with foam, and he thought that it was time now to do something once and for all about Everard. His recovery was nearly complete, and exile from Town had grown tiresome. The fact that he could not visit his mother or any of his other acquaintance was hard. He did not dare look to amuse himself with cards or dice. And instead of visiting Miss Troy and transforming her patent dislike into adoration, he spent his time resting, roaming the beach, and swallowing the vile elixir Dr. Meecham had prescribed. His only occupation had been adding additional chapters to his book on the principles of gaming. He had deliberately left the manuscript in Miss Troy's hands—it provided him with a reason to see her again—but he continued writing, not only because he liked it but because he had virtually nothing else to do.

Thus far he had received no news to encourage him to think that Everard might be brought to reason. Felix's letters from London were full of the man's boasts in the clubs and gaming houses. He had put it about that Charles Hastings had slandered him and then, in the most craven manner, had slunk off to parts unknown. Everard had concluded each boast with a wink and a suggestion that when Hastings attempted to show himself again, Everard would "be ready." One was meant to assume by this, Felix wrote, that the fellow was bent on having his duel, and that he intended nothing short of a duel to the death.

Mr. Hastings shook his head at such folly. If Everard succeeded in killing him, his banishment from England would be assured. He would be obliged to live abroad. If he did return to England, he would find himself persona non grata. Mr. Hastings's vast and loyal acquaintance would make it a point to render his life a misery. He would be cut everywhere and find sympathy nowhere. Yet in spite of this, the man was determined to pursue his revenge. How was one to reason with a fellow like that?

Perhaps, Mr. Hastings thought grimly, he ought to meet the man, pistols at dawn and all that nonsense, and be done with it. If his lordship was going to be obstinate, perhaps it would be better to meet him face-to-face instead of wondering whether his surrogates were hiding around corners and in alleys, prepared to pounce at any moment. He detested hiding out. There was something mean in it. It was beneath his dignity.

It was even more beneath him, however, to let Everard call the tune. He had determined he would extricate himself from this difficulty without recourse to dueling, and he meant to have his way. He laid a wager with himself: before spring, he would have Everard at his mercy, eager to do his bidding, and he would accomplish it without firing a shot. If he won the wager, he would treat himself to a ride in an open curricle with Miss Troy. If he lost—well, there was not much point in thinking what would happen then, was there?

Returning to his cottage, he wrote a letter to Felix, instructing him to learn the identity of the men who had been hired by Everard to dispatch him. He referred Felix to a suitable gentleman, formerly of Bow Street and known for his discretion, cleverness, and most of all, his fealty to the Hastings family. He would be paid shockingly well for his services, and when he had succeeded in tracking down the fellows, they were to be bribed to transfer their allegiance to Mr. Hastings, who would pay them double the sum Everard had promised. In this way, Everard would learn that whomever he hired to carry out his filthy schemes could easily be rendered harmless. If Everard had his mind set on assassination, Mr. Hastings vowed, he would have to do the business himself.

In the letter to Felix, he enclosed a brief one to his mother, saying:

> Be assured that I am well. If Miss Troy is still with you, tell her nothing. It will go easier with her if she is kept in ignorance. You will hear various rumors concerning me. Behave as though you believe them all. Though you are my most beloved mother, I have not forgotten that you are in to me for six buttons. I mean to come in person soon to collect them from your own dear hand.

He then wrote a third letter, to Lord George Moncrief, Berkeley Square, in which he boasted that he had gone to Scotland with "A Lady." He extolled her appetite for pleasures—of the intellect, naturally—but complained that she hadn't the least notion of how to play whist. The combination of exultation and vexation in the letter would, he knew, prove wonderfully convincing to young Moncrief. In conclusion, he asked him to call on Mrs. Buxleigh and make his apologies for not waiting upon her as promised.

> Do not, of course, say what it is that has kept me from her so long! Make what excuse you can. I should like the lady to welcome me with open arms, so to speak, when I return to London. And by the by, you may find yourself admiring the lady a good deal yourself, George. In that case, I shall be happy to turn her over to you when I have done with her.

The callousness of the final sentence would, he felt certain, amuse Moncrief. The young lord would enjoy circulating every word of the letter throughout the clubs. When Everard got wind of it, his pride would be tweaked. News would spread that, far from departing the Town with his tail between his legs, Mr. Hastings had gone off to enjoy a snowbound interlude with a beautiful companion. When Mr. Hastings returned, so the story would go, he would pay court to Lord Everard's mistress. Thus, Everard's boasts would be hooted at. He would be silenced, for the moment.

But a *permanent* solution was needed, one which would render Everard's schemes forever impotent. Unfortunately, none came to mind. Mr. Hastings therefore sought the means of diverting himself. He ventured to the stables, where he hired a horse, a serviceable mare, though not as frisky and sharp as Isolde, his favorite at home. One of the inconveniences of his life in Lyme was having to forgo the use of his own horses. They might be recognized and used to trace his whereabouts. And so he made do with Bluebell, a rich brown three-year-old with sad eyes.

"Yer not ridin' far in this wind, I hope, sir?" said the hostler. His voice sounded a warning. The clouds that had come up threatened a storm.

Mr. Hastings mounted Bluebell and, reining the horse around, tossed the fellow a coin by way of answer. Then he rode off at a reckless pace, the wind at his back, as though nothing would satisfy him but speed and fury. His direction was inland, away from the Bath road, where he might conceivably encounter an acquaintance. When snow began to make its lazy way earthward, he was oblivious. For an instant, he recollected what the physician had said in regard to excessive exertion. Then, with a careless shrug, he spurred Bluebell foreward.

He could not tell how long he rode, but eventually he expended his restlessness and breathed freely. Drawing the horse to a halt at the top of a ridge, he gazed below at a prospect of hills and farms. Though gray and wintry, the landscape seemed delightfully peaceful. It occurred to him that Miss Troy would have liked it as well as he did. In other circumstances, he might have ridden with her by his side, and as she pointed out to him various aspects of the landscape to admire, he would savor the melody in her voice.

Curious to see more, he rode down the ridge and entered the road. Soon he came upon an ancient man on foot who

seemed to make little progress against the wind. Mr. Hastings stopped and offered to take him up behind. Gratefully
the old man accepted. As they headed for a clump of cot-
tages at the end of a lane, the old man talked. Mr. Hastings
smiled to think that he could find amusement in a rustic's
garrulity. A month ago he was sitting in Mrs. Stout's card
parlor feeling sorry for himself because a game of piquet
was dull. The only spark of interest had been Everard's
cheat. And now here he was, content to listen to his companion's ramblings about Arundel Abbey.

All at once, the name struck him as familiar. He drew up
the mare and asked, "Is this Arundel Abbey?"

"Ay has been sayin' it tis, sir, and ay shall be prood to
say it agin, for ay hant never tenanted for a master as just as
Sir Bascomb Troy."

"He has a daughter, does he not?"

"E have many daughters, sir."

"Miss Miranda Troy is his daughter, I believe?"

"Ay would be lyin' if ay said she warnt."

With renewed spirits, Mr. Hastings bade farewell to the
old man at his cottage and thought with satisfaction on his
good luck. Of all the hiding places in the kingdom he might
have chosen, he had chosen one less than an hour's ride
from Arundel Abbey. No longer fearing he would go distracted with boredom, he began to think that his stay in the
neighborhood of Lyme Regis would prove singularly interesting.

At first the dream distressed Miranda. Certain aspects of
it struck her as shocking, others as silly. A little thought,
however, convinced her that the dream was purposeful. It
had shown her her own heart. It had shown her the very
garden she ought to design, one with groupings of rich flo-
ral color. From that moment, she plunged herself into horti-
cultural studies, thinking of nothing but beds, rows, edges,
perennials, annuals, and the like. To Lady Troy's delight,
she spent several afternoons in the company of a fair-haired
gentleman who, she had been informed, was titled and eligible. Her ladyship's disappointment was palpable, how-

ever, when Miranda revealed that she had no interest in the young man beyond his ability to escort her to various hot-houses and introduce her to the head gardeners at the Grove in Hampstead and the Royal Botanical Gardens at Kew.

These were days of high exertion for Miranda. She threw herself into study and observation. Every word Sir Humphrey had uttered had been entered in her journal, and she pondered them as though they had been delivered from Sinai. She could not open her journal, of course, without untying the cravat Mr. Hastings had wrapped around it, and at such times, she could not help wondering how he got on. If Mrs. Hastings had received any communication from him, she had not mentioned it. Mr. DeWitt had called on Mrs. Hastings, but Miranda had been occupied and had never heard anything of the visit that pertained to Mr. Hast-ings. It would have eased her mind to know that he was safe, but, she told herself, had he been found dead, she surely would have heard.

She took herself to task for failing to dispose of his cra-vat. What if Daisy should notice it? What if her mother should see a piece of gentleman's clothing among her pri-vate keepsakes? It was most imprudent for her to have kept it. Worse, it was ridiculous. Nevertheless, she wrapped her journal in it one more time.

One early December morning, while she was sorting through her books and papers for the notes on Repton's de-sign for a trellised enclosure, she came upon Mr. Hastings's manuscript. Curious, she leafed through it, noticing the boldness of his hand and the ease with which he appeared to say what he wished to say without scratching out and in-serting in tiny letters a vast number of corrections. His style impressed her with its forthrightness and wit, and she ad-mitted, now that he was safely remote from her, that she found these attributes singularly attractive. In addition, there was a liveliness, a masculine energy, in the man, that she admired. Yet she had not betrayed any admiration in his company. She had always maintained an air of disapproval and seriousness. Why? she asked herself. Why had she held herself so stiff and unsmiling?

His essay on the Fifth Principle of Gaming, in which he
characterized the various types who devoted themselves to
games of chance, delighted her with its originality and
satire. The final sentences, however, puzzled her. He referred to the gamester who undid himself by falling in love.
It distressed her to think that Mr. Hastings might forbid
himself to fall in love merely because it might distract him
from playing cards.

Then she turned to the next page and, to her amazement,
saw that it contained a letter to herself. On first reading, she
could make nothing of his words. Only one idea pene-
trated—that he did not wish her to destroy his cravat. A
second reading yielded a bit more, namely, that he expected
to see her again, indeed, that he *wished* to see her again.
She was flattered, pleased and alarmed all at once. The high
spirits of the letter recollected the high spirits of the writer.
It came back to her that his presence had made the air
crackle in her bedchamber. The last sentence made her forget to breathe. She was now perishing to know whether he
was all right.

She would have been left to wonder eternally, but a visitor to Queen Street answered her question. Lord Everard
called on Mrs. Hastings, and as Miranda was sitting with
her, reading from Cowper (whose views on the picturesque,
though couched in poetry, agreed with her own), she over-
heard the entire exchange.

His lordship was ill at ease, too ill at ease, in fact, to be
anything but minimally polite. Putting down the book, Miranda studied him. After some minutes, she concluded that
he was the man who had been lurking outside the door on
the day Mr. DeWitt and Mr. Hastings had set out for the
country. But had Lord Everard spotted them? Had he
caught up with them? Had he carried out his threats against
Mr. Hastings? Was Mr. Hastings's corpse lying even now in
a lonely wood or deserted ditch, picked at by hawks and
flies, never to be found or buried or properly mourned? She
shuddered to think of it.

"My dear Mrs. Hastings," said Everard in an impatient
tone, "I wonder if you can tell me where I might find your

esteemed son. I have not set eyes on him these several weeks and have grown anxious on his behalf. Is he quite well?"

Smiling with maternal contentment, Mrs. Hastings replied, "Oh, yes, indeed, he is quite well."

"Then you have lately heard from him?"

"Yes, and I know that he is very well."

"I see. There is a rumor about that he has gone to Scotland. I never heard that he liked the north in winter."

"I believe that rumor is true."

"Rumor also has it that he enjoys companionship which is, shall we say, *enviable*."

Mrs. Hastings's eyebrows rose at the implications of this, but she only said, "That rumor is true as well."

"Indeed?" Everard said.

Miranda noticed a high color in his cheeks. He did not seem at all pleased. He tapped his fingers together and frowned. "If I may speak directly, ma'am, I had heard something to the effect that his companion was a lady."

In great consternation, Mrs. Hastings cautioned him, "It would be most improper to say more on the subject." As she spoke, she rolled her eyes in Miranda's direction, indicating that that young lady's virgin ears were likely to be sullied if she elaborated.

This did not satisfy Lord Everard. He demanded, "Who is the lady?"

Mrs. Hastings rose, furious at this impudence. "It would be most unseemly for a gentleman to discuss such a subject with his mother! And it is most unseemly of you, Lord Everard, to tax me with such a question."

Admonished, Everard made his apologies and shortly afterward he left. The scowl he wore gratified Miranda, as did the inference she had drawn that Mr. Hastings was still very much alive. After all, if Everard had succeeded in sending him off to the nether regions, he would never have paid the call to Mrs. Hastings in the first place.

"You must not let the rumors disturb you, my child," said Mrs. Hastings, interrupting her thoughts.

"You are very kind. I am not disturbed."

Sorrowfully, Mrs. Hastings said, "I thought it might overset you to hear that Charles had gone off with a lady."

"It is merely a rumor, I suppose."

"Alas, it is true."

"True?"

"Yes, all too true."

"How do you know this?"

"I have it from Charles himself. He has written to me."

To her vexation, Miranda experienced a pang. She stood, sat again, stood again, walked to a window to see whether the clouds promised snow, walked to the mantel, the sofa, then sat again. "I suppose," she said, when she had collected herself, "that Mr. Hastings may do as he pleases."

Mrs. Hastings, who had watched Miranda's restlessness with pleasure, said, "I expect that Charles will soon fall out of love with the lady. He never does fancy one for very long. Indeed, I despair of his ever having a lasting attachment."

Abruptly, Miranda stood again and moved to a table. As it contained a miniature of Mr. Hastings, she moved in the opposite direction. She walked about aimlessly, thinking that she ought not to be surprised to hear this characterization of the man. He was a gamester; moreover, he boasted that he was. He had no more notion of fidelity than a rabbit. He was odious, shallow, and careless. One minute he wrote warmly of his esteem for the lady who had risked her reputation to save his life. The next minute he was risking that life to indulge himself in an interlude with a female who was doubtless no better than she should be. She detested his unsteadiness. She could not abide a man who was fickle.

And then she sank into a chair, realizing that she was as fickle as he was, that she had flitted from one suitor to another just as he flitted from one mistress to another, and that just because she now flitted to hobbies instead of gentlemen, she was not any less fickle. It horrified her to find that the single quality she and Mr. Hastings had most in common was the quality in herself she most disliked.

Mrs. Hastings peered at her closely. "Are you going to faint, my dear?"

"I do not believe in fainting," she said with an attempt at dignity.

"Oh," said Mrs. Hastings, somewhat let down, "I thought you might faint when you heard how wicked Charles had been."

Repressing her emotion, she replied, "His wickedness or virtue is a matter of complete indifference to me!" With that, she ran from the saloon.

Mrs. Hastings smiled and did not make any further attempts to induce Miss Troy to faint.

Following Lord Everard's visit, Lady Troy informed Miranda that her father had written to beg them to come home. Although Miranda felt reluctant to leave London, where she had been able to study landscape gardening to her heart's content, she did not demur. She missed her father and her home. Even more, she could not bear any longer to stay in the bedchamber that had been the scene of her dealings with Mr. Hastings. Once she was at home, she might put the entire unfortunate episode from her mind.

Many hours after Mrs. Hastings tearfully bid them goodbye, Sir Bascomb tearfully bid them welcome. That his daughter returned home unmarried, and without any prospects of altering that excellent condition, gave him cause to rejoice. He was prepared, he declared, to give her carte blanche with the estate. She might improve it as much as ever she chose to, as long as she did not spend any money or attach herself to some contemptible fellow. These affectionate avowals went a long way toward allaying Miranda's uneasy spirits. Her anger at Mr. Hastings, though not diminished, was put aside, and she threw herself headlong into preparations for the Christmas holiday.

She was on a stepladder, adjusting candles on the manteltop, when Ragstone entered and cleared his throat.

"A visitor to see you," he said to Lady Troy.

It hit Miranda that the visitor might be Mr. Lloyd, who had threatened to renew his addresses as soon as she returned from town.

Before she could object, her mother desired the visitor to be brought in.

"Oh, Mama," Miranda cried, "I must go at once. If the visitor is Mr. Lloyd, I do not wish to see him."

"You cannot go, my pet. The candles are not straight. You must adjust them to the right. As to Mr. Lloyd, I am sure he is a very eligible gentleman with an excellent income. His lands are very handy to the abbey, you know."

Turning halfway around so that she faced her mother, Miranda said boldly, "I suppose I ought to tell you that he has proposed marriage to me, and I have refused him."

As though a dagger had been plunged into her heart, Lady Troy staggered. "You refused him! Oh, never say so! It is bad enough that you have taken an irrational dislike to Mr. Hastings. Now you have refused Mr. Lloyd, who was your very last chance! Oh, it is insupportable."

Painful words would have passed between mother and daughter then, but they were interrupted by a soft, soothing voice saying, "I hope I do not disturb you."

At the sight of the visitor, Lady Troy's agitation was transformed into a wreath of smiles.

Miranda, for her part, nearly fell off the ladder.

"It is Miss DeWitt come to see us," Lady Troy announced, as though Miranda could not very well see for herself.

In the next few minutes, Miranda observed in bitter silence as her mother made Miss DeWitt welcome, invited her to stay to tea, invited her to stay the night, and invited her to stay the next several weeks, until just past the New Year. All of these kind invitations, Miss DeWitt, with an insufferably gracious smile, was pleased to accept.

At last, Miranda was obliged to break her angry silence and speak up. Otherwise, her mother would have seen to it that, as in former days, the fond schoolmates shared a room and a bed.

ELEVEN

Plotting Against Miranda

A house ought to flow into its grounds; conversely, the grounds ought to connect to the house. Houses which loom over bare lawn, as Arundel Abbey does, seem to dominate their setting rather than to partake of it. This fault may be partially corrected by tearing down the lower wings of the house and building a series of connected rooms which give out on to a conservatory, and from there a gravel walk surrounded by shrubs, and from there a summer garden teeming with carnation, larkspur, monk's hood, petunia, and snap dragon, and from there a sanctuary for birds and butterflies. Papa will not agree to such vast and expensive improvements. Mr. Lloyd, on the other hand, might be brought to agree, but I should then be obliged to marry him, and I will not marry a man merely that I may have his grounds to tinker with.

It was arranged that Miss DeWitt would leave them directly after tea, return to the unnamed friends with whom she presently stayed, and arrive at Arundel Abbey within the next weeks, as soon as she could contrive to get away. Lady Troy was gratified to know that in the coming festive season her daughter would have the companionship of the young lady who had been so skillful as to cure Mrs. Hastings of her blue devils. Meanwhile, as a mother, it behooved her to put aside her wrath against her daughter and inform the housekeeper that they must make preparations to receive a guest.

As soon as her mother was gone, Miranda whirled on Mr. Hastings. "Why have you come here?"

"To see you." He noted that her fair hair and complexion made her susceptible to blushes.

"Are you mad?"

"Very likely." He approached her slowly.

"You will never carry off such a masquerade!"

"Do you wish to place a small wager on that?"

"No! There is only one thing I wish, that you will return to Scotland and never show your face to me again."

"I have not set foot in Scotland these ten months at least."

"I have been assured otherwise. Not only did you go to Scotland, but you were accompanied by your mistress. Thus, while I was in agonies, wondering whether you had recovered from your wound and had devised a stratagem to deal with Lord Everard, you were *enjoying* yourself."

"You were in agonies?"

"That is nothing to the point."

"My dear Miss Troy, I have been quite alone all this time. Alas, there has been no mistress. Who was it that hoaxed you so abominably?"

"Your mother!"

This stopped the gentleman, but only for a moment. He recollected the letter he had sent his mother and the instruction it contained. She must have confirmed to Miss Troy the truth of the rumors concerning his whereabouts. In three strides, he was beside Miranda, holding her hand to his lips. "Thank you," he whispered.

After an unsuccessful attempt to snatch away her hand, she cried, "You *are* mad!"

"Thank you for being jealous." He pulled her into his arms and kissed her.

At first, she was too astonished to resist, then too overcome, then too roused, then too ardent. When he realized that she was kissing him as fervently as he kissed her, he drew back a moment and looked into her brown eyes. Smiling, he kissed her again, holding nothing back this time. At last, he released her and went to the door, saying pointedly, "I will be back to thank you again and again, and again."

Miranda sank onto the footstool, her head in her hands. Remembering how she had abandoned herself to Mr. Hastings's ardor, she despaired. She despaired on his account as well; how anybody could ever take him for anything but a man was beyond her.

To wind up his affairs in Lyme, Mr. Hastings had much to do. He let his cottage to a pair of elderly sisters. Under the name he had assumed, he stayed at several inns in the neighborhood, never the same one twice, so that if Everard was on his trail, he would be led a merry chase. He wrote to Felix, telling him of his invitation from Lady Troy and asking him to send him a great many more of Miss Charlotte DeWitt's dresses, along with a riding habit, a ball gown, bonnets, and the like. Then he added:

> Do not trouble yourself to upbraid me for my folly. I am well aware of it. If you do not choose to send me a full complement of ladies' fashions, I shall be reduced to patronizing a modiste hereabouts, and it shall be said that Felix DeWitt dresses his cousin like a bumpkin. Further, I shall give it out that your behavior toward me has been so vulgar as to force me to leave Marcross and to seek asylum with my dear schoolmate.

Finally, he sent a letter to his butler, Dimpson, with intricate instructions for obtaining from his solicitor his grandmother's very old but very bright emerald and diamond necklace.

Soon he received a lease from the two elderly sisters, signed in due form, a trunk full of ladies' clothes accompanied by a note from Felix saying, "Send word when you are set to leave Arundel Abbey so that I may make arrangements for you at Bedlam," and a plain box containing the precious jewels. With these in hand, and Miss Charlotte's hat on his head, he set out in a hired chaise for what he

trusted would prove a delightful visit with Miss Troy and
her esteemed parents.

He arrived while Sir Bascomb was out supervising re-
pairs on a barn roof. Lady Troy was in Togbury with her
cook, negotiating at the butcher's for a Christmas goose
and suet for plum pudding. Miranda was in a small parlor,
at work on the design for her flower garden. With her
books spread about her and pencils in her hand and hair,
she appeared the picture of studiousness.

As soon as Mr. Hastings was ushered in, dressed in a
mulberry pelisse with fur-trimmed capes, Miranda rose to
her feet. He noticed a sudden change in the air, as though a
lightning bolt had charged it. She must have sensed it, too,
for she moved so as to put the writing table between them.
On her face, he read a variety of emotions. The one he
wished to see—pleasure at the sight of him—was lost
among the uncertainty and dismay. Seeing his intent look,
she lowered her eyes.

When they were left alone by the servant, he said, "Do
not be alarmed. I shall not repeat my late rash conduct. Rest
assured, I shall not kiss you again."

"You ought never to have kissed me. Somebody might
have seen us, and then it would all have been up with you."

He was pleased to know that her objection to being
kissed was founded on her fears for his safety, not on any
repulsion she felt. "I must beg one favor," he said.

She glanced at him suspiciously.

"I have come without a maid, for reasons which I need
not explain. Though I have grown quite adept at wriggling
in and out of my gowns and of hiding myself beneath
shawls, I may require assistance."

"In such a case, you may send for me. However, if you
abuse my generosity, I shall tie your stays so that you cannot breathe."

Her humor pleased him. In spite of herself, she did not
altogether dislike sparring with him. He moved closer.

Quietly, she said, "I do not suppose it will matter to you,
but it really is dangerous for you to have come, more dan-

gerous than you know. My sisters and their families will arrive in a matter of days. What will you do then?"

"The same thing I should do if they did not come—collect my winnings from you."

"Your winnings?"

"We made a bet, you will recall. If my disguise did not succeed, I was to leave you my book, to have it published and reap the profits thereof. But if it did succeed, you were to learn to play piquet."

She smiled a little. "I hoped you had forgotten."

"I have not forgotten a single thing that passed between us in that bedchamber."

Audibly, she caught her breath.

The servant returned to lead Miss DeWitt to her quarters, where her trunks had already been carried, thus putting a period to the conversation. In his sweet Charlotte voice, Mr. Hastings promised to return to her as soon as he was able, and blowing a kiss that was not visible to the servant, bade her au revoir.

Less than half an hour later, he did return but found that Miranda was not alone. She sat with a visitor, Mr. Farris Lloyd, and it was obvious, from the tension in the room, that he had interrupted a tête-à-tête. Mr. Hastings was presented as Miss Charlotte DeWitt, and the three sat in awkward silence. Miranda appeared flushed, and he would have given much to know what her high color meant. Mr. Lloyd was easier to read. He was wishing Miss DeWitt to the other end of the earth. Three minutes' appraisal convinced Mr. Hastings that he had before him a rival for Miss Troy's affections.

"I daresay, you wonder how Miranda and I became acquainted," he said in his Charlotte voice.

From the expression Mr. Lloyd wore, he did not appear to have wondered anything of the sort. Indeed, Miss DeWitt might as well have been invisible. His attention was all for Miranda, who sat with graceful dignity, glancing from one gentleman to the other, smiling painfully. At last, she stood and, explaining that she had obligations elsewhere, excused herself. Mr. Hastings could not tell whether it was his presence or Mr. Lloyd's that had driven her from the room.

When Mr. Lloyd rose and paced, Mr. Hastings debated what course to take. It was tempting to tell the fellow in bold, straightforward language that he himself had his sights set on Miss Troy and that, therefore, he might take himself off, to Perdition preferably, and not intrude on the lady's presence again. However, it occurred to him that such a warning would no doubt seem very odd coming from Miss Charlotte DeWitt, and so he kept mum.

A second, more rational, alternative seemed to be to quit the room and leave the man to his musings. Therefore, he stood and, gathering his skirts, began to make for the door. His doing so evidently gave Mr. Lloyd a start. He blinked, as though he had been roused from a dream, and said, "Miss DeWitt, I hope you will pardon my preoccupation. If I have been discourteous, I apologize. The last thing I wish to do is offend an acquaintance of Miss Troy's, or indeed any member of the gentle sex."

Taking the measure of the man, Mr. Hastings concluded that though he was stiff and not a little pompous, he was not a bad sort. With a gracious nod of the head, which showed the lace ruff of his cap to advantage, he replied, "I am not offended. It is apparent that something troubles you, and I shall not obtrude myself any further on your privacy by seeming to require conversation."

This speech succeeded at once in putting the gentleman at ease. "You are very sympathetic, Miss DeWitt," he said. "You appear to have divined my sensations at this moment without my having said a word."

Mr. Hastings felt an inclination to say that one did not have to be a member of the Royal Society to read his feelings for Miss Troy, that he himself admired her prodigiously, and that it was very much to the gentleman's credit that he knew where it was worthwhile to place his esteem, but he thought better of it. He must, he cautioned himself, speak as Miss Charlotte DeWitt, not as Mr. Charles Hastings. Whereas the latter was male, the former was female. Whereas the latter had formed his character by falling into and out of scrapes, the former had formed hers by putting a dear mother's alarms to rest. Whereas the latter's charms seemed to lie largely in his well-formed face and his skill at cards, the former's seemed to lie in her gentle understanding.

Thus, he answered, "Though we are strangers, Mr. Lloyd, if I may be of assistance to you, I hope you will not hesitate to ask,'" and he would have congratulated himself on the amiability of this offer had it not been accepted with such alacrity. Mr. Lloyd seized his hands, gravely studied the lace gloves that covered them, and said hoarsely, "May I confide in you then?"

Mr. Charles Hastings would have immediately staved off any sentimental outburst, but Miss Charlotte DeWitt smiled patiently and nodded.

While the two men seated themselves on the sofa, Mr. Hastings repressed an impulse to tell his companion to stop making a cake of himself and go to the devil. Instead, he folded his hands primly and cocked his head in the attitude of a sympathetic listener.

"As Miss Troy no doubt has confided to you, I have asked her to marry me."

At this, Mr. Hastings nearly hit him. If he had known that things had gone so far, he would have sent the fellow packing long before now. "Did you kiss her?" he demanded.

"Of course not!" Mr. Lloyd protested. "I think I know what a gentleman owes a lady's honor better than to affront her so."

This answer somewhat allayed Mr. Hastings's irritation. However, he could not rest easy until he knew whether Miranda had accepted him.

"She has refused me."

Relieved, Mr. Hastings contrived to produce several sorrowful murmurs.

"Ah, you are most sympathetic," Mr. Lloyd said, sighing. "Her refusal was something of a letdown, I own. I had offered to make her a generous allowance from her inheritance. At some personal sacrifice, I engaged to allow her space for a garden of her own. Moreover, I showed a willingness to make her my wife in spite of her age and pointed out the logic of conjoining her father's lands with mine. Nevertheless, she said she would not have me."

Mr. Hastings's admiration for Miranda rose a thousand-fold. With complete sincerity, he said, "Mr. Lloyd, I pity you from my heart." No sooner had he said it than he wondered how many foolish things he had said in conversation with women that inspired them to laugh at him in the secrecy of their hearts. In future, he vowed, he would be careful not to make an ass of himself in the company of a lady if he could possibly help it.

Oblivious to whatever Miss DeWitt might be thinking, Mr. Lloyd continued, "I called on Miss Troy today to renew my addresses, but she behaved with such circumspection, such elusiveness, that I did not dare. I am not certain whether I ought to speak to her at all. Perhaps she meant what she said when she refused me and has no intention of changing her mind."

"There are women who do mean precisely what they say, and who say precisely what they mean."

"Are you quite certain?"

"Oh, yes, I have been acquainted with several."

"How can I be certain that Miss Troy is one of them?"

This stopped Mr. Hastings. Had he assumed too much? Was it possible, he asked himself, that Miranda might in fact cherish hopes that Mr. Lloyd would repeat his offer? He dismissed the idea out of hand. The manner in which she had returned his kiss had told him all he needed to know. Besides, she could not possibly be in love with such a ninnyhammer as Mr. Lloyd.

On the other hand, she might find him more attractive as a life's companion than a gamester whose every word and deed seemed calculated to tease and to plague. A Mr. Lloyd might not be as dashing or adventurous as a Mr. Hastings, but he was a vast deal more comfortable. A Mr. Hastings might prove an interesting acquaintance, but he would likely turn out a dreadful husband. "I do not know how to answer you," Mr. Hastings said truthfully.

"Naturally not. Nobody can answer for Miss Troy excepting Miss Troy herself. That is why I have determined to beg a favor of you."

Mr. Hastings eyed him. The man had not displayed any interest whatever in Miss DeWitt. He had not so much as looked her in the eye. He was consumed solely with his own concerns, and yet he thought nothing of begging a favor of her. The effrontery of the man! The selfishness! Mr. Hastings began to see why women wore stays and ties and other instruments of torture—they took one's mind off the ridiculous self-absorption of the male species. However, he kept his thoughts to himself. "What favor?" was all he said.

"Would you sound out Miss Troy for me?"

"No!"

Mr. Lloyd bit his lip and looked most pitiful.

If he had been attired in his smoky blue coat and fawn pantaloons, Mr. Hastings would not have hesitated to give the fellow the heave-ho. But as Miss DeWitt, he felt something akin to compassion for the man. It even occurred to him that in Mr. Lloyd's place he would feel equally unhappy, that his feelings for Miss Troy were such that if she refused him, he would require cartloads of sympathy. Consequently, he relented. "I suppose I might sound her, but only if the opportunity presented itself and only if she truly wished to confide in me."

"In such a case, do you suppose you might say something in my favor? A hint from a trusted friend might go a long way toward furthering my cause."

Though he marveled at the man's impudence, Mr. Hastings said mildly, "I cannot promise anything except that I shall do whatever possible to ensure Miss Troy's future happiness."

To Mr. Hastings's disgust, Mr. Lloyd kissed his hand and thanked him profusely.

The gentleman then rose and announced, "Miss DeWitt, it has been a great pleasure. I shall have the honor of calling upon you soon." With a respectful bow, he took himself off, and Mr. Hastings was not sorry to see him go.

He would have gone, too, but Lady Troy came in and clapped her hands with delight at catching him alone.

"I should like to have a brief word with you, Miss De-Witt," she said conspiratorially. "Will you sit?"

Having little choice, Mr. Hastings sat. Because the bones of his corset had begun to poke him, he did not do so willingly or comfortably. He hoped his hostess had something to say that would reward him for his forbearance.

Leaning forward and smiling maternally, Lady Troy said, "You are perhaps aware that our Miranda, though everything that is amiable and accomplished, is a difficult, headstrong girl."

Mr. Hastings had suspected as much. He could not possibly have conceived such strong feelings for a young lady who was dull and submissive.

"I had hopes of marrying her to Mr. Charles Hastings of London, but the obstinate child will not have him."

He sat straight. "I believe I have heard of the gentleman. He is reputed to be amazingly handsome and charming."

"Yes, he is, to all the world except Miranda, who deems him amazingly loathsome and disgusting."

Irritably, he replied, "Perhaps her first impression was mistaken. Perhaps she will grow to like him in time."

"I should like nothing better, but I fear it is out of the question. She has taken her oath that she detests the man, and once Miranda has made up her mind to a thing, she is as unmovable as a mountain."

Mr. Hastings scowled.

"However, all is not lost. Even if she does not know her best interest, you and I do. *We* shall see to her future happiness, her mother and her most intimate friend."

"Miranda's happiness is very much in my thoughts of late," he said, "but it is difficult to know precisely what to do."

Lady Troy patted his hands. "Then I shall tell you. You must help me persuade her to have Mr. Lloyd."

Standing like a shot, Mr. Hastings said, "She does not love him."

"How do you know?"

He might have proved his contention by mentioning the passion of Miranda's kiss, but as Miss DeWitt he could not do so. Even as Mr. Hastings he could not allude to it. The best he could do was say in his Charlotte voice, "She has never mentioned him to me."

Lady Troy replied, "That is not necessarily a bad thing. At least she does not detest him as she does Mr. Hastings. And there will be time enough after they are married for love and such."

"Do you believe that she would come to love him?"

"Once you know how eligible he is, you will believe it, too." She then proceeded to detail the gentleman's myriad excellent qualities—his steady character, unblemished respectability, noble appearance, substantial wealth, high position, and ancient blood.

The more Mr. Hastings heard, the more restless he grew. He regretted that he had not knocked Mr. Lloyd in the head when he'd had the chance.

"And now, Miss DeWitt," her ladyship said, "will you say you will help me?"

He walked to the window and glared at the bare trees in the deer park. It cost him an effort to reply. "I do not know that I can promise anything, Lady Troy. I am not convinced Miranda will listen to me, or to anybody. Perhaps it is best if she decides for herself."

She stood a little behind him and said softly, "You are possessed of a wonderful gift, Miss DeWitt. I witnessed it in Queen Street. After you left her, Mrs. Hastings was wholly recovered from the oppression of spirits which had overtaken her. I do not know what you said, but the change in her was so startling as to constitute something of a miracle. I implore you to use your gifts in this case as well. After all, you have said you wish to see her happy, and I believe that you love her as much as her father and I do. Is that not so?"

He let out a breath. "Yes."

"I shall tell you something, Miss DeWitt, if you are ever so fortunate as to have a daughter, you will think day and night of her welfare. She will not ask you to think of it; she will not want you to think of it. Being young and hopeful, she will wish to see to her own welfare. But you will not be able to help yourself. You know that she would flourish in the proper circumstances. Hence, you will do your possible to put those circumstances in her way. You will want your daughter to know what it is to enjoy a marriage of equals. You will want her to experience the pleasures of mother-hood. You will want for her all the joys you yourself have known. And it will break your heart to see her turn her back on these blessings for the sake of rearranging the landscape or painting fire screens!" Here Lady Troy's voice broke, and she said no more.

When Mr. Hastings turned to her and saw that tears rolled down her round cheeks, he sympathized. He had been touched a little by Mr. Lloyd's pleas and was now even more affected by Lady Troy's. Her words had given him a glimpse of what his own mother must feel toward him. Instead of viewing Lady Troy as merely another anx-ious mother on the hunt for a son-in-law, he saw her as one who genuinely loved her daughter. It was a feeling he was bound to honor, given that he too loved her.

"May I have your promise to speak to her on Mr. Lloyd's behalf?" she asked, and with such earnestness that he said, "I do not know how to refuse you."

Lady Troy hugged him to her bosom. "You shall not be sorry. Their first child shall be named for you!"

She left him then, and he reflected that thanks to Miss Charlotte DeWitt and her tender heart, Mr. Charles Hast-ings might well lose the woman he loved.

TWELVE

School for Gamesters

Mr. Repton has declared that gardens need no longer stand far from the house. It is not only possible but desirable to have one nearby. One may enter it, he writes, through a meandering walk which leads from the parterre. Papa says he would like to see such a garden and such a walk and such a parterre at the abbey. I have also thought of planting roses in the garden. It appears that new species of pink, crimson, and yellow have recently reached our shores from China, and though delicate, will actually flower on through the summer until the frost. Such roses would be as fragrant as they are beautiful, but it is no use. I cannot think of them or anything else for two minutes together. I can think of nothing but Mr. Hastings, who is all that is odious.

Miranda experienced a surge of thankfulness when Miss DeWitt sent word that she would not join the family for supper and, as she was weary from her journey, would take a tray in her chamber and retire directly afterward. Seeing both Mr. Hastings and Mr. Lloyd in the same room at the same moment had discomfited her almost beyond endurance. That had not been the worst of it, however. The worst had come later, when she had escaped their presence and thrown herself across her bed in an agony of vexation, wishing with all her heart that such a thing as the male species had never been invented, with the exception of her father and Mr. Repton, of course. It had been detestable of Mr. Hastings to have kissed her and thus disturbed her tranquillity. It had also been detestable of him to vow *not* to kiss her and thus disturb her tranquillity even more. It was the height of lunacy, not to say arrogance, for him to come to Arundel Abbey in such a costume and risk his safety merely in order to see her. It was also the most flattering, the most tender, the most thrilling gesture anybody had ever made for her sake. If Mr. Hastings did not cease amusing himself and begin to take Everard seriously, she would positively throttle him. If Lord Everard so much as touched a hair on Mr. Hastings's head, she would positively murder him. These were her sensations as she pounded a fist into her pillow.

At last she calmed a little. It was unlike her, she knew, to contradict herself so wildly. What ailed her? She determined she would not rest until she had discovered the cause of such confusion and restored herself to reason. Sitting on the edge of the bed, she began to sort out her feelings. After a considerable time, during which she reviewed as honestly as she could every encounter she had ever had with Mr. Hastings, she reached a dismaying conclusion, namely, that since meeting him, her days seemed to have keener color and flavor. They were like a garden of rich earth primed for planting. No amount of anger at him or devotion to landscape gardening would diminish the attraction between them. She might fight it, but she could no longer deny it.

Thus her relief at Miss DeWitt's absence. She sat with Sir Bascomb and Lady Troy over supper in the parlor, sipping her tea, picking desultorily at her ham and bread and butter, both dreading and yearning for another meeting with Mr. Hastings.

Meanwhile, her mother extolled the many virtues of Miss Charlotte DeWitt. "You will like her prodigiously," she promised her husband. "Why when she left us, Tabitha was a changed creature. Her spirits were entirely restored. I am excessively grateful to the young lady on that account. Miranda is fortunate in her choice of friends."

"I look forward to meeting her," Sir Bascomb said. "As Miranda's friend, she must be welcome at Arundel Abbey."

With her parents' fond eyes on her, Miranda was forced to smile agreeably. Her smile soon faded, however. Sir Bascomb announced that her sisters and their children meant to arrive earlier than expected, the very next day, in fact. Ordinarily, this would have been welcome news. At this moment, however, it was alarming. Miranda knew that her three sisters would inspect Miss Charlotte DeWitt's face, figure, and style in the minutest detail. How would Mr. Hastings fare under so much feminine scrutiny? At the earliest opportunity, she vowed, she would go and warn him.

Her opportunity presented itself the following morning when it occurred to her that she might knock at his door. If she knocked on *Mr. Hastings's* door, it would cause a ferocious stir, but nobody would remark it if she paid a call on her old schoolmate in her bedchamber. After dressing hurriedly, she knocked and, with her face close to the door, whispered, "Charlotte, are you awake? It is Miranda. May I speak with you?"

Soon the door was opened, though she could not see who had opened it. When it flew shut behind her, she saw Mr. Hastings standing before her, dressed in dark pantaloons and an open shirt. He had not yet shaved and appeared bleary-eyed with sleep.

"I have disturbed you," she said, though it was she who was disturbed. His appearance made her conscious of the strange intimacy they shared.

"No, no," he said repressing a yawn, "it is well you have come. I wish to speak with you." He regarded her unhappily, then studied a painting of a pair of sisters seated with a pair of hounds.

Miranda looked at her hands. It was going to be more difficult than she had anticipated to send Mr. Hastings away. But, she reminded herself, for his sake it had to be done. "I have come to warn you, Mr. Hastings. It is not safe for you to stay at the abbey any longer. You must leave at once."

Apparently he had not heard, for he said, "Both Mr. Lloyd and your mother have asked me to speak with you, and I said I would. That is to say, *I* myself did not promise to speak with you, but Miss DeWitt did, and I find myself in the ridiculous position of having to keep her confounded promises. It is a point of honor with me."

She came near to him, wishing he would look at her, wishing she had the courage to touch his arm. Earnestly, she said, "You do not understand. My sisters arrive today, all three of them. They will look you over, and so closely, I fear, that you will be found out."

He was too engrossed in his own subject to heed her. "It falls to me," he said in a strained voice, "to ask you to consider Mr. Lloyd's proposal of marriage."

"What?" Her brown eyes enlarged as she stared at him.

Over his shoulder he looked at her. "Mr. Lloyd wishes to marry you. Your mother wishes you to accept. I have given them my word I would put forward his case to you."

A moment ago she had flattered herself that if he had any case to make, it would be his own. Now he was pleading for her to have Mr. Lloyd! She studied him through slitted eyes. "By all means," she said acidly, "put it forward."

"I'm afraid I shall not do as well as Charlotte. She always seems to know precisely what to say."

"*Dear,* dear Charlotte."

Stiffly, he said, "Well, then, here it is in a nutshell: the fellow seems a decent sort. He is as rich as a nob, brimful of vintage blood, and, by his lights, prepared to be generous with your money. Therefore, I expect a young lady might do well to accept him, provided she liked him well enough."

With monumental force of will, she contrived to appear tranquil. "Is that all you have to say to me?" It was incredible to her that he could kiss her as he had and then urge her to marry another.

"Yes, except that there may be another whom you like better, and in that case it would be the most natural thing in the world if you refused Mr. Lloyd."

She thrust her face forward so that they stood nearly eye to eye. "Mr. Hastings," she said in something akin to a hiss, "just because you have dressed yourself up as a lady, made yourself out to be the first friend of my heart, and insinuated yourself into the bosom of my family, do not think that you have the right to interfere in my concerns. I feared, when you adopted your disguise, that you might come to great harm. My worst fears have been borne out. You have been transformed into a busybody of the first order! I shall thank you to find another, more suitable place for your officious nose than my affairs. Good morning."

On that grand note, she left him, punctuating her speech with a violent slam of the door. On her return to her own chamber, she repeated to herself every syllable of their conversation. How dare he presume to tell her whom to marry! How dare he make love to her and then put another man forward to her as a husband! He was odious; she had thought so from the start. It was provoking to find herself weeping over such a man, making her eyes red and sore. He was not worth a single tear.

Instead of indulging her tears, she resolved, she would write in her journal, outlining her idea for a rose garden. She tore open the cravat, which had continued all this time to tie the book, and flung it into a corner of the chamber. Opening to a blank page, she applied a new point to her pen and wrote furiously. After a few forced sentences, though, she put the pen down. Her mind continually wandered. It would not obey her command to think of nothing but roses.

Her situation was singularly ironic, she thought. Now that she had fallen in love with Mr. Hastings, he had lost interest in her. He wished to fob her off on Mr. Lloyd, so that he might be rid of her. A day ago, before she had become aware of her feelings, she might have been able to shrug off his inconstancy. Now it was too late. Her case was hopeless.

This state of despair lasted a mere ten minutes, for it occurred to Miranda that all her life she had been fickle, wandering from one pastime to another, one beau to another, one passion to another, unable to stick to anything for very long. Until today, she had viewed that quality as a serious flaw in her character. Now, she saw, it would be the saving of her. In a week, two at the most, she would have forgotten Mr. Hastings. Once she did, he would take his place beside her abandoned novel and a half-dozen useless fire screens.

Mr. Hastings was not any more satisfied with their conversation than Miranda was. Though he had done his duty by Mr. Lloyd and fulfilled his promise to Lady Troy, he could not congratulate himself, for in the process, he had somehow contrived to send the woman he adored fleeing from him in a temper. As if that were not bad enough, she had not uttered one word to indicate that she meant to refuse Mr. Lloyd no matter how many loved ones pressed her to have him, that she did not love him, could not love him, because she loved another man, namely Mr. Charles Hastings. He had waited for her to say so, had even given her an opening, but to no avail.

Perhaps the reason she had not declared a preference for him over Mr. Lloyd was that she did not, in fact, prefer him. Perhaps she fancied that he was as officious as Mr. Lloyd. After his late interference in her affairs, he had to confess that he *was* as officious as Mr. Lloyd, if not more so. Perhaps he was as much at fault as Mr. Lloyd in another way, too—perhaps he thought only of his own concerns and ignored those of anybody else. How much interest had he shown, for example, in her study of landscape gardening? He had read about it in her private journal, but that had happened purely by chance. Their conversation was taken up entirely with him—his wound, his danger, his difficulty with Everard, his disguise, his wagering, his desire to see her despite the risk. He had considered the risk to himself as negligible, but had he considered the risk to her?

Rubbing the stubble on his chin, he rebuked himself for allowing matters to come to such a pass. He ought to have shown interest in those things which interested her, because he *was* interested. There was nothing about her he did not wish to know. He could conceive of few greater pleasures than to ask her a question and hear her answer it in her musical voice. Whatever she had to say, he wished her to say it to him. Yet he had accorded her as much real attention as Mr. Lloyd had accorded Charlotte DeWitt.

He made a wager with himself. Before the week was out, Miss Troy would have spoken to him at length on the subject of landscape gardening. If he won the bet, he would reward himself by telling her straight out that he loved her. If he lost, he would know himself for a fool and leave the field to Mr. Lloyd. The stakes were exactly as he liked them—high enough to spark a determination to succeed.

That evening, despite his heroic vow to show interest in whatever interested Miranda, Mr. Hastings found himself the focus of attention. As soon as the three sisters arrived, with seven children among them ranging in age from six to sixteen, all eyes were fixed on him. Except for Miranda's, they were appraising eyes. It required all his patience to sit in the cedar parlor appearing not to notice that every inch of him was being peered at and judged. He found himself wondering whether his dress, figure, complexion, carriage, coif, and cap would meet the high standards of the fashionable ladies who inspected him, and for a moment, he actually cared. As a man, he had never given a groat for what others might think of his dress and manners. As a woman, he estimated that there was not a single aspect of his appearance that was satisfactory.

At dinner, Susannah mentioned with a giggle that several buttons on his sleeve were misbuttoned. "You really must speak to your maid about it, Miss DeWitt," she advised. "These creatures will grow careless if we do not keep a watchful eye out."

Mr. Hastings would have neglected to show a proper gratitude for such counsel. Luckily, Miss DeWitt knew how to behave and modestly thanked Susannah for her kindness.

Maria was no less kind than her sister in remarking the defects in Miss DeWitt's appearance. When the dinner was eaten and the ladies withdrew, she sat by Mr. Hastings and whispered, "You have been too much in the sun, Miss DeWitt. I see it in the roughness and brownness of your complexion. I shall have my maid prepare for you my favorite mixture of cucumber and rose water, as soon as the season allows. The cucumber must be fresh, you see. You shall put it on your face every morning and night for an hour, and you shall be amazed at the results."

Though Mr. Hastings would not have hesitated to yawn and walk away in the middle of this speech, Miss DeWitt smiled and vowed she could not wait to try out the mixture.

Charlotte was equally patient with Anne, who, after Sir Bascomb had joined the ladies, poured her coffee from the urn and said to all who were gathered, "We must find Miss DeWitt a husband. No female creature should be without a life's companion. It is an offense against Nature for her to have to endure only her own company and that of other women. I wish we might do as much for Miranda."

While Mr. Hastings looked for an escape from so much kind attention, Miss DeWitt modestly lowered her eyes and murmured her gratitude.

He finally lost patience when the sisters turned their attention from Miss DeWitt's deficiencies to Miranda's. While she sat quietly on the sofa embroidering, they derided her study of landscape gardening, declared Mr. Repton's ideas quite out, and inquired if she did not pity herself for having no offspring of her own. As their children were at that instant in the process of noisily tearing around the room in a game of hide-and-seek, Mr. Hastings thought she might declare then and there her intention to live the life of a celibate, but like Miss DeWitt, she answered with astonishing forbearance.

"I am very fond of children," Miranda said, smiling warmly as the littlest one climbed on her.

"Well, you might have had them if you had not turned up your nose at Mr. Hastings," Anne said. "Oh, Mama has told us all about it."

Miranda blushed, glanced quickly at Mr. Hastings, then glanced away. He could see that she was too mortified to make any answer.

Maria added, "I hope you will not be above yourself and refuse Mr. Lloyd as well. He is very likely your last chance."

This was too much for Mr. Hastings. He went to Miranda

and leaned over to whisper in her ear, "This is the outside of enough. We shall not stay in this room another minute."

She regarded him in alarm and would have ordered him to hush, but he stood tall, and speaking louder than the racket kicked up by the children, claimed the attention of everybody in the drawing room. "Miranda and I," he announced, "shall entertain the children in the schoolroom."

So commanding was his voice that nobody demurred. With evil looks and whispered threats, he persuaded the children to gather in a line behind him. Then, fixing Miranda with his eyes, he said sweetly, "Miranda, dear, will you be so good as to show us where we might find the schoolroom?"

Miranda looked at him, then at her sisters, then at Mr. Hastings again. Without another word, she led the way upstairs.

Though the schoolroom was cold—no fire had been lit in anticipation of visitors—it was soon made warm by the seven energetic bodies that began to frolic the instant they entered. The four boys began to pummel each other, cheered and egged on by the three girls. Mr. Hastings pulled the combatants apart and said, "I believe I spy in the corner a game of spillikins. Those of you who play it quietly, I shall reward with half a crown and take them to Togbury to spend it. Those who do not play quietly, I shall chop into little pieces, boil in snake sauce, and feed to the chickens."

This last threat was sufficiently bloodcurdling to spark the children's interest. They grinned, except for the littlest boy, who asked, "Who are you?"

"I am a witch, and I shall eat you myself if you do not do precisely as I say."

The boy burst into giggles and hugged his Aunt Miranda's knees. The other children laughed, hoping that the formidable Miss DeWitt was truly so interesting as to find their little cousin appetizing. Prying him loose, they withdrew to the corner and played, though not very quietly.

Mr. Hastings exhaled in relief and looked at Miranda. He was surprised to find her smiling at him.

"You are very wicked," she said to him.

"And a good thing for you that I am."

She grew serious, as though she had just recollected that she was angry with him. "Well, what are we to do now?" she asked in a cold voice.

He drew her toward a pair of child-sized chairs, where they sat. "You will be so good as to tell me all about landscape gardening."

Baffled, she regarded him. "You are the oddest creature."

"Not at all. It occurs to me that I have had no opportunity to sound you on the subject. It is one which interests me."

"Why?"

"Because it interests you."

She frowned. "You are quizzing me."

Throwing up his hands, he stood. "Why is it so difficult for you to believe that I am perfectly sincere?"

"Is there something you want from me, Mr. Hastings? Are you in need of another favor? Has there been a threat from Everard?"

"No! Confound it, I merely wish you to tell me what I am to do with Clarendon Grove."

"What is Clarendon Grove? I have never heard of it."

"It is my country estate in Dorset. I haven't visited there in years, but the last time I saw it, its grounds were a perfect sight. Its owner neglects them, I fear."

Her expression was still cold and suspicious. "You might hire an improver," she remarked.

"Perhaps I shall, but what is one to do with an improver? Am I to give him a free hand? Am I not to have any preferences of my own?"

"Of course you are to have preferences of your own. The improver must build to suit your taste."

"That is what I hoped. Unfortunately, I have no taste. I haven't the least notion what I like. I suppose you know what you like. I suppose if you had a large flat field covered with weeds and thistle, you would know precisely what to do with it, but I do not."

He could see her forming a picture in her mind. With more enthusiasm than she had shown previously, she said, "There are a great many things you might do with it."

Sitting again, he drew his chair close to hers.

"You will want to begin by seeking out 'the genius of the place,' as Mr. Pope says. Ask yourself what truly suits that particular expanse, and as you do, consider utility as well as beauty."

He thought for a moment before replying, "Perhaps a cascade would do. I expect I should like the sound of the water."

"It is true, water has a very pleasing sound, but a cascade would require your forming hills and cliffs out of flat ground. It is best to defer to nature here rather than to force or distort her. Use what she has already provided."

"I do not see that she has provided much of anything. What is one to do with an uninteresting, unvaried lowland?"

"Well, you might, for example, build a fountain garden in the Italian style."

His eyes were fixed on her animated face. He smiled, impressed not only by her taste but also her good sense.

"Your improver might form a rectangle in the field, or some other configuration natural to the shape of the ground. It might be surrounded by shrubs and trees for privacy, and in the center, might rise a fountain of marble or rougher stone, with carved fishes and frogs, sprinkling into a pool at various intervals. The water might rise gradually to a height, then cease, then slowly rise again. And surrounding this fountain might be a series of circular and square pools containing smaller fountains. The rise and fall of the water might be synchronized, so that the fountains achieved the effect of a ballet."

The idea appealed to him enormously, especially if she would agree to walk in the fountain garden on his arm. She was smiling at him now, fully engrossed in planning the project.

"Mr. Lloyd has a somewhat similar garden," she enthused, "if you would care to see it. Of course, in winter, you could not experience the full effect of the fountains, but you could gather some notion of the possibilities for Clarendon Grove."

He glanced at a spot on the distant wall that seemed to have affronted him. "I expect you admire Mr. Lloyd's fountain garden excessively," he said.

With high color in her cheeks, she said, "Whether I admire Mr. Lloyd's fountain garden, which is small and not at all well kept up, is none of your affair. I shall admire which gardens I choose, and not those which I am told fit the mold of the picturesque!"

Not knowing what to make of this answer, except that he had put her in a temper again, he asked, "Will you help me build a fountain garden at Clarendon Grove?"

She suddenly noticed how close they were sitting and drew away. "I think you would do best to hire an improver."

"I shall need you to explain the design to him."

Shaking her head, she replied, "Landscape gardening is merely my passion of the moment. I daresay, by the time you are set to make your improvements, I shall have tired of the subject."

"Perhaps not. Perhaps if you were encouraged to pursue it, you would stick to it. Perhaps if your family did not belittle your interest, urging you to think exclusively of marriage, you would not abandon it."

He fancied he had hit the mark, for her face grew swollen with emotion. She rose, walked to the corner where the children played, said a few soft words to them, then stared at the wall. Though he was not a patient man, he waited patiently for her to say something. When she did not, he approached her, certain now that he had given her pain.

"Might I," he inquired gently, "have a cascade somewhere on the property?"

She faced him. Her expression was strained. "I am sure you might do anything you liked. You always do."

"From what you say, it would require a rolling, hilly prospect. And the waterfall must appear offhanded, as though nature had meant it to flow there. I believe it might look very well next to the fountain garden."

The absurdity of the notion made her laugh in spite of herself. "I fear the two are not compatible," she said. "The fountain garden would be formal, elegant. The cascade would be situated in a wild, rustic setting."

He stood very close to her. "Do you know, I am the sort of fellow who might be formal and elegant one moment, and wild and natural the next. Why can I not have both styles?"

What she saw in his eyes, he could not tell, but it compelled her to swallow hard. "I shall see what Mr. Repton has to say on the subject," she replied breathlessly.

"Then we shall speak again?"

The servant came in then to announce that the children's mothers wished them to be put to bed. From their corner, they groaned and protested, but Miss DeWitt cheered them by saying they had earned their reward and might look forward to a walk to the village the next day. Pulling their Aunt Miranda along with them, they left Mr. Hastings alone in the schoolroom.

Curious to know how Mr. Hastings would comport himself with a passel of noisy children, she accompanied them on the walk to Togbury. The day was freezing, and, though Miranda carried the littlest one, Clive, and Mr. Hastings carried the other little ones in turn, they complained until Miss DeWitt distracted them with the story of the disagreeable children who were captured by a giant whose eyes and nose oozed phlegm and who forced them to live in a cave with no clothes on their bones and nothing to eat but pease porridge and slugs. They demanded more details of the giant's hideousness, and it took him the entire distance to the village to appease their thirst for gore.

Once in Togbury, Mr. Hastings presented each of the five older children with half a crown and set them loose to buy what they liked with it. They were to meet him in front of the linen draper's in an hour. Those who did not appear in time would be left to freeze in the cold and snow, their bodies—stiff and blue—to lie undiscovered until the spring thaw.

Miranda cautioned, "Their mothers will not approve their being allowed to run free."

"Excellent," he replied. "Children always have a better time when they know they are doing what their mothers will not approve."

She watched the children scatter in various directions, crowing with the joys of freedom and wealth. When Mr. Hastings invited her to accompany him and the two smallest children to the baker's, she accepted. She noted that he glanced at her sidelong with satisfaction.

"I think you are in charity with me again," he said as they walked.

"I have always liked Miss Charlotte DeWitt," she replied, smiling. "In the case of Mr. Charles Hastings, however, I must reserve judgment."

"A pity, for he likes you very well."

His directness stopped her pulse. She found herself wishing to believe him with all her heart.

At the baker's, he put half crowns in the children's tiny hands so that they might purchase tarts of every kind. He permitted them to eat the sweets right away, filling their cheeks to capacity and smearing their faces with sugar and jam.

From there, they proceeded to the confectioner's, where he bought enough angelica to make him a permanent favorite.

Miranda forbore to reprimand him as her sisters would have done, for his carefree indulgence had good results. The older children returned to the linen draper's in good time with their purchases, boasting that they had made a pact to save a portion of their money for next time. The younger children obeyed his every utterance as though they feared he would gobble them up; yet they snuggled contentedly into his bosom whenever he lifted them into his arms. It warmed her to see how well he got on with them; it also dismayed her. The more she saw, the more she liked him; at this rate, it would be a very long time before he took his rightful place among her other discarded pastimes.

On their return to the house, the children were fed and made to rest, but they clamored so earnestly and noisily to visit the schoolroom with Miss DeWitt that their mothers relented.

"What spell do you suppose Miss DeWitt has cast on them?" Susannah inquired irritably.

"Oh, she is a worker of wonders," said Lady Troy. She then detailed the miraculous change that had come over Mrs. Hastings after her interview with the young lady.

Word was sent to Miss DeWitt begging her presence in the schoolroom. Miss DeWitt graciously replied that she would comply, as long as Miranda agreed to accompany her. Given a choice between an evening of sisterly censure and two hours with Mr. Hastings and her nieces and nephews, Miranda had no hesitation selecting the schoolroom.

Entering, she found them all seated at a long table. She could tell that they had been waiting for her. Mr. Hastings rose and led her solicitously to the head of the table. Meanwhile, the children watched her with large eyes.

"What have you plotted this time?" she whispered to Mr. Hastings.

"You shall see," he said, seating her gallantly.

"We are going to play piquet," little Clive announced.

She stood bolt upright, horrified. "It is impossible," she protested. "The children are too young to learn such a game. Their mothers will cry out against the impropriety. You and I shall catch blame and be banned from their presence for having set up a school for gamesters. And even if they were to approve, I could not learn such a game. It is true I lost the wager and am obliged to learn piquet, but I have scarcely learned casino. Surely you do not expect me to make such a leap so soon. The children can tell you, I have no skill at cards. I shall appear a fool and spoil your play. Oh, Mr. Hastings, I mean, dear Charlotte, you are not serious. You cannot really mean to make me play piquet."

This breathless speech over, Mr. Hastings smiled at her tenderly and said, "Would you care to place a small wager on that?"

THIRTEEN

Fever

Hastings's Sixth Principle of Gaming: The greatest
sin in gaming is to fail to bet high during a run of
luck. A gamester must always ride with a winning
streak, pushing it to the furthest extremity. He who
will not wager may retain his blunt, but he will not
be able to look at himself in the glass each morning
and know that he is a man.

The younger children had fallen asleep with their heads on
the table by the time Miranda could say with confidence
that she understood the principle and practice of declaring.
Mr. Hastings was so well pleased with her progress that he
taught her the method of scoring for carte blanche, point,
sequence, and sets, a lesson that put the older children to
sleep as well.

When the servant came to bustle the seven off to bed,
they rubbed their eyes, yawned, and complained that Aunt
Miranda had got ahead of them while they slept. This state
of affairs was intolerable, as previously she had been perfectly cowhanded at cards and always lost to them. Miss
DeWitt was obliged to promise to resume the lesson on the
morrow.

"And if you pay very strict attention," Mr. Hastings announced, "we shall learn the play of the hand and the taking
of tricks."

Hearing this, Miranda cried, "Do you mean to say there
is more to piquet than what I have learned tonight?"

"Oh, a great deal more," he replied cheerfully.

The children applauded and went off with the servant in high spirits.

Miranda sat down with a disheartened sigh. "I shall never learn it," she said.

He sat next to her. "You are sinking, I collect."

Wearily, she gazed at him.

"To 'sink' is to refrain from declaring a combination you think will not win. You evidently regard yourself as such a combination."

She put up a hand to ward off any more talk of cards. He took hold of the hand, an impulsive gesture that succeeded in bringing her fully awake.

"Sinking may be useful at times," he said, smiling. "On the other hand, it is well to remember that if you choose to sink, you cannot later claim the combination, even if it would have won. That is to say, there are times when it is best to venture forth, even when you are uncertain as to the result."

She gazed fixedly at their locked hands.

He followed the direction of her eyes, then drew closer. A sudden sense gripped her that he was going to kiss her, but he stood and inquired, "What have you decided to do in regard to Mr. Lloyd?"

The abruptness of the question brought her to herself. It reminded her that she had not a single ally in her determination to refuse her neighbor's offer of marriage. Even the man she wished to accept pressed her to accept the other. It was a bitter circumstance. Compared to it, playing piquet was a stroll in a garden.

The reference to Mr. Lloyd did not anger her as it had done in the past. However, it grieved her. Blinking back tears, she bade Mr. Hastings good night and went away.

When she was gone, he lifted his skirt to reveal a delicately shod foot and kicked the door shut.

The following days were divided between herding the children to the village and entertaining them at cards. They thought piquet was ripping, and Miss DeWitt, who taught them how to cheat at it, "top of the trees." Aunt Miranda, they had to allow, had a certain skill but she lacked the proper pugnacious spirit. Mr. Hastings too remarked that if she played more energetically, she might win more often, and she might actually enjoy herself. At such moments, Miranda regarded them bleakly, saying that it would be better if she left them to their game and amused herself elsewhere. This provoked an outcry. The children liked their aunt's company too well to permit her to leave and thereby please herself instead of them.

Miss DeWitt was equally reluctant to part with her erstwhile schoolmate, so much so, in fact, that the next day she produced sketch paper and pencils and invited Miranda to teach them all something about landscape gardening.

"We cannot always be playing piquet," Mr. Hastings said in his Charlotte voice, "else we should become weary of it, and as Dr. Johnson has said, 'When you are weary of piquet, you are weary of life.' "

Miranda laughed. "Dr. Johnson said, 'When you are weary of *London*, you are weary of life.' He said nothing about piquet, as you very well know, Charlotte dear. Besides, I fear the children will find the subject of landscape gardening tedious."

"You are sinking again," Mr. Hastings admonished, finger raised.

"Oh, don't sink," little Clive begged her. "You mustn't lose heart."

Knowing it was useless to argue against such earnestness, and that if she did leave them she would be obliged to sit with her sisters, she agreed to teach them all something about landscape gardening. "Not long ago," she said, "fences were generally made of brick or stone and kept one in or out, as the case might be. We are fortunate to live in a time when fences have become less obtrusive. They may be painted green or brown, blending with the surroundings in such a fashion as to seem invisible. They may be made of wicker, chain, or iron railing, and built low enough to see over. At the same time, they may be curved and wrought into shapes that are as pleasing to the eye as the greenery which surrounds them."

"May one jump over them?" Clive inquired.

"Of course," she said, and invited them to draw a fence, using any number of curlicues, trims, lattices, and bars. Soon they were all at work on their designs, Mr. Hastings included, and when they had finished, they exhibited their creations proudly. The next day, the children demanded to be allowed to draw gates for the fences.

Thereafter, the days included lessons in landscape design as well as piquet and excursions to Togbury, and so the time passed quickly, as pleasant times have a way of doing. Unhappily, they were not quite so pleasant for Mr. Hastings as they were for the others. He was obliged to maintain a correspondence with Felix, who had little of a cheerful nature to report. Although the Bow Street gentleman had successfully bribed Everard's henchmen to trade their loyalties to Mr. Hastings, Everard himself was more of a threat than ever. He had nursed his grudge to the point of obsession, and wherever he went, he hinted that he had devised a plan to avenge himself on Mr. Hastings in bloody fashion.

The most recent communication from Felix contained the disagreeable news that Everard had been to Lyme Regis. Mr. Hastings had been identified as a guest at two local inns in the vicinity. The elderly ladies who had let his house had offered a sufficiently detailed description of Mr. Hastings to put Everard on the scent.

"You had better go hotfoot from Arundel Abbey as far as Miss Charlotte's legs can carry her," Felix warned in his letter.

Mr. Hastings read that warning as the family took its morning meal in the breakfast parlor. Thoughtfully, he folded the letter and tapped it against his cheek.

Lady Troy marveled, "How devoted your cousin is, Miss DeWitt. What an extraordinary correspondent. I declare, I do not know another gentleman who is so attentive to his relations as Mr. DeWitt."

Aloud, Mr. Hastings cordially agreed; to himself, however, he wished that Felix was attentive to better purpose. The last thing he intended to do was quit Arundel Abbey. An explorer did not abandon his climb just when he was within reach of the peak. A general did not sound the retreat just when he was on the brink of conquest. A whist player did not leave the table just when he was about to trump his opponent's ace. And he was not about to leave Arundel Abbey just when he was near discovering whether Miranda could love him.

He thought it best to say nothing to her of Felix's warnings. It would have been impossible to look her in the eye and explain his reasons for staying on at the abbey at the risk of his life.

Christmas arrived, making it necessary for the children, like the servants, to dress up in their very best clothes, file into the drawing room, and watch in reverent silence as blue, green, yellow, and red candles were lit. Stories were read, decorations admired, and presents dispersed. Miss DeWitt was affectionately scolded for giving far too many confections to the children.

After the afternoon feast, during which outsized quantities of goose and pudding were consumed, the four sisters presented their parents, Miss DeWitt, and each other with little gifts—books, trinket boxes, handsome bottles filled with scent, sweetmeats, and gloves. Among these gifts was one marked for Miranda; the giver was not identified. All gathered around to see what the small rectangular box contained.

More agitated than excited, Miranda began to untie the ribbon. She could not shake an odd sensation that the gift was from Mr. Hastings. Lifting the lid from the box, she uncovered a necklace of diamonds and emeralds. The gasps that went up from her family added to her uneasiness. Speculation was rife as to the name of the giver, especially as all in the room took their oath that neither the credit nor the blame for the magnificent present could be laid at their door. Each of the sisters took her turn at trying on the necklace and exclaiming over its exquisiteness. Sir Bascomb estimated the bauble's worth at over a thousand pounds. Lady Troy declared that she had seen nothing to equal it, except perhaps a diamond and emerald necklace her dear friend

Tabitha had worn at her come out. "Oh, but the two are nothing alike," Lady Troy declared. "This one is ever so much prettier."

Demurely, Miss DeWitt said that Miranda looked very well in the necklace and hoped she would have much pleasure in it always.

Miranda fingered the gems in considerable awe.

The mystery of the giver was thought to have been solved that same evening, when Mr. Lloyd paid a Christmas call on his neighbors.

"You sly thing," Susannah charged him. "You thought we would not find you out, but we have!"

Mr. Lloyd furrowed his brow. "You have?"

"It was most improper of you to do such a thing!" Lady Troy admonished him. "If I did not know you as well as I do, I should be very angry. I shall insist that Miranda give it back, and with a scolding."

Squinting at them, he said, "I beg pardon if I have done anything amiss."

Maria cried out, "Oh, Mama, do not upbraid him for his generosity. Say rather that you hope he will be rewarded by his lady fair, and in a manner to make all of us happy."

Lady Troy was adamant, and taking the necklace from Miranda, she put it in Mr. Lloyd's hands.

He looked at it in bafflement, shaking his head. "I hope you do not think that *I* gave this to Miss Troy!"

"We do not think it. We know it!"

"I am shocked that you should think so little of me. I believe I know a gentleman's duty better than to make an improper gift to a lady, especially one I esteem as highly as I do Miss Troy." Here he bowed to Miranda and assumed an air of virtuous indignation.

Reluctantly, Lady Troy took back the necklace. If Mr. Lloyd would not own his generosity, she could not very well foist the thing on him. As her daughters pointed out, she had no choice but to permit Miranda to keep the gift.

Meanwhile, Miranda observed Mr. Hastings, who in his turn observed the proceedings without expression. He appeared so subdued, so indifferent, that for a moment she thought it possible that Mr. Lloyd had indeed given her the present. One glance at him, however, told her otherwise. It was not the sort of thing Mr. Lloyd would do. He was everything that was proper. He never would have taken such a risk. To Mr. Hastings, in contrast, risk was mother's milk.

Maria waved a finger at Mr. Lloyd as though he were a naughty child. "You came tonight expressly to see how well the necklace looked on Miranda and to be thanked. You may as well confess it."

"Truly I did not," he protested. "I came to invite you all to the assembly at Togbury. Squire Rowdy has determined that we shall celebrate the New Year at a public ball, and he asked me expressly to extend to you an invitation."

The necklace was forgotten. An assembly, even if it was a public one, was a gift to them all, not just one of their number. Hence, it was cause for more excitement than an old necklace. The sisters accepted at once, saying that they would write to their husbands, insisting they come down for it. Sir Bascomb and Lady Troy beamed at the prospect of so much gaiety in their midst. It had been some time since all their family had been gathered around them on an occasion of harmony and joy.

Mr. Lloyd approached Miranda, who sat on a settee next to Miss DeWitt. "May I," he asked her, "have your promise for the first two dances?"

She felt the eyes of her family on her. Their loving gazes and expectant smiles made her ache inside. Instinctively, she turned to Mr. Hastings. He seemed to regard her with unusual intensity, but what that intensity meant, she could not guess. She knew only what she wished it to mean.

"What do you think I ought to do, Charlotte?" she asked him.

The fire in his eyes blazed for a moment. It seemed he would say something startling. But he collected himself and, smiling a ghastly smile, said, "You must give Mr. Lloyd your promise, Miranda dear, and you must go to the assembly. You must dance all the dances and drink champagne. Above all, you must be sure to wear your new necklace, for then all the gentlemen will not be able to help falling in love with you."

Hurt, Miranda looked at Mr. Lloyd, nodded, and accepted his invitation.

During the next seven days, she endeavored to corner Mr. Hastings. She had three questions to pose: First, what did he mean by throwing her at Mr. Lloyd's head? Second, what had he done in all this time about Everard? And third, did he like her as much as her heart told her he did, or had her heart told her merely what she wished to hear? Of course, she did not intend actually to ask the last question, but she hoped that in the course of an earnest conversation with the gentleman concerning the other two points, a favorable answer would spontaneously slip out.

The only thing that slipped, however, was Mr. Hastings, who proved as slippery as an eel. Wherever he went, he had children about him for protection. There was no getting at him in the schoolroom. As to the dining parlor and drawing room, he was forever excusing himself to see to one errand or another or to tend to one of the children who was sick or pouting or bored.

Undeterred, she knocked on his chamber door, calling, "Oh, Charlotte dear, may I come in? It is Miranda."

Mr. Hastings called back, "Oh, Miranda dear, I am afraid I am indisposed."

Evidently, he was aware that she meant to question him and meant to avoid being questioned. She resolved therefore to push him to the edge. The next time the family gathered around the fire to decide who should drive to the assembly in the various carriages at their disposal, Miranda said loudly, "Oh, we must not forget dear Charlotte. We must be certain she is noticed at the assembly, and we must each of us promise to procure her a dancing partner."

The glare Mr. Hastings darted her way gave her immense gratification. Her three sisters also gratified her by naming gentlemen of the neighborhood who were eligible and who would make creditable dancing partners for Miss DeWitt.

"I do not think I ought to attend the assembly," Mr. Hast-

ings murmured in his most modest Charlotte voice. "Somebody will be wanted to stay with the children, and I should
be pleased to fill that office. I do not like to dance."

A roar of protest went up. Miss DeWitt must not deny
them the pleasure of her company. She had sacrificed her
own comfort too often for the sake of the children. It was
now time for her to think of her own pleasure. If she did not
have a suitable gown, they would be happy to fit her out
with one of theirs. She might also borrow any brooch or
earrings she fancied. Indeed, they would come to her chamber to help her dress and assist her maid in dressing her
hair. Yes, they must positively do something about Miss
DeWitt's hair. That yellow shade was awfully distinctive, to
be sure, but it wanted elegance. It must be powdered a trifle
to tone down its brightness, and curled with more care to
appear less scraggly. She must be given a cap more fetch-
ing and less droopy. Why it covered half her face! Moreover, Miss DeWitt, for once in her life, must leave her
shawl at home. She was forever concealing her figure under
it, which was certainly a pity, for surely she possessed a tolerable form and, with the aid of proper stays and a chemise,
might show it off to advantage. They would come and help
her dress, and so she need not fear looking outré.

Miranda heard these kindnesses with a smile; Mr. Hastings, with a groan. The groan was silent, of course, but she
heard it as clear as the chime of the mantel clock. *Miss De-
Witt* might be gracious in her thanks to her friends, but *Mr.
Hastings* was as furious as a bull.

Miranda's stratagem had its desired effect. On the night
before the assembly, Mr. Hastings sent a message to her by
way of a servant.

"Miss DeWitt begs you will come to her in her chamber," the girl said, dipping a curtsy.

After tidying her hair and adjusting her bodice, Miranda
went to his room and knocked.

The door opened and she was pulled unceremoniously
inside. Mr. Hastings took hold of her arms and pinned her
to the wall. Dressed as himself, in a half-buttoned shirt and
pantaloons, he was almost menacing. He blasted at her,

"Miss DeWitt has no intention of attending the assembly, as you well know. You also know that it is impossible for her to attend without Mr. Hastings's identity being uncovered. I do not know why you have determined to tease me on this matter, but from this moment, it shall stop!"

She wrestled to get free but could not. "It shall stop," she shot back, "if you will stop propelling me into Mr. Lloyd's arms!"

He froze. He frowned. He opened his mouth as if to say something, then evidently changed his mind. Gently, he removed his hold on her. He smiled and appeared to relax. "Nothing easier," he said with a bow. "From this moment forward, I shall not propel you into anybody's arms, and especially not Mr. Lloyd's."

"And you will not promise my mother or Mr. Lloyd to press me further on the subject of matrimony."

His smile broadened, giving him a somewhat rakish look. "The gentleman's name shall not pass my lips again."

She exhaled in relief. "And you will not oblige me to dance with him or have anything more to do with him."

With his hand on his heart, he swore, "May I never win another bet if I commit either of those offenses."

"Very well, then," she said, pleased, "we have a bargain. I shall support your wish to beg off attending the assembly. In your turn, you shall cease interfering in my affairs."

He put up his hands in the manner of one swearing an oath before heaven. "Absolutely, except for one small proviso."

Her eyes narrowed.

"I must insist that you wear the necklace to the assembly."

This reference reminded her that he had put himself in jeopardy by making her such a present. "How could you have been so reckless?" she upbraided him. "And such an expensive gift! If my family had believed Mr. Lloyd's protestations of innocence, it might well have been all up with you."

"I gave you the necklace because I promised it to you. I said in my letter that I would give you a fitting sign of my gratitude for having saved my neck. Now you have it. All I ask is that you return my cravat."

Her mind leapt to the cravat, which she had forgiven long ago and had returned to its place around her journal.

"You have not destroyed it, have you?" he asked.

She colored. "You shall have it," she said, wondering whether she would grow as attached to the necklace as she had to the cravat.

"Well, then," he said, looking into her eyes contentedly and giving no indication that he intended to stop before the century was out. "Well, then."

She was aware of feeling awkward. His position in front of her prevented her moving away from the wall and away from him. In order to do so, she would have had to edge around a table on one side or a looking glass on the other. In her present state, she would not have been able to execute such a maneuver without knocking something over. But if she stayed where she was, she would soon grow faint from want of air. "I expect we ought to bid one another good night," she said breathlessly.

He stepped aside and opened the door for her. "Good night, Miranda," he said.

"Good night, Charles."

It was not until the next day, when she was in the act of taking her tenth trick and Mr. Hastings was smiling at her warmly over the cards, that she realized what name she had called him.

A line formed at the foot of the staircase so that the children, the servants, and Miss DeWitt might behold the family trimmed out in all their finery. Sir Bascomb and Lady Troy descended first, their faces wreathed in smiles. They kissed their grandchildren and wished the servants all that was proper at the new year. To Miss DeWitt, they expressed their regret at having to forgo her company at the assembly. She assured them that nothing would make her happier than to entertain the children that night.

The sisters followed in turn, each on the arm of her husband, a trio of agreeable looking gentlemen who were, as far as Mr. Hastings could see, interchangeable in their blandness. Last came Miranda. Her animation was evident in her smile and step. The instant she spied Mr. Hastings, however, she paused. Something in his gaze caused her to lower her eyes.

She wore a white, unadorned Grecian robe. The neck was cut low, and above it sparkled the emeralds and diamonds he had given her. Although she liked earrings, her ears were bare, as if she meant to take nothing away from the brilliance of the jewels on her breast. Her lush froth of hair was done up in the Grecian style, swept high and frizzed on the forehead, but unadorned by ribbons or lace. This stark simplicity affected him powerfully.

He noticed for the first time that her graceful neck curved delicately to her shoulder. Her gown clung to her legs. She appeared so lithe that if he took her around the waist, he suspected, she would yield toward him like a young tree. Up to that moment, he had thought he knew all the shades of her appearance. Now, he saw, it would take a lifetime to learn all he wished to know.

Because she seemed to be experiencing a high degree of consciousness under his hot gaze, he forbore to speak to her. He waved good-bye to them all equally and wished everybody a happy new year without any particularity. Soon the door closed and he could no longer see her; nevertheless her image stayed with him. But he did not have the luxury of enjoying it, for the children clamored for his attention and pulled him to the schoolroom. There he spent a full half hour refining their skills at brag and striving manfully to contain his restlessness. At the end of that time, he sent for Ragstone.

"I fear I am suffering a fever," he whispered to the butler. "I do not wish to alarm the children, but neither do I wish them to be exposed to any contagion if I should catch cold. Perhaps you might suggest a solution."

Because the butler liked nothing better than to be applied to for advice, he assured Miss DeWitt that he would see to it that the children were cared for. She, meanwhile, must go to her chamber and rest herself.

"I shall do as you say," Mr. Hastings murmured in his most submissive Charlotte voice. "I shall go to sleep straightaway."

"A night of rest is the best restorative," Ragstone said.

Taking leave of the children was no easy matter, for they raised a howl at having to relinquish their favorite companion after having just relinquished their favorite aunt. Ragstone came to his rescue, rebuking them all so soundly for their selfishness in keeping Miss DeWitt from her sickbed that they were brought to the edge of tears. Sniffling, they waved good-bye to her and reconciled themselves to an evening of piggyback, gingerbread, and hallooing at the top of their lungs.

In his chamber, Mr. Hastings located a trunk that the maid had not unpacked. From it he took a fine deep blue coat and a pair of ivory breeches. For an instant, he regarded them wistfully. It had been some time since he had worn anything so comfortable. They were creased here and there, but they would do. With decision, he dressed, covering his elegant ensemble with a greatcoat and hat.

Carefully, he opened the door. Ascertaining that nobody was about, he made his way down the stairs and along the corridor to the rear of the house, and from there to the stable. Because the carriages were gone, the hands had gathered in the warmth of the kitchen. The sole attendant lay asleep in one of the stalls, a bottle of gin in his hand. As quietly as possible, Mr. Hastings led a gelding to the yard, saddled, and mounted him. Then, with a whisper of, "Now noble steed, get me to Togbury before I come to my senses," he rode off at a gallop.

The road to Togbury was so familiar to him by now that he traveled it in excellent time. He had heard it mentioned that the assembly was to be held at the Guildhall, but for the sake of discretion, he tied up his horse at the back of the chandler's shop and went the rest of the way on foot. The flicker of bright light and the sound of music and merry-making assisted him in finding his way to the Guildhall.

After depositing his coat and hat, he made for the entrance, where he encountered Lady Troy. Her astonishment at the sight of him rendered her speechless, but only for half a minute. "Mr. Hastings," she cried loud enough for others to hear, "you are the last creature on earth one would expect to see in Togbury."

He treated her to his most charming smile. "I hope you are not sorry to see me, Lady Troy."

"Gracious, no! It is only that I am astonished. I thought that as you and Miranda, that is to say, as we have not seen you since that disastrous, what I mean to say is, I had given over all hope of seeing you, but surely you know that Tabitha Hastings's son is ever a welcome sight in my eyes." In her confusion, she fanned her bosom furiously.

Smiling, he raised her free hand to his lips. "You are very kind," he said. "May I call upon you and your excellent daughter during my stay in the neighborhood?"

He spoke with such charm that she fanned herself all the more. "We shall expect you," she breathed.

He bowed, then moved toward the crowded center of the room.

This exchange had caught the attention of several couples standing close by. Observing the handsome stranger dressed in the style of the Town, they elbowed their neighbors and whispered, "Who is that gentleman?"

"That is Mr. Hastings," Lady Troy answered, still in amazement.

"Nonsense," Squire Rowdy told her. "Mr. Hastings is in Scotland. He has taken a lady there. It was the latest *on-dit* in London just last week. My sister writes me all the gossip."

"I believe I know Mr. Hastings when I see him," Lady Troy snapped. "He is the son of my bosom friend, after all. I can assure you he is not in Scotland; he is here, and searching for somebody particular. There, do you see how he looks this way and that? I wonder who it might be."

By this time, a substantial crowd was watching Mr. Hastings, admiring his style, whispering his name to anyone who would listen and waiting to see who it was that he had come to find. Oblivious to the stir he had created, he moved through the crush. The room began to quiet as all eyes observed him. The crowd parted to let him through. He stopped when he spied Miranda, whose back was to him. She was engrossed in conversation with a gentleman who, remarking the sudden silence in the hall, looked about him curiously. Noticing her companion's inattention, Miranda also looked about. Mr. Hastings saw her back go rigid. It seemed she had stopped breathing. She knew he had come; he was sure of it. What he was not sure of was what would happen when she turned and saw him.

FOURTEEN

Wooing

Whenever I study a scenic painting by Mr. Poussin, I
see in his landscape the very attribute I wish to
achieve in my own gardens—tranquillity. Arundel
Abbey, indeed, the entire countryside in the south of
England, generally lends itself to improvements
which result not so much in the creation of peaceful
prospects as in the enhancement of a tranquillity
already inherent. Nothing can be so soothing to an
anxious heart as a rolling lawn under snow dotted
with yew and bare poplar, or an orchard of cherries
and plums in fragrant bloom, or a fishpond reflecting
an arbor under floating vermilion leaves. But to
imagine such perfect scenes is perhaps unwise, for
one is likely to be disappointed in proportion to the
size of one's hopes. We learned this morning that
during the night the storm had blown down several
elms lining the deer park. It is an omen, my father
says, and I fear he may be right.

Though she knew she would see Mr. Hastings, Miranda was
not prepared to see him as he was, looking for all the world
like a hero out of books. The casual elegance of his dress,
the warmth of his smile, the light of mischief in his eye daz-
zled her. She suddenly saw why it was that his Charlotte disguise, while convincing to others, was so thoroughly
unconvincing to her—she was conscious of his presence in
a way that nobody else was. Regardless of his costume, she
was drawn to him.

Looking at him now, she scarcely knew whether to throttle him for putting himself in danger or to throw herself

into his arms. As it developed, she did neither. The others in the room observed her every move, her every flicker of expression. She must be on guard. With a slight nod of the head, she acknowledged Mr. Hastings's existence. The slightness of the gesture indicated that his sudden appearance affected her scarcely at all and the crowd might as well go on about its business.

His gray eyes congratulated her on her composure. Drawing close, he said, "Miss Troy, may I have the honor?"

Placing her hand in his, she went with him to the bottom of the set. The violins struck the beginning notes of a reel, the dancers straightened their lines, and the crowd soon lost interest in Mr. Hastings and his doings. They danced in silence. Whatever they had to say was expressed in their eyes. Each time he took her hand for a turn or a circle, she felt a surge of electricity.

The next dance was slow and stately. She put her hand in his, and they performed a circle. At that moment, Miranda had the opportunity to whisper, "What are you doing here, Mr. Hastings?"

"I came on a bet," he said, turning her under his arm.

She sighed. "I ought to have known."

"I made a wager with myself, you see. If I could induce you to talk to me of landscape gardening, I would confess that I love you."

At that instant, they were obliged to dance in opposite directions with other partners. Miranda nearly forgot to move, so stunned was she by what he had said. She wondered if she had heard him accurately. Nevertheless, doubt did not stop her heart and her hopes from swelling.

Soon the dance required them to return to their original partners and the music signaled an end. She gave him a smile meant to convey all that she felt. He bowed a polite adieu and withdrew to a table of brimming wineglasses, where he helped himself, never taking his eyes off her. Their stares might have caught the notice of others in the hall had not Miranda's attention been summoned by Mr. Lloyd.

"May I beg the favor of a word with you, Miss Troy?" he asked.

She glanced at Mr. Hastings, who was sipping his wine. He watched her without seeming to.

"Oh, I hope you do not mean to be serious tonight, Mr. Lloyd," she said lightly. "I do not think I would comprehend anything serious that was said to me in such a setting."

"I have made up my mind to speak to you this very evening," he said in what seemed to her rather an inexorable manner. "If you fear too much for your reputation to accompany me to the anteroom, so that we may converse privately, then I shall speak here, where every creature may see that I mean no affront to your person or dignity."

Miranda felt it would be kinder to refuse the gentleman when they were alone than to mortify him in earshot of so many of his neighbors. She therefore submitted to be led to the anteroom, hoping that Mr. Hastings would not misinterpret her disappearance, and hoping too that he would still be there when she returned, which she intended to do within thirty seconds.

The anteroom was snug with low burning candles, a warm fire, and a cozy settee in front of it. Resisting the charm of the atmosphere, Miranda insisted upon standing. Mr. Lloyd deferred to her, saying, "I honor you, Miss Troy, for your attention to propriety."

Remembering what had passed in her bedchamber in London, she required considerable presence of mind to accept this compliment.

"Miss Troy," he commenced, "has Miss DeWitt spoken to you in regard to my intentions?"

"Yes, she has, but—"

He seemed pleased. "Kindly permit me to continue. Not long ago, I asked you to take my hand and heart in marriage. You could not return my feelings at that time but assured me that there was no other upon whom you had bestowed your affections, and so I vowed that I would renew my addresses to you at a subsequent time. That time has now arrived." He paused so that she might absorb the importance of what was about to befall her.

"Please, Mr. Lloyd, it is not necessary—"

"Oh, but it is," he cut in. "You see, I have an added inducement to persuade you to have me, one I was unable to offer when I spoke to you earlier, and that is that I have observed your attachment to your schoolmate, Miss DeWitt, and as I respect the lady greatly myself and as I am in her debt, I should not object if you wished her to come and visit us frequently, or even to live with us."

Miranda did not know whether to laugh or to moan.

"I should like us to be married in the early spring. At our time of life, it does not do to prolong matters. Lengthy engagements may be perilous, and there is every reason to get right to the business of being husband and wife before the planting season begins." He lifted her hand to his lips and would have planted a kiss there, but Miranda pulled away.

She saw a shadow fall across the room and heard a footfall.

"Miss Troy cannot accept your kind offer," Mr. Hastings said, coming inside.

Indignant, Mr. Lloyd inquired, "Who, sir, are you, and why may she not accept me?"

"Because she is to marry me."

Miranda had all she could do to keep from crying out with pleasure.

Mr. Lloyd looked his rival up and down with scorn. Turning to Miranda, he said, "This gentleman, who, rumor has it, is Mr. Hastings, presumes upon your good nature and mine. One word from you, and I shall show him the door."

"No!" she cried.

He refused to credit it. "You cannot love him," he insisted. "He is a gamester and a flirt. He cannot offer you what I offer—a quiet life, a steady husband, and an estate adjoining Arundel Abbey. You said yourself you had no desire to meet him. You cannot really mean to marry him."

Gently she replied, "Oh, Mr. Lloyd, I will wager that I do mean exactly that!"

* * *

Miranda's acquaintance would never have described her as shy, but once Mr. Lloyd had left the anteroom, she was overcome with an excruciating shyness. Not knowing what else to say, she fell back on the obvious. "It was dangerous for you to have come," she said unsteadily.

"It is your own fault, you know." As he spoke, he approached. "When I saw how splendidly you wore my grandmother's necklace, I knew I could not stay away."

Melting, she looked at him.

He caught her in his arms and pressed her to him with an enveloping strength. After brushing his cheek against hers, he kissed her resolutely on the mouth. "I wanted to do that in London," he confessed. "Unfortunately, I saw so many Mirandas at the time that I would not have known which pair of lips to aim at."

Reluctantly, she freed herself from his hold. "Somebody will come in and see us," she said. Walking to the mantel, she leaned her forehead against its coolness.

He came up behind her and slipped his arms about her waist, causing her to stand close against him. "And what is the worst they can do to us if they do see us?" he asked, nuzzling her ear. "Force us to marry each other?"

"We cannot marry, Charles," she said, turning. "You know we cannot."

"I do not know any such thing. In fact, I am willing to wager my heart, my body, my soul, and my bachelor's freedom that we can."

"We cannot marry while Everard still carries his grudge."

He pulled her close and caressed the bareness of her shoulder with his lips. "Ah, yes, Everard," he murmured. "He shall no longer be an obstacle, my love. I give you my solemn word."

She put him at a distance so that she could see his face. "Then you will put the matter to rest?"

He nodded. As he smiled into her brown eyes, he stroked her hair. Slowly, he drew away and blew out the candles one by one. Coming close to her again, he held her to him. For a time—neither could gauge how long—they stood together in the darkened parlor, brightened and warmed by the blazing fire.

Three days after the assembly, Sir Bascomb and Lady Troy waved good-bye to three daughters, three sons-in-law, and seven grandchildren. The subsequent quiet in the house pleased Sir Bascomb, who was fondest of children when they lived at a distance, and instead of actually witnessing their alarming energy with his own eyes, he might hear of it by the post. With his home restored to peace, he would have napped blissfully by the fire, but a winter storm had roared through the neighborhood the night before, leaving the fields white, the roads muddy, and his heart troubled. During the storm, several of the abbey's noblest elms had succumbed to heavy wet snow, buffeting winds, and advanced age. It was, he declared, an omen of bad things to come, though when pressed, he could not say what bad things he feared. While his wife embroidered and his daughter, together with her schoolmate, played at cards, Sir Bascomb dozed restlessly, awakened by fits and starts.

Lady Troy was also ill at ease, though for a different reason. She addressed Miranda and Miss DeWitt in a tone of vexation, saying, "Why has Mr. Hastings neglected to call? I vow, he made it a point to say he wished to call upon me and my excellent daughter—he did say my *excellent* daughter. But he has not shown his face. What can he mean by it?"

Miranda looked at Mr. Hastings, inviting him with her eyes to invent an answer.

"Perhaps he is indisposed," Mr. Hastings said in his most lulling Charlotte voice.

"Or perhaps he never meant to call at all," Miranda said, giving him a teasing look. "Perhaps the gentleman has gone off to Scotland with an unnamed lady."

"Poof!" said her ladyship. "Mr. Hastings came to the assembly expressly to find you, my pet. There was no mistaking his intention. If you do not believe me, you may ask anybody in Togbury. He likes you. I only wish you could find it in your heart to like him a little. Perhaps he was odious to you when you met, but you must learn to forgive. Odious men oftentimes make the best husbands."

Miranda laughed. "Gracious, Mama, do you still have hopes of marrying me to Mr. Hastings? I thought you wished me to have Mr. Lloyd. As I cannot have both, you had best make up your mind who it is I am to have."

Flustered, Lady Troy replied, "I put Mr. Lloyd forward when it appeared that you would have none of Mr. Hastings. But I have always preferred Tabitha's son. Not that my preferences have ever weighed with you, more's the pity."

"Poor Mama. You are cursed with an obstinate daughter, and now you wish either Mr. Hastings or Mr. Lloyd to be cursed with an obstinate wife."

"It is not for me to interfere," Lady Troy said loftily. "Tabitha and I have taken our oaths that we will no longer interfere. But it is very hard, my pet. Perhaps you do not appreciate how hard it is, but I am certain Miss DeWitt does. She is as softhearted a young lady as I have ever met. Indeed, if you should ever wish to learn how to behave in a manner befitting a sensible female, you will take a page from Miss DeWitt's book."

Mr. Hastings threw Miranda a significant look.

Lady Troy sighed and went on, "Do you not think, Miss DeWitt, that Miranda ought to at least try to return Mr. Hastings's regard?"

Miranda knew it would be catastrophic to catch his eye. Therefore, she peered fixedly at her cards.

Mr. Hastings answered tranquilly, "I really cannot venture an opinion, Lady Troy. I have never met the gentleman."

"Ah, yes, you remained at home the night of the assembly and suffered that dreadful fever. I do hope you are quite recovered."

"Yes, though I do experience recurrences of fever from time to time." The smile he gave Miranda nearly caused her to laugh out loud.

"It is too bad you were unable to come with us," Lady

Troy said, "for then you might have seen how handsome a gentleman Mr. Hastings is."

"Oh, is he handsome?"

"Very handsome. Has Miranda not told you?"

"Miranda never breathed a word to me. Well, Miranda dear, is it true? Is your Mr. Hastings handsome?"

Clearing her throat, Miranda said, "Tolerably. That is to say, he does not squint and he has no pockmarks."

"Miranda!" Lady Troy cried, causing Sir Bascomb to shudder in his sleep. "You cannot be so prejudiced against Mr. Hastings that you will refuse to believe the evidence of your own eyes?"

Taking a breath, Miranda said, "Oh, very well, I suppose he is handsome." She looked up to exchange a smiling glance with Mr. Hastings.

"He is not merely handsome, Miss DeWitt. And he is not merely rich, though he is very very rich, to be sure. I am a mother, Miss DeWitt, and I should never marry a daughter of mine to a man merely because he was handsome and rich. Mr. Hastings has other qualities to recommend him. He is the son of excellent parents. His father was a man of estimable character. His mother is a woman of compassion and charity."

Miranda observed Mr. Hastings's face grow serious. He was listening intently.

Lady Troy continued, "Oh, you might argue that the goodness of a gentleman's parents does not necessarily guarantee his own character, and I should agree with you, but Mr. Hastings is devoted to his mother. From the time his father died, he has cared for her. As a child, he took on the burdens of a grown man for her sake. He has never considered it unmanly to indulge her and dote on her. And as a gentleman treats his mother, so shall he treat his wife."

Abruptly, Mr. Hastings stood. Miranda could see that he was moved by what had been said and could not hear more. "Surely the gentleman has some defect," he remarked in his Charlotte voice. "Even the best of men have faults."

Lady Troy, who noticed nothing out of the way, continued blithely, "If he has a fault, it consists in not calling the

day after a party, as a gentleman ought to do. He neglected
to call on his mother the day after her soiree, and now he
neglects to call on us. Apart from that, however, he is without defect."

Her ladyship's speech was interrupted here. Ragstone entered to announce a visitor.

"It is Mr. Hastings!" she cried ecstatically. "I knew he
would come."

Her cries woke Sir Bascomb, who rubbed his eyes and
endeavored to find out what calamity had befallen.

Meanwhile, Ragstone presented Lady Troy with a salver
containing the gentleman's card. Her face fell when she
read it. "Oh, it is only Lord Everard."

Miranda gave Mr. Hastings a look of horror. In return, he
smiled.

"Deny us to him, Ragstone," Miranda said. "Tell him we
are indisposed."

"You shall say no such thing, Ragstone," Mr. Hastings
said in his sweet Charlotte voice. "He will know it for a
ruse. An entire family cannot possibly be indisposed, after
all. The gentleman will merely call again."

"Very sensible, Miss DeWitt," Lady Troy said.

"It would please me beyond anything if you would call
me Charlotte."

"I shall call you Charlotte, and you shall be as much a
daughter to me as Miranda, for you are a delightful girl.
Ragstone, desire Lord Everard to come inside."

As soon as Ragstone left them, Miranda threw her cards
down and stood. Fixing Mr. Hastings with a look of an-
guish, she mouthed the words, "He has found you!"

Mr. Hastings answered with a cheerful nod.

Lord Everard was ushered in. He did not sit; nor did he
trouble himself with polite preliminaries. He interrupted the
introduction of Miss Charlotte DeWitt by demanding,
"Where is Mr. Charles Hastings?"

"Gracious!" Lady Troy responded. "We were wondering
the very same thing."

An ugly frown distorted Everard's face. He seemed to

Miranda to have grown years older. His expression struck her as savage.

"Miss Troy knows his whereabouts, I'll warrant."

Miranda shuddered. Luckily, her mother spoke before she was obliged to answer.

"What are you implying, sir?" Lady Troy asked, offended.

"I imply nothing. I say it directly. Miss Troy is engaged to Hastings."

"Engaged!" Lady Troy clapped her hands and rose to embrace Miranda. "Can it be true?"

"Engaged!" Sir Bascomb repeated. "Ah, I knew those elms boded ill."

Everard said, "The engagement is spoken of everywhere. I have just had it from the mouth of Mr. Farris Lloyd. It appears that Miss Troy refused him in order to accept Mr. Hastings. She then spent the better part of the ball alone with him in an anteroom."

Sir Bascomb grew red-faced and pushed himself to a standing position. "You may leave my house at once, sir," he shouted to Everard. "Any man who accuses my daughter of impropriety is unwelcome here."

Lady Troy ran to Miranda, clasped her to her heart, and called her her sweet, sweet pet.

At this juncture, Miss DeWitt, who had remained quiet all this time, stepped in to soothe everybody's nerves, from Sir Bascomb's affronted ones, to Lady Troy's joyful ones, to Miranda's terrified ones, to Everard's jangled ones. In his Charlotte voice, he coaxed the baronet and his wife into retiring to their respective chambers, where they might bring themselves to calm and reason and then reconvene at a later time to ascertain whether any impropriety had been committed. He invited Miranda to avail herself of this opportunity to collect her thoughts in her bedchamber and decide whether she was in truth engaged. Meanwhile, she, Miss DeWitt, would be glad to entertain Lord Everard.

Sir Bascomb and Lady Troy thought it a sensible plan, but Miranda would not budge.

"Dear Charlotte, I should not dream of leaving you alone with Lord Everard," she said firmly.

"I do not know why you should be afraid, dear Miranda," he said. "I am well past the age of requiring a chaperon. Besides, my cousin Felix has spoken often of Lord Everard. I feel as though we were already acquainted." With his eyes, he signaled his wish that she leave the room.

Stubbornly, she shook her head.

While Sir Bascomb and Lady Troy occupied Lord Everard with polite good-byes, Mr. Hastings reached to the deck on the table and drew a card, which he showed to Miranda. It was the four of hearts. With a gesture, he invited her to take a card, which she did, darting him a look of defiance. She held her card up for him to see. It was the deuce of spades. Mr. Hastings, who had drawn the high card, waved good-bye to her.

Miranda imagined that a hideous clash of wills, fists, and weapons would take place the instant she left the two men together. But being an honorable loser, she did at last withdraw.

"You are well acquainted with my cousin, Mr. Felix DeWitt?" Mr. Hastings inquired in his softest Charlotte voice. He approached Lord Everard, daring the man to recognize him.

Everard shrugged, "Well enough."

Mr. Hastings guessed that Charlotte was not handsome enough to interest his lordship. Or perhaps his preoccupation with finding his quarry had robbed him of the ability to think of anything else. He certainly bore the marks of a man preoccupied. His eyes were ringed with signs of sleeplessness. He spoke impatiently, as though he could not spare a moment for civility. In Mr. Hastings's view, he looked almost wild. He could see why Miranda had been frightened.

"I have stayed long enough. I shall return another day." Everard began to make for the door.

"Do stay, Lord Everard."

"What the devil for?"

"I believe I may assist you." Mr. Hastings picked up a fan and waved it daintily at his neck.

"Who the deuce are you?"

"We have already been introduced. I am Charlotte De-Witt, cousin of Felix DeWitt, with whom you are acquainted."

Disgusted, Everard waved his hand in the air. "What in Jove's name has that to say to anything?"

"I am Miss Troy's schoolmate. More to the point, I am in her confidence."

As Lord Everard paused to consider this information, Mr. Hastings observed that the man's expression was gradually transformed. In a short time, he grew as pleasant as he had formerly been rude. He sat next to Miss DeWitt on the sofa and asked, "Does Miss Troy know where I might find Mr. Hastings?"

Putting his nose close to Everard's, Mr. Hastings whispered, "Perhaps yes, perhaps no."

The irritation Lord Everard experienced could scarcely be contained. "You are gulling me!"

"Not in the least. I believe she does know where he may be found, but I also believe she has taken her oath to keep the location secret."

"I shall persuade her to tell me," he vowed. His fists were clenched.

"I do not think you will succeed."

"Why not? She cannot dislike me. We are scarcely acquainted."

"I believe she has been sworn to secrecy. Rumor has it that Mr. Hastings has an enemy who wishes to do him in. My dear friend Miranda will go to any lengths to protect him."

Everard squirmed. After a pause, he said, "Perhaps it would help if I gave her a gift," he said. "Presents have a way of loosening a woman's tongue, you know."

Mr. Hastings favored him with one of Charlotte's most delighted smiles. "How clever of you to think of it. Yes, you have hit upon the very thing. You must make her a present."

Everard chewed on a fingernail. "I have come this far. I shall not stick at making her a present of some gewgaw or other."

"It must be a very fine present. After all, Mr. Hastings has just given her an elegant necklace. It has, shall we say, raised the level of Miss Troy's taste in gifts."

"I thought a locket might do."

"Mr. Hastings gave her diamonds and emeralds."

"Hastings is a knave and a fool."

"You may well be right, but she is in love with him."

"Well, then, I shall give her my mother's brooch."

"Does it contain jewels?"

"It is a ruby set in gold filigree with pearls."

"Not paste, I hope."

Everard looked murderous. "Not paste."

"Miss Troy will like it very well then. If you will return when you have the brooch in hand, you shall have your answer."

Everard jumped up. "I cannot wait as long as that."

Miss DeWitt smiled. "Patience, dear man, patience. A lady's confidence is not won in an hour, or even in a day."

"Patience be damned!" he growled. But having no other recourse, he was at last brought to be patient.

He took his leave then, after which Miss Charlotte DeWitt, in a shocking display, pulled up her skirts and danced a jig.

Because she had been peeking out the door of her bed-chamber, Miranda knew the instant Mr. Hastings returned to his. She was inside the door before he could stop her. "I have worked it all out," she said breathlessly. "You shall take my mare—Delilah—and you shall ride east. Then, doubling around, you may escape to Ireland. My father has a farm there. I shall send a note which will assure your comfort. I shall help you pack a valise."

She would have pulled his shifts and skirts from the wardrobe on the spot if he had not taken her by the shoulders. "I have no intention of going to Ireland," he told her with an engaging smile.

"But you must escape!"

"And miss the fun? Not likely, my love."

"Don't you understand, Charles. Everard is here!"

"Naturally, he is here. I sent for him."

Her jaw fell.

"Well, I did not send for him precisely. But I knew that as soon as I showed myself at the assembly, word would get out that Mr. Hastings had been spotted in Togbury, courting Miss Troy. I knew it was merely a matter of days before he turned up."

She viewed him through slitted eyes. "Is that why you danced with me and made love to me? So that word would get out? So that you might 'send for' Lord Everard?"

He pulled her tightly to him. "I expect you are violently in love with me. Otherwise you would not be in such high dudgeon."

As her face was buried in his chest, her answer was muffled.

"I hope you just said that you do indeed love me, because I love you and I promise you, I do not mean to make you a widow before you are even a bride."

Lifting her tear-streaked face, she asked, "How will you stop him?"

"I shall not stop him."

"Oh, Charles. You do not mean to give yourself up to him?"

"Not in the least. Charlotte shall stop him. And you shall assist her. With two such estimable ladies at my side, I cannot possibly fail."

FIFTEEN

The Betrothal

Hastings's Seventh Principle of Gaming: In the
course of every great man's life, in the course of
every great woman's life, indeed, in the course of
every life, great or ordinary, there comes a critical
turning point when a gamble must either be taken or
refused and everything hangs on the choice. If one's
luck is out, the result may be disaster or even death.
If it is in, the result may be happiness ever after. In
either case, Fate will have her way. Of course, skill,
perseverance, self-possession, and, most important,
deviousness go a long way toward assisting her.

Lord Everard lost no time in obtaining the brooch and pre-
senting himself at Arundel Abbey with his treasure in hand.

"You have brought it?" Mr. Hastings greeted him when
he entered the cedar parlor. His Charlotte voice was soft
and soothing.

"Here it is."

Taking the small leather sack from Everard, Mr. Hastings
opened the drawstring and removed the bauble. He turned it
over and over, held it up to the light streaming from a
nearby window, bit the gemstone, and observed it closely
through the lens of Sir Bascomb's glass, which he had bor-
rowed for that very purpose.

Everard paced impatiently. "I assure you, it is real in
every aspect."

With an ingratiating smile, Mr. Hastings replied, "I do
not doubt you, sir, but Miss Troy will. I must be certain she
will not find you to be a fraud, a cheat, a liar, a bamboozler,
a sharp, a disher, a diddler, a chiseler, or a doer."

At this catalog of epithets, his lordship glared.

"I do hope I have not said anything amiss," Miss DeWitt simpered.

"Where is Miss Troy? I shall give her the brooch and have my answer from her."

"Gracious you are an impetuous creature!" Mr. Hastings said. "Ah, there is something so virile, I think, in the sight of an impetuous man."

Everard regarded Miss DeWitt with evident distaste.

"But do not be impetuous with Miss Troy, I beg you, my lord. It will only frighten her. Do you know how to be civil?"

"What the devil do you mean by that? Of course, I know how to be civil."

"Then by all means put your civility to use now."

Mr. Hastings rang for the servant to fetch Miss Troy, and in a half a minute, Miranda entered the parlor.

Taking Miss DeWitt's hint, Everard greeted her with polite expressions. He talked on unexceptionable topics—the weather, the condition of the roads, the gossip from Town. When it appeared that Miss Troy was very much at her ease, he asked whether he might offer her a token of his esteem.

"I am obliged to refuse you, sir," Miranda intoned. "A proper lady does not receive gifts from a gentleman, unless they are to be married."

Everard threw a look of vexation at Miss DeWitt, who merely nodded pleasantly and went on with her work, which was to poke a needle into a cloth and pretend to be embroidering.

"However," Miranda said, "I should be pleased to look at the present."

He removed the brooch from its sack and planted it in her palm.

Miranda turned it over and over, held it up to the light, tested the ruby with her teeth, and, after obtaining Sir Bascomb's glass from Miss DeWitt, observed it closely through the lens. "It is excessively pretty," she declared, holding it against her yellow dress to gauge the effect. "A pity I cannot accept it."

He rose and would have taken it from her hand but she said softly, "But if you were to leave it here by accident, I should find it, and not knowing the owner, I should be obliged to keep it. It would be too bad not to keep such a handsome thing."

He regarded her suspiciously. "I am not in the habit of losing expensive jewels, Miss Troy, not unless I receive something in return of equal value."

Miranda smiled at him. "I take your meaning, my lord. And I also take your brooch." She pinned it to her bosom and demanded that Miss DeWitt admire it.

"It looks very well," Mr. Hastings said placidly.

"The devil with the look of the thing!" Everard shouted. He took Miranda by the shoulders and shook her. "Tell me where the villain hides himself."

Immediately, Miss DeWitt set down the embroidery and intervened. With a strength uncommon in a respectable woman, she parted the two.

Miranda let forth a shriek, put her hand to her brow, and ran headlong from the parlor. Piteous sobs were heard as she dashed up the stairs.

With arms crossed and head wagging, Mr. Hastings said to Everard, "What am I to do with you? You will be impetuous, you naughty man, despite my warnings. Now you have the result."

Irritated with himself, Everard raked his hair. "Damn the woman. She took my brooch. She ought to have repaid me in kind."

"You shall be paid in kind, sir. Indeed, you shall be paid with interest, but not if you go and spoil it."

"Very well, what is it you advise me to do?"

"You must visit Miss Troy and befriend her, engage her in conversation, invite her to play a game of cards with you, desire her help in some matter or other. Nothing pleases a female so much as to be useful."

"I do not require her help. What the deuce would I ask her to do?"

"I have the very thing. Implore her to assist you in composing a letter—a love letter. Young ladies like nothing better than love letters."

"I have never written a love letter in my life."

"That is precisely why you require her help, don't you see?"

"Will she tell me where Hastings is?"

"I can promise you she will."

"Well then, I shall return tomorrow for chitchat, cards, and love letters." He rose to take his leave. At the door, he turned, saying, "I do not know why you should be so generous with your help and advice, Miss DeWitt. We are certainly not very well acquainted, and there is no love lost between myself and your cousin."

Mr. Hastings scanned the room to see whether anybody might be listening. When it was clearly safe, he confided, "I do not wish Mr. Hastings to marry Miss Troy."

Everard nodded. "You have a grudge against him?"

"In a manner of speaking. He is a gamester. I believe no man is so unlikely to be made into a husband as a gamester. Moreover, he is a flirt. Why, he even had the audacity to trifle with *me*! But worse than that, he keeps a mistress so flagrantly that he is sure to break my poor Miranda's heart."

His lordship looked the lady over incredulously. "Are you certain Hastings flirted with you?"

Chin high, Mr. Hastings replied, "He said he should like nothing better in all the world than to see me stripped forever of my stays and shift!"

Everard shook his head. "I expect that blow to the head has affected his mind."

"What blow to the head?"

"Never mind that. I am satisfied that we both have the same object in view, to learn where Hastings has gone to and to get rid of him for good and all."

Miss DeWitt gave him her gloved hand. "How do you contrive to phrase your words so cleverly?"

Once again, he looked her over. "I vow, you are not so bracket-faced as I had thought at first," he said.

She rewarded him with a glowing smile.

He shrugged and then was gone.

When he appeared the following day, he found Miranda and Miss DeWitt seated at a table, sorting dried herbs. Miranda wore the brooch. She greeted him warmly and left Miss DeWitt at the table so that she might sit near her visitor before the fire.

"Charlotte has explained to me your behavior of yesterday," Miranda cooed, "and I have quite forgiven you. You poor man. I had no idea you were in such a state of distraction over a lady. But I must keep mum. It is to be a deep secret. I am to say nothing about it. We shall speak of other things. Is that not right, Lord Everard?"

"Yes, I thought we might converse."

"What a delightful notion. What shall we speak of?"

He threw Miss DeWitt a peevish look, but there was no help for him in that quarter, for she was preoccupied with her herbs. At last he hit upon an idea. "I should like you to select the subject."

"Well then, I should like to talk of gaming."

He laughed cynically. "What do you know of gaming?"

"A great deal. You see, Mr. Hastings has written a book on the subject, and I have committed his principles to memory." She then treated his lordship to a recital of *Hastings's Principles of Gaming*. With each one, his brow grew darker and his lips thinner.

"We have had enough conversation, I think," he said when she finally paused. "What say you to a game of cards?"

"I should be pleased."

They adjourned to the table and seated themselves at a distance from Charlotte.

"What is your game?" Everard asked with a forced politeness.

It was a wonder to Miranda that the man did not jump out of his skin, for he was stretched as tightly as a chicken skin glove. "Piquet," she answered.

For the first time, Everard relaxed. His expression turned sly. "I am only too happy to oblige," he said.

"Oh, but you mustn't let me win, my lord. If I am to win, I must do it by my skill, not your generosity."

Everard's smile broadened. "As you wish, Miss Troy. I am yours to command." He glanced at Miss DeWitt, who nodded approvingly.

The game commenced, and though Miranda played well, she was no match for his lordship.

"I count myself lucky we do not play for money," she said to Lord Everard. "Would it not be delightful if you and Mr. Hastings were to play? That would be an even match."

Everard appeared to have learned his lesson from the previous day. Instead of pouncing on the lady's words, he said, "In point of fact, I *have* played piquet with Mr. Hastings. As a result, I am in to him for a great deal. But I cannot pay him what I owe, for I do not know where he has gone to."

Miranda answered with a modest smile.

His lordship pressed his point. "As his affianced bride, you do know, I expect."

Reluctantly, she nodded.

Everard leaned forward. "Will you tell me where he is? I shall not rest easy, I assure you, until I have repaid him in full."

"I cannot tell. It is a secret."

His impatience was so intense that he stood and might have said something offensive, but Miss DeWitt stepped in to say, "Perhaps you have grown weary of card playing, dear Miranda. Perhaps there is some other pastime you might enjoy instead." On that, she leveled a look at Everard, who, after a few seething moments, took the hint.

"Miss Troy," he said with feigned politeness, "would you be so good as to help me write a letter?"

Miranda treated him to a smile. "I shall be honored."

Miss DeWitt happened to find pen and paper conveniently lying nearby. She brought them to the table, then left the two to themselves. Before she quitted the room, she nodded her approval to Everard.

"What sort of letter do you wish to write?" Miranda asked his lordship.

He inhaled and rolled his eyes. "A love letter, I suppose."

Miranda clapped her hands. "Ah, there is nothing I like so well as a love letter." She handed him a sheet of plain paper. Dipping his pen, she handed it to him as well. "Now, how shall you begin?"

"I had hoped you would advise me."

"I suggest you open with 'My darling.' It demonstrates your attachment without appearing overly sentimental."

He wrote, 'My darling.'

"And now you must tell her of all the qualities in her appearance and character which have made you love her. What are they?"

"I haven't the least notion."

"Surely you have noticed something about the lady that you like?"

"A lady is a lady. One is much like another."

Miranda had all she could do to keep from grinding her teeth. "I can see why you require assistance," she said sweetly. "Never mind, then. I shall dictate you a letter," and she proceeded to invent a missive that Cupid himself would have been proud to bear to its object. It extolled the lady's gentle heart and gentle hands, her supple limbs and supple lips, her sweet breath and her sweet bosom. It lauded her character, her virtue, and her forbearance in allowing these humble addresses. It closed with the hope that they would one day be united in matrimony and that he might carry her off and make her his own for all eternity.

When it was done, Everard looked it over, scowling.

Miranda smiled. "It is very little, I know, to what you would wish to say, but I think she will like it well enough."

"Now that we have conversed, played at cards, and written a love letter, I must ask you again, Miss Troy, where is Mr. Hastings to be found?"

Bowing her head, she kept silent.

"I gave you the blasted brooch," he shouted. "You owe it to me to tell!"

Insulted, she replied, "I do not accept expensive presents

from gentlemen with whom I am barely acquainted. I found the brooch. It was left in this room by accident!"

This so incensed him that he rose and pulled her from her chair. He had put his hands to her throat and was on the point of squeezing, when Miss DeWitt entered.

"Fie, sir!" she scolded. "Fie! Is this how you follow my advice?"

He backed to the wall, panting hard and glaring at Miranda wrathfully.

While Miranda fanned her bosom and appeared on the verge of fainting, Miss DeWitt bustled his lordship to the door. "You have very nearly ruined everything," she whispered. "Come back tomorrow. I shall have matters set to rights by then. Do not fail me again, sir, or I shall be obliged to desert you and leave you to your own pitiful devices." Without a farewell, she pushed him out the door.

Inside the parlor once more, Mr. Hastings exchanged a smile with Miranda. "The man is so enraged," he said, "that he has transformed himself into the easiest pigeon I ever marked."

"Come," she said, "have a look at his letter. I think you will be pleased."

Mr. Hastings laughed as he read. He was so delighted that he paid homage with a bow to its creator. He then lifted her high and swung her around the room.

"There is only one way you may redeem yourself," Miss DeWitt informed Lord Everard the next day when he came to call.

"I vow, I am out of patience with the lady."

"And she mistrusts you. She suspects you of being the one who wishes to do Mr. Hastings an injury."

His eyes burned at this news.

"Naturally, I told her you had no such plan in view."

"I am obliged to you."

"Indeed you are, my lord, for to win Miss Troy's trust again after your appalling rudeness to her, I was forced to tell a fib. It was very distressing to me to tell an untruth. My whole ambition is to be honest with all the world.

Those who represent themselves as something they are not are my abhorrence."

"I would be obliged, Miss DeWitt, if you would come to the point."

"I told her we were engaged."

His lordship was too stunned to speak.

"It was the only way to regain her trust. Knowing that you are engaged to her dearest friend in all the world, she will naturally think well of you. In point of fact, she already thinks well of you. I have explained that you are a gentleman of an impetuous nature and that is one of the manly qualities which I so much admire in you."

"And she believed you?"

"She has no reason to doubt me. I have always been truthful with her in the past. But now you must do your part, my lord. You must act as though we are betrothed. When Miss Troy or any member of her family are present, you must dance attention on me, gaze at me longingly, and do the pretty. If they are not convinced, all will be lost."

Everard's misery at this news was palpable.

At this juncture, Miranda and her parents entered the cedar parlor. They made polite greetings to Lord Everard, and Miranda giggled at him conspiratorially, while Sir Bascomb and Lady Troy invited him to sit.

"You have not come to insult my daughter again, I hope," said the baronet to his lordship.

"I beg pardon if I offended," Everard said stiffly. "I was not myself."

"I have not been myself for weeks and weeks," remarked Miss DeWitt with a heavy sigh.

"What ails you, dear Charlotte," Lady Troy cried. "Has your fever returned?"

Miss DeWitt hid her face. She suddenly betrayed an unaccustomed bashfulness. "Oh, do not ask me! Do not! Oh, I am mortified!"

Sir Bascomb and Lady Troy exchanged a puzzled glance. They turned to Miranda for an explanation of her friend's flutters. Never before had they seen Miss DeWitt, who had always been a thoroughly sensible young lady, behave so strangely.

Miranda giggled, then burst out with, "Charlotte is engaged, Mama! Oh, Papa, is it not wonderful? She is in love!"

The baronet and his lady were indeed pleased for the young woman, for they had grown attached to her. "And who is her betrothed?" Lady Troy asked.

Moving to Lord Everard and slipping her hand through his arm, Miss DeWitt replied, "This gentleman, Lord Everard."

The baronet and his lady strove mightily to appear happy for dear Charlotte.

"I congratulate you," Sir Bascomb said dubiously.

Lady Troy began to weep. "Oh, I wish you very happy, Charlotte. I know that you are a wondrous maker of miracles, having transformed Mrs. Hastings from a sorrowful creature to her former self. I only hope you will transform Lord Everard as well. My lord, you are to be congratulated. You have won a treasure."

Miss DeWitt poked her affianced husband in the ribs so that he would make a suitable response. After a moment's hesitation, he lifted her gloved hand to his lips and said, "I shall endeavor to deserve my good fortune." Smiling lamely, he thanked Miranda and her parents for their good wishes. "Is there something I might fetch you?" he asked Miss DeWitt solicitously. "You need only name it, and it shall be yours."

Charlotte simpered. "In your love letter, you addressed me as your 'darling.' I should like you always to address me as your 'darling.' "

Though he looked daggers at her, Lord Everard said, "My darling."

"We mean to be excessively jolly after we are married, do we not, Everard?" Charlotte squealed.

He rolled his eyes. "Whatever pleases you, my darling."

Sir Bascomb and Lady Troy witnessed this scene with undisguised heartache. Miranda viewed it with every appearance of contentment.

Folding her fan, Charlotte tapped Lord Everard on the cheek. "And now you must run along, my love. Tomorrow, when you return, I shall have a gift for you."

"What sort of gift?"

Giving out with a tinkling laugh, she rapped his cheek with her fan so that it smarted. "It is a secret. You shall learn everything tomorrow."

"Deuce take it! Another tomorrow!"

Miss DeWitt turned to the others and beamed. "He is such an old grumbletonian, is he not? Oh, but he is adorable. Do you think I am adorable, too, Everard?"

As his lordship had already made his escape, it was up to Charlotte to assure everybody that he thought her perfectly adorable in every way.

As soon as Miss DeWitt left them, floating away on a cloud of love, Sir Bascomb and Lady Troy cross-examined Miranda.

"Is she aware that Everard is the worst bounder, the lowest insect, the most vice-ridden, ramshackle care-for-nothing in Britain?" Sir Bascomb raged.

Tranquilly, Miranda replied, "I believe she does know it."

"Oh, never say she marries him for the sake of his title!" Lady Troy implored. "She is too fine to marry for such a reason. And she certainly cannot like him for his riches, for he has gambled them all away."

Going to each of her parents in turn, Miranda kissed them tenderly. "You are good to fret about Charlotte. You are fond of her, are you not?"

"We have come to love her," said Lady Troy.

"I do not like to see sensible girls leave a perfectly comfortable house," said Sir Bascomb glumly, "especially when they mean to go to such a one as Everard. I had hoped Miss DeWitt would stay here at the abbey. I knew it was an evil omen when the elms fell."

"All will be well," Miranda assured them. "Our dear Charlotte has everything well in hand."

* * *

As instructed, Lord Everard presented himself the following day. Miss DeWitt sat quite alone, reading a novel, when he was ushered into the parlor. She looked up at his appearance. "I have learned the secret," she informed him.

"Miss Troy told you where Hastings is to be found?"

"It is all written down plainly." She handed him a note.

He opened it and read. When he finished, he gazed into space wearing the oddest expression, one that Mr. Hastings had never before viewed on his lordship's face. At first Mr. Hastings could not make it out. Then gradually he came to recognize it. It was a genuine smile.

CONCLUSION

Piqued, Repiqued, and Capotted

It is incredible. I have finished a design for a garden. It is complete in every detail, and I am hugely pleased with it. But I am not to think of executing my design at Arundel Abbey. Mr. Hastings says he wishes to have it at Clarendon Grove. He is also good enough to say that as I improve the estate, I may as well improve its owner. I am good enough to reply that its owner requires no improvement. He is good enough to insist that he requires at least one—the addition of a wife. And we go on like that, perfectly foolish, perfectly happy. It is a wonder I have not wearied of landscape gardening. It is an even greater wonder that I have not wearied of Mr. Hastings. He vows that he will run me such a merry chase all the rest of my days that I may grow exhausted but never bored. I do believe him on both counts.

Because the weather had turned unseasonably warm, fog rose up from the snowy countryside, couching the wood in a haze. The dawn gave hints of a sunny day to come. Mr. Hastings stood by a beech, waiting for the sunrise. He wore his own clothes—a pair of black pantaloons, such as he might have worn to Brooks or Boodles, a pair of polished Hessians, a dark green coat with black velvet collar, an ivory waistcoat, and a white shirt and cravat. His appearance was immaculate.

Miranda stood next to him, also dressed in Mr. Hastings's clothes—a pair of breeches, white stockings, overlarge boots, and other accoutrements that were hidden by an outsized greatcoat. Her luxuriant hair was contained under a tall hat, and she wore a firm expression that she imagined was masculine.

Several yards away stood Lord Everard, loading his weapon. When he was satisfied as to its lethal capabilities, he signaled to his enemy that he was ready to begin.

Seeing the signal, Mr. Hastings said softly to Miranda, "Pray that my luck is in this morning," and walked slowly toward Everard.

When the two faced each other, the doctor Mr. Hastings had brought along came forward. Addressing Everard, he asked, "Where is your second, my lord?"

"I shall not require a second." He did not look at the doctor but only at Mr. Hastings. It was clear he could not wait to get down to the business at hand.

The doctor shook his head gravely. "Mr. Hastings has brought a second. You see, there is Mr. Smith, ready to act for his friend." With a gesture, he indicated Miranda.

Lord Everard did not look at her. He could see only Mr. Hastings. "The devil take Mr. Smith," he snapped.

"Begging your pardon, my lord, but there are rules to be observed here. One must have a second. An affair of honor is not to be undertaken without seconds."

Everard favored the doctor with a contemptuous glance, then continued staring at Mr. Hastings.

The doctor shook his head, convinced that only tragedy could be the result of such havey-cavey doings. With a helpless shrug, he went to his gig, climbed up to the seat, and watched.

Mr. Hastings, who had not moved, answered Everard's murderous glare with a slight smile. The two men stood knee-deep in fog. Everard carried a heavy pistol. Mr. Hastings's hands were empty.

In her guise as Mr. Smith, Miranda approached. "Gentlemen," she said gruffly, "I shall count off twenty paces. Each of you shall be entitled to a single shot."

"Thank you, Mr. Smith," said Mr. Hastings. "And now you will kindly get out of the range of fire."

She stood her ground. "Swear to me, Mr. Hastings, that you will not get killed."

Everard was growing jittery. He raised and lowered the pistol.

"Mr. Smith!" Mr. Hastings demanded. "Stand clear."

"Promise me!"

"You are devilishly obstinate for a wo—, for a wooden-head."

"Indeed, I am. Promise!"

Everard licked his lips. "Are you deliberately delaying the proceedings, Hastings?" he sneered.

Mr. Hastings smiled, and though he looked at Everard, he answered Miranda. "I promise I shall not get killed. Now will you do as I say?"

"I love you," she whispered in his ear, and moved to the tree, from where she instructed the gentlemen to turn and count off their paces.

At the count of twenty, each pivoted and faced the other. Everard raised his weapon and took aim at Mr. Hastings's head.

"I say, Everard, before you shoot," Mr. Hastings said amiably, "I am obliged to mention that you have made a fool of yourself once again."

A fierce look flashed across Everard's face. "Where the devil is your weapon?" he demanded.

Mr. Hastings raised his hands to show that he had none.

"You are a coward!"

"Not in the least, but I saw no reason to wave a pistol about when I had already defeated you."

"I shall shoot, whether you are armed or not."

Mr. Hastings went on as though Everard had said nothing. "You see, my lord, when you fancied you were making love to Miss Charlotte DeWitt, you were in fact making love to a man."

It took several seconds for this to penetrate. The moment it finally did, Lord Everard put his head to one side. "You are raving."

"My dear Lord Everard," said Mr. Hastings in his soothing Charlotte voice, "you have engaged yourself to me, your sworn enemy, Charles Hastings. You have written me a love letter in your own fair hand. You have made me a present of an exquisite ruby brooch belonging to your esteemed mother. You have kissed my hand and made up to me and plighted your troth in the presence of Sir Bascomb and Lady Troy and their daughter. If the news of such a courtship should get out, you would be a laughingstock."

Hatred swelled in Everard's countenance. "If it is true as you say, then you are the ugliest damned female I ever set eyes on." He cocked the pistol and aimed it at Mr. Hastings's heart.

"Is that any way to speak to the lady, that is to say, the gentleman, you pledged to marry? Fie, sir. Fie."

"I shall shoot you, and then the news shall not get out."

In his own voice, Mr. Hastings replied, "You are mistaken. It will get out. If anything at all should happen to me, word will spread over London like the Great Fire. I have sent instructions to Miss Charlotte's dear cousin Felix. He will see that word gets out."

Everard licked his dry lips. "What if you should be shot by somebody else, or should meet with some unfortunate accident?"

"It does not matter how I come to my end—the word will be spread the instant my demise is even so much as suspected."

Something seemed to die in Everard then. The fire of hatred that had burned in his eye dimmed. He stood still for some time, frowning into the distance, then walked deliberately toward the tree where he had tied his horse, intending to ride away.

Nearing the beech where Miranda stood, he stopped. With a lurch, he seized her from behind. She suppressed her impulse to cry out, for she did not wish to give herself away. Instead, she tore at his hands and kicked him, but he overpowered her. Using her as a shield, with the pistol aimed at her head, he once more approached Mr. Hastings.

"If I cannot kill you," Everard said, "I shall be obliged to kill your Mr. Smith."

"It would be better if you did not," Mr. Hastings said in a

voice that was so steady, so low that Miranda grew even more alarmed, if that was possible. She had never heard such seething wrath in him.

Mr. Hastings continued, "Perhaps I ought to have added that if any of my friends or family should meet with an untimely accident, it shall be laid to your door. Felix will act as though you had shot me. I expect you shall have to spend the rest of your life taking prodigiously good care of me and mine, making certain we come to no harm, if you wish to remain in England, that is."

Knitting his brow, Everard seemed uncertain as to what to do. While he was deciding, Miranda, who had been pulling away, now stepped backward, thrusting the weight of her body, and her elbow in particular, into her captor's abdomen. He doubled over. She dove to the steaming earth while Mr. Hastings dove for Everard.

Looking up, Miranda saw the two men struggle. They stood, arms raised, battling for possession of the pistol. At last, Mr. Hastings forced Everard to let it go. It dropped, disappearing into the yellowed grass. The instant it hit the earth, it fired.

At the sound of the shot, the doctor came scurrying up with his bag of implements. Lord Everard sat on the ground, nursing his foot. Mr. Hastings knelt by Miranda, making sure she was unharmed, wiping mud from her cheek. When he was satisfied that she was well, he helped her to her feet.

Everard looked at Mr. Hastings. "I shall take my leave of England," he said. He spoke as though he tasted vinegar mixed with bile. "I shall go abroad."

Mr. Hastings bowed. "Then I shall wish you bon voyage, my lord."

Mr. Hastings and the doctor assisted Lord Everard to rise and walked with him to the gig. Miranda followed. Catching up with Mr. Hastings, she tucked her hand in his. Both watched the gig drive off.

"I could almost pity Lord Everard," she said. "It was bad enough to have engaged himself to a man, but to have shot himself in the foot as well—it is too mortifying."

He smiled at her. "Save your compassion for dear Charlotte. She deserves it."

"Why does she deserve pity?" She looked up at him earnestly. "Charlotte is an excellent creature, and an excellent friend, the best I have ever known."

"Yes, but Lord Everard has broken her heart. The scoundrel has jilted her, and though she is better off without him, still, she must flee to Wales and hide herself there until she can bear up under her disappointment."

Miranda lowered her head. "I am sorry. I shall miss her."

"I shall miss her as well. She has taught me a great deal. I shall never again see things as I used to. I shall see them as a woman might see them, as well a man."

"What will become of poor Charlotte?"

"Oh, eventually she will marry and have children. Her wifely and motherly duties will keep her at home, I fear, and she will not be able to visit us, but she will write to your parents, of whom she has grown very fond, and we shall go and visit her, whenever one of your sisters threatens to visit us at Clarendon Grove."

"What will become of Mr. Hastings?"

"He will wed Miss Miranda Troy and when they tire of billing and cooing, they shall play hazard."

"I do not know how to play hazard."

"It is a game of dice. I shall teach it to you."

"I'll wager you will not."

"I'll wager I will."

"What will become of your second, Mr. Smith, whose clothes fit so ill?"

"He shall go home and rip them off, and I shall be glad to assist him in that enterprise if he permits."

"I'll wager he shall *not* permit."

"What are you willing to wager?"

Sir Bascomb and Lady Troy were at breakfast when Miranda came in with Mr. Hastings. Both of them exhibited such lively spirits and exchanged such affectionate smiles that the baronet frowned, as though the premonition he had had of evil tidings had been borne out. Lady Troy, who could read tidings as well as her husband, clapped her hands together in raptures.

"So it is true," mourned Sir Bascomb. "You are engaged."

"So it is true!" rhapsodized Lady Troy. "You are engaged!"

"We are engaged," Miranda said, and going to the table, she kissed each of her parents on the brow. She was followed by Mr. Hastings, who kissed his future mother-in-law's powdery cheek and then put out his hand to Sir Bascomb. With a sigh, the baronet gave it a limp shake.

"Tabitha will be so pleased!" her ladyship sniffed through joyful tears.

"I hope you will learn to be pleased, too, sir," Mr. Hastings said kindly to Sir Bascomb.

"Do you love my daughter?" the baronet asked.

Mr. Hastings took Miranda's hand and pressed it to his heart. "More than the air I breathe. More than life itself. More even than piquet."

"I love him, too, Papa," Miranda said. Turning to Mr. Hastings, she put her hands around his neck and kissed him. He did not require any encouragement to return the kiss in full measure.

Sir Bascomb shook his head gloomily.

Lady Troy scolded him. "How can you be so tiresome? It is evident that they were meant for each other. I knew it from the beginning, from the time they were born, as did Tabitha. They are excellent children. Excellent. Why, look to what lengths they have gone merely to please their mothers."